PENGUIN BOOKS

STORM IN THE VILLAGE

'Miss Read', or in real life Mrs Dora Saint, is a teacher by profession who started writing after the Second World War, beginning with light essays written under her own name mainly for *Punch*. She has written on educational and country matters for various journals, and worked as a script-writer for the B.B.C.

'Miss Read' is married, with one daughter, and lives in a tiny Berkshire hamlet. Her hobbies are theatre-going, listening to music and reading. She is a local magistrate and, of course, a manager of the local village school!

'Miss Read' has published numerous books including *Village School* (1955), *Village Diary* (1957), *Thrush Green* (1959), *Fresh from the Country* (1960), *Winter in Thrush Green* (1961), *Miss Clare Remembers* (1962), an anthology, *Country Bunch* (1963), *Over the Gate* (1964), *The Market Square* (1966), *Village Christmas* (1966), *The Howards of Caxley* (1967), *Fairacre Festival* (1968), *News from Thrush Green* (1970), *Tyler's Row* (1972), two books for children, *Hobby Horse Cottage* and *Hob and the Horse-bat*, and The Red Bus Series for the very young. Her most recent books are *Farther Afield* (1974), *Battles at Thrush Green* (1975), *No Holly for Miss Quinn* (1976), *Villahe Affairs* (1977), *Return to Thrush Green* (1978), and *The White Robin* (1979).

Many of 'Miss Read's' books are published in Penguins.

'MISS READ'

Storm in the Village

PENGUIN BOOKS

Penguin Books Ltd, Harmondsworth, Middlesex, England
Penguin Books, 625 Madison Avenue, New York, New York 10022, U.S.A.
Penguin Books Australia Ltd, Ringwood, Victoria, Australia
Penguin Books Canada Ltd, 2801 John Street, Markham, Ontario, Canada L3R 1B4
Penguin Books (N.Z.) Ltd, 182-190 Wairau Road, Auckland 10, New Zealand

—

First published by Michael Joseph 1958
Published in Penguin Books 1973
Reprinted 1975, 1976, 1977, 1979, 1981

—

—

Set, printed and bound in Great Britain by
Cox & Wyman Ltd, Reading
Set in Monotype Garamond

To Douglas

CONTENTS

PART FOUR
Calm after Storm

PART ONE

Straws in the Wind

1. The Two Strangers

MISS CLARE's thatched cottage lay comfortably behind a mixed hedge of hawthorn, privet and honeysuckle, on the outskirts of Beech Green. The village was a scattered one, unlike its neighbour Fairacre, where Miss Clare had been the infants' teacher for over forty years, only relinquishing her post when ill-health and the three-mile bicycle journey proved too much for even her indomitable courage.

The cottage had been Miss Clare's home for almost sixty years. Her father had been a thatcher by trade, and the crisscross decorations on the roof still testified to his skill, for they had been braving the weather for over twenty years, and stood out as clearly now, on the greying thatched roof, as they had on the first day of their golden glory. It was true that here and there, particularly round the squat red-brick chimney, the roof was getting a little shabby. Miss Clare often looked at it ruefully, when she went into the back garden to empty her teapot or to cut a cabbage, but as long as it remained weatherproof she had decided that it must stay as it was. It would cost at least two hundred pounds, she had been told, to rethatch her home; and that was out of the question.

One breezy March morning, when the rooks were tumbling about the blue and white sky, high above the cottage, Miss Clare was upstairs, making her lodger's bed. A shaft of sunlight fell across the room, as Miss Clare's thin, old hands smoothed the pillow and covered it squarely with the white honeycomb quilt which had once covered her mother's bed.

No one would call Miss Jackson tidy, thought Miss Clare, as she returned books from the floor to the book-shelf, and retrieved shoes from under the bed. It was one of the few things that grieved her about her young lodger. Otherwise she was thoughtful, and very, very clever with the children.

Miss Clare imagined her now, as she tidied the girl's clothes, standing in front of her class of young children, as she too had done for so many years, at Fairacre School. Prayers would be over, and as it was so fine, no doubt they would be getting ready to go out into the playground for physical training. Often, during the day, Miss Clare would look at the clock and think of the children at Fairacre School. The habits of a lifetime die hard, and to have the present infants' teacher as her lodger, to hear the school news, and the gossip from the village which, secretly, meant more to her than the one in which she lived, was a source of great comfort to her.

She picked a small auburn feather from the floor: A Rhode Island Red's feather, noted Miss Clare's country eye, which must have worked its way from the plump feather bed.

Outside, the birds were clamorous, busy with their nest building, and reconnoitring for likely places in the loose parts of the thatched roof. Miss Clare crossed to the window and let the feather float from it to the little lawn below. Before it had had time to settle, three excited sparrows threw themselves upon it, squabbling and struggling. Miss Clare, sunning herself on the window-sill, smiled benevolently upon them, and watched her feather borne off in triumph to some half-made nest nearby.

It was then that she noticed the men.

There were two of them, pacing slowly, side by side, along the edge of Hundred Acre Field which lay on the other side of Miss Clare's garden hedge.

It was one of several unusually large fields which formed part of old Mr Miller's farm. Harold Miller had lived at the farmhouse at Springbourne all his life, and had farmed the same land as his father before him. Now, at eighty, he was as spry as ever, and nothing escaped his bright, birdlike eye. His two sons, much to his sorrow, had shown no desire to carry on the farming traditions of the family, but had sought their fortunes, with fair success, elsewhere, one as an engineer and the other as an architect.

Hundred Acre Field and its spacious neighbours were among the more fruitful parts of Mr Miller's farm. Many of his acres were on the bare chalk downs which sheltered his home from the northerly winds. Here he kept a sizeable flock of sheep, rightly renowned for many miles around. At the foot of the downs the plough soon turned up chalk, and on a dry day, the white, light dust would blow in clouds from these lower fields. But those which lay furthest from his farm, near Miss Clare's cottage, had at least two feet of fertile top soil, and here old Mr Miller grew the oats and wheat which Miss Clare watched with an eye as keen and as appreciative as their owner's.

At the moment, Hundred Acre Field was brushed with a tender green, the tiny spears of wheat showing two or three inches above the soil. Beyond this field had lain a large expanse of kale, on which Mr Miller had been feeding his flock during the hardest months of the winter.

The two men walked slowly towards the kale stumps, stopping every now and again, to bend down and examine the soil among the wheat rows. Miss Clare's long-sighted eyes noted their good thick tweeds approvingly. The wind was still keen, despite the bright sunlight, and she liked to see people sensibly clad. But their shoes grieved her. They were stout enough, to be sure; but far more suited to the pavements of Caxley than the sticky mud of a Beech Green field. And so beautifully polished! Such a pity to mess them up, thought Miss Clare; and what a lot of mud they would take back into that neat little car that stood on the green verge of the lane, quite near her own front gate!

What could they be doing? she wondered. There they stood, with their backs to her, gazing across the grand sweep of the fields to the gentle outline of the hazy downs beyond. One had drawn a paper from his pocket and was studying it minutely.

'What a busybody I'm getting!' said Miss Clare aloud, pulling herself together.

She took a last look round Miss Jackson's room, then crossed the little landing to her own at the front of the cottage.

She had just finished setting it to rights and was shaking her duster from the window, when she saw the two men again. They were standing now by the car and, Miss Clare was glad to see, they were doing their best to wipe the mud from their shoes on the grass.

'Though why they don't pick a little stick from the hedge and dig it all away from their insteps, I really don't know,' said Miss Clare to herself. 'They *will* make a mess in that nice little car!'

She watched them climb in, turn it adroitly, and move off in the direction of Fairacre.

'Curiouser and curiouser!' quoted Miss Clare to the cat, who had arrived upstairs to see which bed had a pool of sunlight on it, and would be best suited to his morning siesta. But his luck was out, for his mistress headed him firmly to the stairs, and followed him into the kitchen.

'Ministry of Agriculture, I should think,' continued Miss Clare, lifting the cat on to his accustomed chair near the stove, from which, needless to say, the outraged animal jumped down at once, just to assert his independence.

His mistress was gazing, somewhat uneasily, out of the kitchen window. She was still preoccupied with the arrival of the two strangers.

'I wonder who they can be? And what are they going to do in Fairacre?'

At that moment, in Fairacre, as Miss Clare had surmised, Miss Jackson and her young charges were pretending to be galloping horses in the small, stony playground of Fairacre School.

'Higher, higher!' she urged the leaping children, prancing among them spiritedly, and her excited voice floated through the Gothic window, which was tilted open, to my own class.

As headmistress of Fairacre School I have taken the older children now for several years; while first Miss Clare, then Miss Gray (now Mrs Annett), and finally Miss Jackson, held sway in the infants' room. Miss Jackson, to be sure, could be a thorn in the side at times, for she was still much influenced by her college psychology lecturer and apt to thrust that good lady's dicta forward for my edification, much too often for my liking. But she had improved enormously, and I was inclined to think that her serene life with Miss Clare had had a lot to do with this mellowing process.

My children were busy with sums, working away in their

exercise books, with much rattling of nibs in inkwells and chewing of pen holders. I walked to the window to watch the progress of Miss Jackson's galloping horses.

The sun was dazzling. The weather cock glittered, gold against the blue and white scudding sky, on the spire of St Patrick's church, which stood, a massive neighbour, to our own small, two-roomed building. The children cavorted madly about, their faces rosy and their breath puffing mistily before them in the sharp air. Their short legs worked like pistons and their hair was tossed this way and that, not only by their own exertions but also by the exhilarating wind which came from the downs. Miss Jackson blew a wavering blast on her whistle, and the galloping horses stopped, panting, in their tracks.

It was at this moment that the little car drew cautiously alongside the school wall, and one of the two men inside called to Miss Jackson.

I could not hear the conversation from my vantage point at the window, but I watched the children edge nearer the wall, as Miss Jackson, leaning well over, waved her arms authoritatively and presumably gave directions. Inquisitive little things, I thought to myself, and then was immediately struck by my own avid curiosity, which kept me staring with fascination at the scene before me. There's no doubt about it – we like to know what's going on in Fairacre, both young and old, and there's precious little that happens around us that goes unobserved.

The men smiled their thanks, appeared to confer, and Miss Jackson turned back to her class, who were now clustered tightly about her, well within earshot of her conversation. One of the men got out of the car and made his way towards the centre of Fairacre, Miss Jackson resumed her lesson, and I, with smarting conscience, set about marking sums, much refreshed by my interlude at the school window.

'They had a flat tyre,' vouchsafed Miss Jackson, over our cup of tea at playtime, 'and wanted to know if they could get some coffee anywhere while they had the wheel changed. I told them to try the "Beetle and Wedge", and to call on Mr Rogers at the forge about the wheel. They seemed very nice men,' she added, a trifle wistfully, I thought.

I felt a slight pang of pity for my young assistant, who had so little opportunity of meeting 'very nice men'. There are very few men in Fairacre itself, and not many more at Beech Green, and buses to Caxley, the nearest town, are few and far between, even if one felt like making the effort to join the Dramatic or Musical Society there. Occasionally, I knew, Miss Jackson went home for the weekend, and there, I sincerely hoped, she met some lively young people with her own interests. Unfortunately, it appeared from her chance remarks that Miss Crabbe still held first place in her heart, and if she could ever manage to visit this paragon I knew that she did so.

When I took my own class out for their P.T. lesson, later in the morning, the little car was still there, and both men were busily engaged in changing the wheel themselves; so presumably, no help had been forthcoming from Mr Rogers at the forge. Before the end of my lesson, the job was completed. They wiped their hands on a filthy rag, looked very satisfied with themselves, and drove back on their tracks towards Caxley.

'See them two strangers?' shouted Mrs Pringle, an hour or so later, crashing plates about in the sink. Mrs Pringle, the school cleaner, also washes up the dinner things, and keeps us in touch with anything untoward that has happened in Fairacre during the morning.

I said that I had.

'Up to a bit of no good, I'll bet!' continued Mrs Pringle sourly. 'Inspectors, or something awkward like that. One went in the butcher's first. I thought pr'aps he was the weights and measures. You know, for giving short weight. They has you up pretty smartish for giving short weight.'

I said I supposed they did.

'And so they should!' said Mrs Pringle, rounding on me fiercely. 'Nothing short of plain thieving to give short weight!' She crashed the plates even more belligerently, her three chins wobbling aggressively, and her mouth turned down disapprovingly.

'*However*,' she went on heavily, 'he wasn't the weights and measures, though his suit was good enough, that I must say. But he was asking for the forge. My cousin Dolly happened to be in the shop at the time, and she couldn't help overhearing, as she was waiting for her fat to be cut off her chops. Too rich for her always – never been the same since yellow jaundice as a tot. And the butcher said as he knew Mr Rogers was gone to Caxley, to put a wreath on his old mother's grave there, it being five years to the day since she passed on. As a nice a woman as I ever wish to meet, and they keep her grave beautiful. So this fellow said was there anywhere to get a cup of coffee? And the butcher said no harm in having a bash at the "Beetle", but it all depended.'

She turned to the electric copper, raised the lid, letting out a vast cloud of steam, baled out a scalding dipperful of water, and flung it nonchalantly into the flotsam in the sink.

'I passed him on my way up to the post office. Nicely turned out he was. Beautiful heather mixture tweed, and a nice blue shirt with a fine red line to it – but his tie could have done with a clean – and his shoes! Had a good polish first thing, I don't doubt, but been tramping over some old ploughed field since then! Couldn't help but notice, though I hardly give him a glance; I never was a starer, like some in this parish I could mention!'

She bridled self-righteously and dropped a handful of red-hot forks, with an earsplitting crash, on to the tin draining board.

'Was that his car?' she bellowed, above the din. I nodded.

'They'd got a new-fangled satchel thing – brief-case, ain't it? – in the back. Two strangers, poking about here with a brief-case and a lot of mud on their shoes,' she mused. 'Makes you think, don't it? Might be Ag. men, of course. But you mark my words, Miss Read, they was up to a bit of no good!'

Mr Willet, the school caretaker, verger and sexton of St

Patrick's next door, and general handyman to all Fairacre, had also noted the strangers.

'Nice little car that, outside here this morning. Them two chaps from the Office?'

The Office, which is always spoken of with the greatest respect, referred in this case to the divisional education office in Caxley, from which forms, directions and our monthly cheques flutter regularly.

'No,' I said, 'I don't know who they were.'

'Oh lor'!' said Mr Willet, blowing out his moustache despairingly. 'Hope it ain't anything to do with the sanitary. They're terrors – the sanitary! Ah well! Time'll tell, I suppose – but they looked uncomfortable sort of customers to me!'

He trudged off, with resigned good humour, to sweep up the playground.

But it remained for the Reverend Gerald Partridge, vicar of Fairacre and Beech Green, to say the last word on this mysterious subject.

'Did you have visitors this morning?' he asked, after he had greeted the children. I told him that we had not seen anyone strange in school.

'I noticed two men in a little car outside here, as I drove over to see about poor old Harris's funeral at Beech Green. Now, I wonder who they could have been?'

I said that I had no idea.

'Who knows?' said the vicar happily. 'We may look forward to having some new people among us perhaps?'

As it happened, the vicar had spoken more truly than he knew.

2. Fairacre's Daily Round

By next day, of course, the two strangers were forgotten. Life, particularly in a village, has so many interests that each day seems to offer more riches than the last.

Miss Clare turned her attention to a magnificent steak and kidney pudding, which simmered gently on her stove from two o'clock onwards, for her lodger's, and her own, supper together at eight o'clock. It filled the little house with its homely fragrance, and Dr Martin, who called in hopefully about half past three for a cup of tea with his old friend and patient, noticed it at once.

'That's the stuff!' he said approvingly, rubbing his hands, and he cast a glance at Miss Clare's spare frame. 'You're putting on weight since that girl came. Good idea of yours to have a lodger!'

It had not been Miss Clare's idea at all, as they both knew very well, but Miss Clare let it pass. It was Dr Martin who had engineered Miss Jackson's removal from her headmistress's house to Miss Clare's; and he could see that young company as well as an addition to her slender housekeeping purse was doing his patient all the good in the world.

'Have a ginger nut,' said Miss Clare, pushing the massive biscuit barrel across to him.

'I'll have to dip it. My new bottom set's giving me hell!' said the doctor, with disarming frankness. 'We're getting old, Dolly, that's our trouble.'

They smiled across at each other, and sipped their tea in comfortable silence. The steak and kidney pudding sizzled deliciously on the stove. The fire warmed their thin legs, and though indeed, thought Miss Clare, we're both old and white-haired, at least we're very happy.

Mrs Pringle was busy washing out the school tea cloths at her own sink. This was done every day, but on this occasion Mrs Pringle was particularly engrossed, for it was the first time that she had used what she termed 'one of these new-fangled deterrents'.

A staunch upholder of yellow bar soap, Mrs Pringle had set her face against the dazzling array of washing powders which brightened the grocer's shop. On a wooden shelf, above her sink, were stacked long bars, as hard as wood, which she had stored there for many months. This soap was used for all cleaning purposes in the Pringle household. The brick floors, the stout undergarments and Mrs Pringle's dour countenance itself were all scoured with this substance, and when one piece had worn away, Mrs Pringle fetched her shovel, laid a bar on a piece of newspaper on the kitchen floor and sliced off another chunk to do its work.

But the gay coupons, all assuring her of their monetary value, which fluttered through Mrs Pringle's letter-box from time to time, gradually found a chink in her armour. The day, came when, slightly truculent, she handed one across the counter, and put the dazzling packet in her basket. She was careful to cover it with other packages, in case she met neighbours who, knowing her former scorn of these products, would be only too pleased to 'take a rise out of her' if they saw that she had finally fallen.

And so, on this day, Mrs Pringle washed her tea cloths with a critical eye. The packet had been tucked away behind the innocent bars of soap, for Mrs Pringle had no doubt that her husband and grown-up son could be as equally offensive as her neighbours about this experiment, if they caught sight of the soap powder.

'Hm!' said Mrs Pringle grudgingly, as she folded the wet tea towels, and put them into her laundry basket. 'It don't do so bad after all!'

With some pride, she trudged up the garden and began to peg out the cloths on the line. When she had done this, she propped the line up with a sturdy forked hazel branch, and surveyed the fluttering collection.

'Might be something to be said for these deterrents, after all!' she told herself, returning to the cottage, 'and it do save chipping up the soap – that I will give 'em!' It was, indeed, high praise.

Miss Jackson, in the infants' room at Fairacre was embarking on the most elaborate and artistic frieze yet attempted by her class. It was to go all round the room, fixed with drawing pins to the green-painted matchboarding, and it was to represent Spring.

The children were busy snipping with their blunt-nosed little scissors – which were always much too stiff for small children to manage properly – at gummed paper, in all the colours of the rainbow.

'Make just what you like!' Miss Jackson had exhorted them. 'Flowers, leaves, lambs, birds, butterflies – anything that makes you think of Spring!'

Most of her class had flung themselves with abandon into this glorious snipping session, but there were, as always, one or two stolid and adenoidal babies who were completely without imagination, and awaited direction apathetically.

'Make grass then!' had said Miss Jackson, with some exasperation to the Coggs twins, who sat with glum, dark eyes fixed upon her. Ten minutes later, she found that a large mound of green snippings lay on the desk between them, while, with tongues protruding, and with a red ring round each hard-working thumb, the grass-makers added painfully to their pile.

Anyway, thought Miss Jackson, that's far better than making them go, step by step, drawing round tobacco tins and paste jars to make horrid little yellow-chicks-in-a-row, for an Easter frieze! For she had found just such a one – made by her predecessor Mrs Annett – and had looked scornfully upon its charming regularity. The children, needless to say, had loved it, but Miss Jackson favoured all those things which were written in capital letters in her own teaching notes – such as Free Art, Individual Expression, Untrammelled Creative Urge, and so on, and anything as formal and limited as poor Mrs Annett's despised chicks were anathema to her.

And so the children snipped and hacked and tore at a fine profusion of gummed papers. Mrs Annett's and Miss Clare's frugal eyes would have expressed concern at the large pieces which fell to waste on the floor. But Miss Jackson, seeing in her mind's eye the riotous glory which was to flower around her walls so soon, and with a fine disregard for the ratepayers' money, smiled upon her babies' efforts with approval.

In the churchyard, next door to the school playground, Mr Willet was having a bonfire. He had made himself a fine incinerator by knocking holes in a tin tar barrel. This was set up on three bricks, so that the draught fairly whistled under it, and inside Mr Willet was burning the dead flowers from the graves, stray pieces of paper, twigs, leaves and all the other rubbish which accumulates in a public place.

He had had some difficulty in getting the fire to start, for the débris was damp. But, having watched Mrs Pringle returning to her home after washing up the school's dinner plates, he had made a bold sortie to the school woodshed, and there found a paraffin-oil can, which Mrs Pringle fondly imagined was known to her alone.

He sprinkled his languishing bonfire lavishly, and stood back to admire the resulting blaze.

'Ah! that's more like!' he said with satisfaction. He bent to retrieve the oil-can and stumped back to the woodshed.

'And if the old Tartar finds out, 'tis all one to me!' he added sturdily, tucking it behind the sack which shrouded it.

Meanwhile, the vicar was polishing his car, and doing it very badly. It wasn't that he was lazy about it. In fact, he was taking the greatest pains, and had an expensive tin of car polish, half a dozen clean rags of various types, ranging from a soft mutton-cloth to a dashing blue-checked duster which he had found hanging on the banister.

Mrs Willet, who was helping with the spring-cleaning at the time, was much perplexed about this duster. It had vanished while she had fetched the feather mop for the top of the spare room wardrobe, and was never seen by her again.

But despite his armoury and his zeal, the vicar's handiwork was a failure.

'I must admit,' said the vicar aloud, standing back on his gravel path to survey the car better, 'that there are far too many smears.'

'Gerald!' called his wife, from the window. 'You did remember to ask the Mawnes to call in for a drink this evening?'

'Well, no!' answered the vicar unhappily. 'To be truthful, it slipped my mind, but I have to take a cheque to Mawne for the Church Maintenance Fund. I'll ask them then.'

'Good!' said his wife, preparing to close the window. The vicar forestalled her.

'My dear!' he called. The window opened again. 'What do you think of the car?'

'Smeary!' said his wife, closing the window firmly.

'She's right, you know,' sighed the vicar sadly to the cat which came up to rub against his clerical-grey legs. 'It definitely *is* smeary!'

With some relief he turned his back on the car and went into the house to fetch his biretta. He would visit the Mawnes straight away. An afternoon call would be much more satisfying than cleaning the car.

The smoke from Mr Willet's most successful bonfire began to blow into my classroom during history lesson, and I went to the window to close it.

I could see Mr Willet, his shirt-sleeves rolled up, forking dead vegetation into the smoking mouth of the incinerator. He turned, as he heard the window shut, and raised his hands in apology and concern.

I shook my head and smiled, waving my own hands, hoping that he would accept my grimaces and gestures as the verbal equivalent of 'Don't worry! It's doesn't matter!'

It appeared that he did, for after a minute or two of further dumb show, he saluted and returned to his fork; while I gave a final wave and returned to my class.

The slip-shod spelling in the older children's history essays had roused me to an unaccustomed warmth and I had been in the midst of haranguing them when I had broken off to close the window. I returned to the fray with renewed vigour.

'Listen to this Patrick, "There were four Go-urges. Go-urge the Frist, Go-urge the Scond, Go-urge the Thrid, and Go-urge the Froth."And to make matters worse, I had put "George" on the blackboard for you, and spent ten minutes explaining that it came from a Greek word "Geo" meaning earth.'

Patrick smiled sheepishly, fluttering alluring dark lashes. I refused to be softened.

'Who remembers some of the words we put on the blackboard, beginning with "Geo"?'

There was a stunned silence. The clock ticked ponderously and outside we could hear the crackling of Mr Willet's bonfire. Someone yawned.

'Well?' I said, with menace.

'Geography,' said one inspired child.

'Geology,' said another.

Silence fell again. I made another attempt to rouse them.

'Oh, come now! There were several more words!'

Joseph Coggs, lately arrived in my room, broke the silence.

'Je-oshaphat!' he said smugly.

I drew in a large breath, but before I could explode, his neighbour turned to him.

'That's Scripture, Joe!' he explained kindly.

I let out my breath gently and changed the subject. No point in bursting a blood-vessel, I told myself.

Mrs. Annett had asked me to tea that afternoon.

'And stay the evening, please!' she had implored on the telephone. 'George will be going into Caxley for orchestra practice, and I shall be alone. You can help me bath Malcolm,' she added, as a further inducement.

The thought of bathing my godson, now at the crawling stage, could not be resisted, so I had promised to be at Beech Green schoolhouse as soon after four as my own duties would allow.

It began to rain heavily later in the afternoon. I saw Mr Willet, his bonfire now dying slowly, scurry for shelter into the church. By the time the clock stood at a quarter to four, the rain was drumming mercilessly against the windows, and swishing, in silver shivers, across the stony playground.

We buttoned up the children's coats, turned up their collars, tied scarves over heads, sorted wellington boots on to the right feet, and gloves on to the right fingers, before sending them out to face the weather. One little family of four, somewhat inadequately clad, had the privilege of borrowing the old golfing umbrella from the map cupboard. So massive is this shabby monster that all four scuttled along together, quite comfortably, in its shelter.

'I'll give you a lift,' I said to Miss Jackson. 'I'm going to Beech Green for tea, and you'll get soaked if you cycle.'

I sped across to the school house to put things to rights before leaving my establishment. Tibby, my black and white cat, turned a sour look upon me, as I shovelled small coal on to the fire, and put up the guard.

'And is this meagre warmth,' his look said, 'supposed to suffice? Where, pray, are the blazing logs and flaring coals best suited to the proper warming of a cat's stomach?'

I escaped from his disapproving eye and got out the car.

The downs were shrouded in rain clouds, and little rivers gurgled down each side of the lane as we drove along to Beech Green.

'Betty Franklyn told me that she was going to live with an aunt in Caxley,' Miss Jackson said, speaking of a six-year-old in her class. 'I wonder if that's right? Have you heard?'

'No,' I answered, 'but it would be the best thing, I should think. She'll be looked after properly, if it's the aunt I'm thinking of.'

Betty's mother had died early in the year, and the father was struggling along alone. I felt very sorry for him, but he was a man I had never taken to, sandy-haired, touchy and quick-tempered.

He was a gamekeeper, and lived in a lonely cottage, in a small copse, on the Beech Green side of Fairacre. He brought the child to school each morning on the cross-bar of his bicycle, and sometimes met her, when his work allowed, after school in the afternoon.

It must have been a cheerless home during the last two or three months, and the child had looked pathetically forlorn. I hoped that this rumour would prove to be true. The aunt had always seemed devoted to her little niece, and, in Caxley, the child would have more playmates. I felt certain that the aunt had offered to have the child as soon as her mother had died; but the father, I suspected, was proud and possessive, and would look to his little daughter for company. He was certainly very fond of her, and probably he had realized that she would be far happier in Caxley, and so given in to persuasion.

I said as much to Miss Jackson, as we edged by a Land-rover which was drawn up on the grass verge by Hundred Acre Field. Despite the sweeping rain, old Mr Miller, a small, indomitable figure in a trench coat and glistening felt hat, was standing among his young wheat surveying his field. He appeared oblivious of the weather, and deeply preoccupied.

'It will be a good thing for Betty,' I said, 'I shouldn't think her father's much company.'

To my surprise, Miss Jackson replied quite sharply.

'I should imagine he's very good company. He's always very nice when he brings Betty in the mornings. I've found him most interesting, and very well read.'

I negotiated the bend near Miss Clare's house in silence.

'And what he doesn't know about trees and birds and woodland animals!' continued Miss Jackson warmly. 'He's suggested that I take my class to the wood for a nature walk one day, and he'll meet us there.'

'Will he, indeed?' I said somewhat taken aback.

'And when you think of the lonely life he leads, since his poor wife's death,' went on my assistant, her face quite pink with emotion, 'it really is quite shattering. How he must have suffered! And he's a sensitive man.'

I drew up outside Miss Clare's cottage. She waved through the window from behind a pink geranium, and beckoned me in.

'I'm going to tea with Isobel,' I bellowed in an unladylike way, 'so I mustn't stop!' She nodded and smiled, and watched her lodger, who was alighting, still pink and defensive.

'Good-bye, and thanks!' said Miss Jackson, somewhat shortly, pushing open the wet gate.

I drove off slowly and thoughtfully.

'It looks to me,' I said aloud, 'as if Miss Crabbe will soon be supplanted in Miss Jackson's heart. But not, heaven forbid, by that Franklyn fellow! I know a scamp when I see one!'

3. Mrs Annett Has Doubts

'HELLO, hello!' called Mr Annett bursting out from his school door as he heard my car forge its way slowly into the playground.

'Put it under cover! Up in the shed,' he shouted, through the pouring rain. I edged carefully under the corrugated iron roof of the playground shelter. The drumming of the downpour was thunderous under here.

Two small boys, ostensibly tidying up some gymnastic apparatus, watched my manoeuvres with interest.

'Best leave 'er in gear, miss,' advised one. 'Nasty slope back if the 'and brake give up the ghost!'

'I'll stick a brick by your back wheel,' said the other. 'Don't do no harm, if it don't do no good! And don't forget your ignition keys, miss!'

By this time Mr Annett had joined us, and overheard my mentors.

'Those two,' he told me, when we were out of earshot, 'are supposed to be educationally sub-normal.'

'They may not know how many beans make five,' I returned, 'but they know a good deal more about my car than I do. You see, they'll find a niche, soon enough, when they leave school!'

We made our way across the streaming playground, to a little gate let in the side fence of Mr Annett's garden. As he closed it behind us I looked at his trim beds and lawn and compared it sadly with my own.

A fine clump of white crocuses, sheltered from the rain by a glossy rhododendron bush, were a joy to see; their pure white cups lit from within by their dazzling gold stamens. Nearby, a speckled thrush was diligently hammering a snail on a large knobbly flint, that glistened in the rain. He was far too engrossed with his task to bother about us, although we passed close to him as we made our way to the back door.

A warm odour of freshly baked scones met us from the kitchen. Isobel, flushed and cheerful, was busy buttering them, while Malcolm, strapped securely in his high chair, out of temptation's way, was shaking a bean in a screw-topped jar, and singing tunelessly as an accompaniment.

'The tympani chap in a jazz band,' said his father, nodding towards him. 'That's what he's going to be!'

'And very nice too,' I said. 'I've always wanted to have a go at that myself.'

Tea was set in the dining-room, which looked out on to the back garden. Beyond the lawn lay Mr Annett's kitchen garden, and I could see that his broad beans were already standing in sturdy rows. In the distance, I had a glimpse through the budding hawthorn hedge, of the school pig sties and chicken houses in the field beyond; for Mr Annett was a firm believer in rural pursuits for his older boys, and his practical methods had become much admired, and emulated, by other local teachers.

Tea was a hilarious meal, much enlivened by young Malcolm, who preferred to eat his neat strips of bread and butter by squeezing them well in his plump hands. When the food emerged, as a revolting squish, between his fingers, he devoured it with the greatest relish, covering his face and his duck-decorated bib with rather more than half. His father watched with disgust.

'Loathsome child!' he said sternly.

'Take no notice!' said his wiser mother. 'He wants us to make a fuss about it.' She passed the scones to me, her face carefully averted from her offspring, and I tried to wrench my own gaze away from my god-child's unpleasant handiwork.

'It must be very hard work,' I observed. 'All that kneading and squeezing. I wonder if it's nicer that way?'

'Don't you start, for heaven's sake!' said Mr Annett with alarm. 'Here, have some honey, and don't go getting ideas in your head!'

He began to talk about the two boys who had been so interested in my car.

'The smaller one tells me that there's talk of a housing estate in Hundred Acre Field,' said he. 'Heard anything about it?'

I said I hadn't.

'There was a tiny paragraph in the *Mail* or the *Telegraph* a week or two ago,' said Mrs Annett. 'Something about two or three thousand new workers coming to the atomic place. They've had some new plant put in, haven't they?'

'And is this housing estate for them?' I asked, somewhat alarmed. 'Good lord, it surely won't be built at Beech Green? It's miles from the atomic station!'

'Well, I don't know. There'd be work buses, I suppose.'

'Not that we're likely to have a huge estate here,' said Mrs Annett. 'That field is excellent farming land. Surely, it wouldn't be built on?'

We ate, for a few minutes, in silence, turning over this uncomfortable rumour in our minds. Mr Annett broke the silence.

'Come to think of it, there were two men sizing things up over there one morning last week—'

'So there were!' I broke in. 'We thought they were just Agmen!' For it is by this euphonious term that officials of the Ministry of Agriculture are known here.

'Never mind,' said Mr Annett boisterously. 'Think of all the children! Beech Green Comprehensive School, we'd have here, and Fairacre would have a couple of new wings and a bathing pool and a nursery block—'

'And if Mrs Pringle's going to look after that lot, my life won't be worth living!' I retorted. 'Let's pray that we hear no more of housing estates in this peaceful spot!'

Alas! My prayer was not to be answered.

When Mr Annett had driven off to his orchestral practice in Caxley, in his shabby little car with the 'cello propped carefully in the back, Isobel and I enjoyed ourselves putting young Malcolm to bed.

We enveloped ourselves in mackintosh aprons for bathing the energetic baby, for he was a prodigious splasher, screaming with joy as he smacked the water, and drenched the bathroom.

When we had dried him and tucked him firmly into his cot, we tiptoed downstairs.

'Not that we need to bother,' said his mother, 'he'll be standing up again by now, ready for half an hour's jumping!

He's just like George – never still. I'll go and cover him up when he's fallen asleep with exhaustion, but that won't be yet?'

Sure enough, we could hear the rhythmic squeaking of Malcolm's cot springs as he jumped spiritedly up and down, letting off the final ounce or two of energy that still quivered in his plump frame.

'Let's forget him!' said his mother, leading the way into the drawing-room, where a bright fire burned.

'George is looking very well,' I said, when we were settled.

'I'm so glad to hear you say that,' said young Mrs Annett earnestly. 'You know, I often wonder if he's really happy. It's not easy to be a second wife. One always imagines – wrongly, I'm sure – that the first wife was a paragon of all the virtues, and that one is a very poor second best.'

'What an idea!' I exclaimed.

'Well, there it is! I can't talk about it to George, naturally, and there's really no one else I've ever felt I could say anything to; but it doesn't stop these nagging doubts, you know, just to keep quiet about them.'

I felt very sorry for the girl. She was obviously worrying about a non-existent problem, as I set about explaining. But, once she had started to tell me her confidences, more came in quick succession and I began to wonder, with some trepidation, what further disclosures Isobel might make. As an incorrigible spinster I very much dislike being the confidante of married ladies, and marital troubles, imparted to me in low tones whilst their husbands are temporarily from the room, fill me with the greatest alarm and foreboding. Fortunately, Isobel's good sense and reticence spared me any major discomfort.

'Of course, I know I'm foolish to think such things,' went on Mrs Annett, poking the fire vigorously. 'And I should feel better about it if George and his first wife had been married long enough to have had a few healthy rows. But to be killed – when they'd only been married six months – well, it does cast an odour of sanctity over the whole thing, doesn't it? And George really did adore her. You must admit that a second wife's got a good bit of leeway to make up!'

She sat back on her heels, brandishing the poker and looking so fierce that I burst into laughter.

'Listen!' I said, 'If you've got the sense to see it all as squarely as that, then you must also have the sense to see that you're an addle-pated ass! And why not give George credit for a little intelligence too? He married you because he wanted to – and the first wife just doesn't come into the picture now, poor soul!'

'I do see that really,' admitted Isobel, 'but I'm here alone such a lot that I think too much and imagine things. You see, I've always had people round me – at school, at college, and then when I taught with you at Fairacre. The day seems quite long with George over at the school, and although I'm terribly busy with Malcolm and the house and meals – somehow one's mind goes rattling on, and I get these idiotic ideas.'

It was the first time that I had realized the possibility of young wives being lonely, but I saw now, in a flash, that that very simple circumstance was, possibly, the reason for a number of troubles in early married life. Isobel went on to tell me more.

'And then, of course, I worry far too much about our finances. When I was earning, I bought anything I took a fancy to – within reason – and if I were short at the end of the month, well, that was my own affair and I took the consequences. But now I feel that it is George's money, and that I must use it to the best advantage for the three of us. It really is shattering at times! And there are so many things I see when I go to Caxley – pretty things, you know, like flowers and china and blouses and bracelets – that I would have bought for myself before, and had no end of a thrill from – but now, I feel it's extravagant and go without, and it is distinctly depressing!'

I was becoming more enlightened, each minute, about the terrific adjustments that a young female of independent means has to make when she throws aside her comfortable job and takes on the manifold duties of a wife and mother.

'And another thing,' continued Mrs Annett, now in full spate, 'I enjoyed teaching and knew that I could do it well. I felt sure of myself – but now, I can't tell whether I'm making a good job of housekeeping or not. There's no one to tell me if I am, and, I must say, I feel full of doubts.'

'Don't forget,' I said, 'that you've suddenly taken on about six skilled jobs and have got to learn them all at the same time. Catering, cooking, looking after Malcolm, keeping George happy, laundry work, entertaining, and all the rest of housekeeping will take months and years to learn. I think you're doing jolly well. The only thing is – I feel you do it all for twenty-four hours out of the twenty-four, seven days a week, and have no time to stand away from the job and see how nicely it's getting along.'

'I suppose that's it, really. It's impossible for us both to go out together unless we get a reliable sitter-in, and Malcolm's a bit of a handful at the moment, so we don't do it often. But I do miss the orchestra!'

'Then I'll come definitely every orchestra night,' I promised. 'I should have thought of it before. It's the least a godmother can do.'

Mrs Annett's face lit up.

'Do you mean it? Won't it be an awful tie to you? I'd just love to go, but I feel it's too much to ask anyone.' She broke off suddenly.

'Listen!'

We sat rigidly, mouths open. I could hear nothing but the gentle gurgling of the rain down an outside guttering, and an occasional patter on the pane.

'He's stopped jumping!' said Malcom's mother, leaping to her feet. 'Let's go and cover him up.'

Collapsed, face downward, at the end of his cot lay Malcolm Annett. With bated breath we turned back his blankets, scooped the warm bundle to the right end, and covered him up all over again. This time he lay still, and we tiptoed downstairs again, leaving him to his slumbers.

When I returned home, I found that a note had been put through the door. It said –

'FAIRACRE FLOWER SHOW

A committee meeting of the above will be held in the school at 7 o'clock on Friday next, March 30th. Your attendance is requested.'

'Well, Tibby,' I said to the cat, who was curling round my legs luxuriously, 'that'll be a nice comfortable evening, cramped up in small wooden desks.'

But, as it happened, Fate decided otherwise.

The rain which had been so torrential on the Tuesday when I had visited Beech Green, gave way to clear skies and high winds.

The children were excited and boisterous, as they always are when the weather is windy. Doors slammed, windows rattled, papers blew from desks, and the gale roared so loudly in the elm trees that border the playground that at times it was difficult to make my voice heard in the classroom.

On Friday morning the wind reached unprecedented force. The weathercock shuddered at the top of St Patrick's spire, my lawn was scattered with petals torn from the prunus and almond trees, and the gay clumps of crocuses lay battered in the garden beds, like bowed dancers in satin skirts.

I was busy correcting Eric's arithmetic at his desk at the back of the classroom when the rumbling began. The children looked up in alarm, for the noise was terrifying. I had only just time to realize that it must be a tile slipping down the roof, when with a deafening crash, it reached the skylight, smashed the glass into a hundred tinkling fragments, and fell thunderously on to my desk below. It was, in fact, a large piece of the curved ridge of the roof, and had I been sitting in my accustomed seat, would doubtless have caused me a trip to Caxley hospital.

The children were much shaken – and so was I, for that matter. Miss Jackson burst in from the infant's room to see what the trouble was, and stood appalled on the threshold. It was Joseph Coggs who first recovered.

'Best clear the mess up,' he growled huskily, and set off for the lobby, returning with the dust-pan and broom. I lifted the heavy lump of masonry and staggered with it to the playground, while Miss Jackson wielded the broom, and the children, having recovered from their fright, began to cluster round and thoroughly enjoy this sensational interruption to their peaceful labours.

Mr Willet, who had been setting out his seed potatoes ready for sprouting, in shallow wooden boxes, in his own quiet kitchen, had somehow been informed of the disaster, by the mysterious bush telegraph which works so well in every village, and had rushed straight to the scene, pulling on his jacket as he pounded up the village street.

'Accident! Up the school!' he had puffed to curious quest-ioners, without slackening his pace.

It was not surprising, therefore, to find that Mr Willet was accompanied by four agitated mothers when he arrived, in an advanced state of breathlessness, at the school door.

'You all right?' he gasped out.

I assured him that we were all unharmed and indicated the smashed skylight.

'Lord!' breathed Mr Willet, with awe. 'That's done it!' The four mothers edged round the door, their eyes goggling. I let them feast on the scene before them for a minute, and then decided that it was time for them to depart.

'No harm done!' I said firmly. 'And now that Mr Willet's here we shall soon clear up the mess!' I shepherded the reluc-tant quartet towards the lobby.

'Poor little mites! Might have been struck dead!' said one, with relish.

'I always said that skylight was a danger!' asserted the next.

'Tempting Providence to have glass in a roof!' said the third.

'Proper upset I be!' said the fourth, somewhat smugly. 'And if our Billy has the nightmares, I shan't wonder! Poor little toad, and him so high strung! I've a good mind to take him back home with me!'

She glanced sidelong at me to see how I would take this dis-play of maternal concern.

'Take him by all means!' I said. 'But I think you're being very silly. It will only make Billy think he's been in far more danger than he has. We shall all finish our lessons in the infants' room, while the skylight is being seen to.'

'Maybe that's best,' agreed the woman hastily. It was quite obvious to me, and to the rest of the mothers, that she had no real intention of being burdened with her son's presence for the rest of the day. Now that she had paraded her maternal rights she was quite prepared to give way.

'Perhaps you'd be good enough to tell the other mothers, if you happen to see them, that all's well here, and there's nothing to worry about.'

Full of importance, and heavy with the dramatic tales which they would be able to unfold, they hastened away, chattering among themselves, and I returned to Mr Willet.

He was standing on my desk, surveying the ugly splinters of glass which protr ded from the edges of the skylight's frame.

'I'll have to pull they out,' he said slowly. At every shuddering blast of wind, the skylight rattled dangerously, and it was obvious that we should have another shower of glass before long.

'Best do it from the roof,' advised Joseph Coggs, who had taken a workmanlike interest in these happenings. 'If us does it underneath us'll get glass cutting us!'

Mr Willet surveyed the small boy with respect.

'You're dead right, son.' He turned to me. 'I'll get down to Rogers at the forge and we'll bring his long ladder and get up on the roof.'

'I'll take the children out of your way,' I said, opening the dividing door in the partition, and shooing my children into their younger brothers and sisters.

''Twould be best to nail up a bit of sack, I reckons,' continued Mr Willet, still gazing aloft. 'Catch the bits, like, and keep some of the weather out. Cor! What a caper, eh? What actually done it?'

I told him about the lump of tiling and he stumped out into the playground to inspect it. His face was full of concern when he returned.

'You shouldn't 'ave 'liften that, miss! Might've raptured

yourself. Easy enough to get a rapture, heaving rocks like that!'

I said meekly that I was only trying to clear the place up.

'Ah! I daresay!' said Mr Willet gravely, 'but you wants to give a thought to your organs now and again.'

I promised that I would give my organs every consideration in the future and Mr Willet seemed mollified.

'I'll get this straightened up, and old Rogers and I'll fix something up on the roof this afternoon, till them Caxley chaps can do their bit of glazing.'

He bustled away, and I thought as I watched him go how fully he was enjoying our small upheaval. To Mr Willet, with all the time in the world, this was no annoying interruption to his potato sorting. It was an exciting happening, a bizarre quirk in the gentle pattern of his day, and a challenge to be met with courage, common sense and joyful zest.

It was Mrs Pringle who reminded me about the committee meeting in the evening.

'Can't have it here, in this glory-hole,' she said, looking at the debris with distaste. 'All catch your deaths! The vicar's bronical enough as it is!'

'That's all right,' I said, 'we'll have it at my house. I'll put a notice on the door here, and we'll send messages after school by the children. There's only about six of us on the committee.'

'At *your* place?' exclaimed Mrs Pringle. If I had suggested the school coke-pile for our rendezvous she could not have sounded more taken aback.

'Yes,' I said, 'in the dining-room. The fire's going, and there's plenty of room, and I've even got a drop of sherry somewhere.'

Mrs Pringle surveyed me morosely.

'I'd better come over and put your place to rights, when I've done this lot,' she said, as one who knows where her duty lies, no matter how unpleasant. 'Can't have the gentry in that dining-room, with that brass of yours in the state it's in. Noticed it through the windows – and they could do with a wipe over!'

I rallied as best I could under this blow, and thanked her humbly.

'That's all right,' she answered graciously. 'Flared-up leg, or no flared-up leg, I'll do you!'

'And it isn't as dirty as all that,' I felt compelled to point out, still smarting slightly from this surprise attack. 'Anyone would think I lived like a pig!'

'Hm! There's pigs and pigs!' boomed Mrs Pringle enigmatically. And limping heavily, she made a triumphant exit, before I could retaliate.

4. Reviving the Flower Show

BY seven-twenty the committee members of the Fairacre Flower Show were assembled in my freshly furbished dining-room, enjoying, I hoped, some of my sherry, and the dazzle of my unusually clean brass.

'This really is most pleasant – most pleasant,' said the vicar from the head of the table. 'We really are indebted, Miss Read, for your hospitality.' He dropped his leopard-skin gloves, now in an advanced state of moult, on to the table, and I watched a light shower of fluff settle gently on Mrs Pringle's newly polished surface.

'Nice to be able to stretch your legs,' agreed Mr Roberts, the farmer, who is over six feet tall and has to sit on, and not in, the school desks at most committee meetings.

John Pringle, Mrs Pringle's only son and a keen gardener, made the third man, and Mrs Bradley, Mrs Mawne and I made up the rest of the committee.

Mrs Bradley, in her eighties and a person of determined character, might have been known as the mother of Basil Bradley, a popular novelist, if she had not been such a dominant personality in her own right. It was she who had pressed for the revival of Fairacre's Flower Show, and it was apparent that, despite her age and deafness, she intended to play a vital part in its organization.

Mrs Mawne was a newcomer to Fairacre, although her husband, a retired schoolmaster and keen ornithologist, had lived in the village for a year or two. They had lived separately for some years, but had recently composed their differences and appeared to be peaceably settled (somewhat to the village's disappointment!) among us.

She was a large woman, as used to getting her own way, I suspected, as Mrs Bradley, and I surmised that a clash would soon arise between these two ladies. We did not have long to wait.

We had safely sketched out the different classes, such as 'Six Roots' and 'Six Onions' and so on, and had come to the more delicate task of deciding on the specific requirements of the Table Decoration class.

'Vawse of sweet peas,' said Mr Roberts. 'Can't beat sweet peas for the table.'

Mrs Bradley snorted.

'No scope! We must give people a chance to show their talents. What about a colour qualification? Say, in blue and pink?'

Mrs Mawne smiled deprecatingly and spread her hands.

'A little obvious, don't you think?' she suggested.

Mrs Bradley fell back upon her invaluable weapon of deafness.

'What say? I didn't hear you, Mrs Mawne!' she bellowed, though the dangerous glitter in her beady eyes belied her words.

Mrs Mawne, though a trifle discomfited, joined battle.

'I said,' she shouted menacingly, 'that I thought the colour idea a little obvious!'

'Oh! You did!' replied Mrs Bradley, her neck growing very red. 'Well, have you any better suggestion?'

'Indeed I have,' answered Mrs Mawne, with maddening composure. 'Several, in fact. When I was in Ireland I organized a most successful Flower Show and the table decorations fell into three classes –'

'Pshaw!' muttered Mrs Bradley testily, and fidgeted with her gloves. The vicar began to look very unhappy, and Mr Roberts and I carefully avoided each other's eye.

'One decoration to be not higher than four inches,' swept

on Mrs Mawne, enunciating with infuriating emphasis close to Mrs Bradley's unwilling ear, 'the second to be composed of the flowers of one natural order – ranunculaceae, I believe it was; and the third to be made entirely of dead flowers.'

'*Dead* flowers?' jerked out Mr Roberts, with extreme surprise. 'Oh, I don't like *dead* flowers! They smell, for one thing.'

Mrs Mawne ignored him. As a sweet pea lover he had damned himself as a Philistine for ever in her eyes.

'That sort of thing may impress the Irish,' retorted Mrs Bradley, with octogenarian vigour. 'Poor, ignorant peasants as they are – but for enlightened Fairacre folk, it just won't do. In any case,' she added, switching abruptly, 'whatever could you get, in July, four inches high?'

'Chickweed!' suggested Mr Roberts, guffawing at his own shaft of wit. Both ladies glared at him, but he was oblivious of their fury, as with his huge head tipped back he roared out his merriment.

'Perhaps we'd better leave – ' began the vicar timidly, just as I was saying:

'Annuals in a soup-plate?' in an apologetic query. The vicar fell upon this well-worn suggestion avidly.

'Excellent!' he said cheerfully, and scribbled on his little pad. 'Table decoration then, "Annuals in a Soup Plate". All agreed?'

Six hands were raised in silence, and the rest of the programme was completed in outward harmony.

'Have you heard anything about this housing estate?' queried Mr Roberts, as the ladies were collecting their gloves and handbags, and the vicar was putting his papers away in an envelope much too small for them.

'Housing estate?' said he, looking up from his task. 'Where?'

'Only a rumour, I expect,' said Mr Roberts. 'Heard it in "The Bell" at Caxley last market day. Wasn't there a bit in the papers, about new houses being needed for the atomic station?'

'But that's miles away,' said Mrs Mawne.

'Ugly great rubbishy thing!' pronounced Mrs Bradley. 'Spoiling the view!'

'And are they building a new estate there?' pursued the vicar.

'More likely here,' answered Mr Roberts.

'*Here!*' squeaked the assembled company in six different keys. The vicar was the first to find his breath.

'My dear Roberts, are you serious?'

Mr Roberts began to look uncomfortable.

'Look! I shouldn't have said anything. It's just a rumour I heard that the atomic people may choose a site near Fairacre. Someone said that Miller's land might be picked on. Hundred Acre Field, I believe – but don't spread it round.'

John Pringle now spoke in his slow, measured burr.

'I heard that too. There was two chaps looking at it recently – and it's my belief all the tittle-tattle started from that. Nothing in it, I don't suppose.'

'I certainly hope it's not true,' said the vicar decidedly. 'It's a wonderful piece of country just there – a real beauty spot.'

'Dan Crockford made one of his best pictures of the downs from the edge of Hundred Acre Field,' said Mrs Bradley, naming a local artist of some fame, who died a few years ago.

'Dan Crockford!' commented Mrs Mawne, with some scorn.

'It is a most beautiful picture, Mrs Mawne,' the vicar assured her earnestly, 'and hangs now in the Caxley Town Hall. It was in the Royal Academy early in the century.'

'And so were dozens of other quite dreadful things!' responded that lady decisively, pulling on a glove with great vigour. Mrs Bradley seized this golden opportunity.

'Dan Crockford,' she began with deadly precision, 'was one of my dearest friends, and once did me the honour of proposing marriage.' She omitted to add that this had happened after the Hunt Ball of 1902 when the exuberant young Dan had offered his heart and hand to no fewer than six ladies within an hour.

Mrs Mawne had the grace to look abashed.

'I'm sorry, Mrs Bradley. I withdraw my remarks!' Mrs

Bradley gave a stiff nod, and turned to say her farewells to me, when the vicar spoke.

'If this dreadful business does come to anything, perhaps your son might be willing to draft a few strong letters to the papers –'

'Basil would do all he could to protect his native land,' asserted the old lady militantly, and I felt extremely sorry for the unsuspecting novelist, who, I had heard, was engaged on his seventeenth historical novel and would doubtless loathe to be dragged from some elegant and urbane past century to struggle with the affairs of the twentieth.

Basil Bradley's novels had steady sales, for they mixed love, duels and history in very unequal proportions, and had the whole displayed in attractive dust jackets, showing ladies in Empire gowns reclining on those uncomfortable bolster-ended sofas which are usually upholstered in striped damask in pastel shades.

The ladies were invariably unhappily married to squat, square men, much older than themselves, with purple complexions and the gout. By about page 352, however, each heroine in turn decided that she must renounce her lover and tread the stony path of duty with her unloved husband, thus leaving four or five pages for a tearful farewell scene written in unbearably tender prose. As all Basil Bradley's books were illustrated, by a man who had been a friend of his at Oxford, this touching finale gave the artist a chance to let himself rip over the intricate wrought-iron balcony from which the heroine, with draperies fluttering, waved good-bye to the gallant and diminishing figure on horseback. Unkind critics of the artist's work had not failed to point out a noticeable feature – that of horses so far distant as to be almost incapable of recognition, the animal either being held by grooms in murky shrubberies while the hero was duelling, or else cantering with such speed that a cloud of dust obscured all but the rider's wig. They had further observed, in the captious way that critics will, that the artist was incapable of drawing a horse at all. But these waspish comments luckily made no difference to Basil Bradley's admirers, who as soon as they saw the latest reclining lady in dampened muslin, swooped upon the book and, horses or no horses, knew that here they would find several hours' pleasant entertainment.

'Well, let's hope there'll be no need for letters to the papers,' said Mr Roberts heartily, 'but if you do get a few hundred people coming here to live, you'll have some fine congregations, vicar!'

The vicar's face glowed.

'Of course, they would be in my parish! It would mean a great deal of visiting, but most interesting, most interesting. I wonder how they would get on with the village folk?'

'They'd never mix!' said Mrs Mawne. 'Nothing in common. Town dwellers mainly, and would spend their time in Caxley.'

'They'll have to have a few more buses running then,' commented Mr Roberts. 'Liven us all up, wouldn't it?'

Mrs Bradley had the last word.

'There won't be a housing estate on Dan Crockford's landscape. There could never be the slightest possibility of such a monstrous project!'

We made our farewells in the little hall, and Fairacre's Flower Show Committee made its way out into the windy night.

But despite Mrs Bradley's brave words a most unsettling occurrence was taking place at that very moment.

Far away, beyond the roaring elms and the wind-swept young wheat of Hundred Acre Field, old Mr Miller stormed vigorously up and down his firelit drawing-room. He had just returned from an evening with friends in Caxley, and had found a letter, in a long official envelope, propped up on the mantelpiece.

It was the contents of this letter which had thrown the peppery little man into such fury. His wife, still in her coat and hat, watched him with concern from her armchair.

'Come to bed! Do now, dear. Sleep on it!' she urged.

'Sleep on it! I'll never sleep!' shouted her enraged husband. He shook the letter in her face as he passed.

'Lot of jumped-up jacks-in-office! "Might come to some

fair agreement", they dare to say! Hundred Acre Field's been in our family for over a century. Do these people think I'll part with it? That they'll ever get it, while I'm alive?'

He stopped his agitated pacing and eyes blazing, he shook a fist at the ceiling.

'Let 'em try!' he roared. 'Let 'em try!'

5. Rumours Fly

NEWS of Mr Miller's letter from the Atomic Energy Authority spread rapidly. People shopping in Caxley High Street shook their heads over the affair, and the folk of Fairacre and Beech Green, between whose two villages the new housing estate would be, dropped their everyday discussion of births (unduly premature), marriages (not before time) and deaths (always whole-heartedly regretted), and turned to this more meaty fare.

Mr Miller had written a spirited reply to the letter, flatly refusing to part with an inch of land and adding a page or two of scurrilous remarks about the authority concerned, that made Mr Miller's cautious solicitor blench when he showed it to him. By the time it had been recast into language comprehensible only to the legal mind, and Mr Miller's plain refusal had been hedged about with clauses, parentheses and a whole hatful of 'heretofores', 'whereases' and 'inasmuchases', the reply ran into four pages of typing on quarto-sized paper, and was enough to make poor, frustrated Mr Miller beat his octogenarian brains out on his solicitor's desk.

'All I wanted was "No! And damn you!",' protested the fiery little man. Mr Lovejoy, who, to tell the truth, had had a most trying morning with this client, smiled placatingly.

'I can assure you,' said Mr Lovejoy, spreading his pink, smooth hands, 'that this is worded in the strongest possible manner.' He would like to have pointed out that he had just saved Mr Miller from almost certain charges of defamation of character, slander, libel and quite a dozen other obnoxious things, but he did not feel up to it. Gratitude he was not so

43

silly as to look for from this elderly firebrand, common civility he hardly dare expect in his present state of mind, and personal assault would not have surprised him.

He was relieved when Mr Miller, glancing at the clock, said he had an appointment at eleven, and made for the door.

'We'll do our very best for you in this matter, Mr Miller,' said Mr Lovejoy as his client shot through.

Exhausted, he returned to his desk, and rang for his morning coffee.

'Black, today!' he said.

April was being as warm and lovely as March had been rough and wet. The gardens in Fairacre were at their best, full of colour and fragrance, and Mr Willet's little cottage garden was one of the loveliest.

I had spent the first part of the Easter holidays with friends by the sea, but returned to Fairacre about a week before term started to do a little spring-cleaning, with Mrs Pringle's grudging assistance, some gardening and odds and ends of shopping which are difficult to fit in during term-time.

Amy, my old college friend, who lives at Bent on the other side of Caxley, spent two days with me, whilst James, her husband, was away on business, and we talked so much that we were quite hoarse.

'The trouble with you,' said Amy severely, watching me look up Mr Roberts' telephone number in the book, 'is that you don't train your mind. In some ways, you've got quite a *good* mind,' she continued, more kindly, 'but you don't *apply* it.'

I said I didn't quite follow this.

'Well, fancy wasting all that time looking up a telephone number that you must want dozens of times during the year! You should remember it!'

'But I can't!' I protested.

'You could!' insisted Amy, prodding me quite painfully with her knitting needle.

'Two, one, three!' I said, having found Mr Roberts' name.

'There you are,' said Amy triumphantly, 'what a simple

44

one to remember! Two, halve the first number, and add the two together for the third! Child's play!'

'But I've got to remember "Two" to begin with,' I argued. 'Supposing I thought of six, and halved that, and added it, and all the rest! Why, I'd probably get Caxley Swimming Bath!'

'Tchah!' said Amy. 'It's just a matter of association. For instance, I always remember my mother's number 237, because the 23 bus goes by the door, and the house is number seven.'

'Well, Mr Roberts doesn't have any buses passing his house, and the farm's called 'Walnut Tree Farm,' so that doesn't get us very far!'

'Of course, if you're going to be plain *naughty* –' said Amy loftily.

'There's always the book,' I pointed out.

'What's your car number, d'you know?' shot Amy at me.

'Yes,' I said promptly, 'It's – .' I stopped short. 'No, I don't know. I would have known if you hadn't put it out of my head by asking.'

'And what would you do,' said Amy, with heavy sarcasm, 'if a policeman asked you?'

'I'd get out and walk round to the back of the car and tell him,' I responded.

'If you hadn't *got* the car,' shouted Amy rudely.

'Then I doubt if the occasion would arise,' I answered with maddening insouciance.

Amy was on the point of gibbering, when the idiocy of the conversation overcame us both, and we laughed so much that it was some minutes before I could ring Mr Roberts. By that time I had to look his number up all over again.

We walked down to Mr Willet's cottage after tea. It was a perfect evening, sunny and still. The young leaves were more golden than green in the evening sunshine, and the birds were singing their hearts out.

Mr Willet's cottage is a thatched one, and has an uneven old brick path from the gate round to the back door. The bricks have weathered to a soft rose colour, and have brilliant emerald streaks between them where the moss grows, smooth and close as velvet ribbon. The path to the front door is seldom used. The knocker is encrusted with paint and is difficult to lift, but I remembered the story told of Arthur Coggs, our village reprobate, who had wielded that knocker energetically late one night when, afire with beer and missionary zeal, he had attempted to arouse Mr Willet's religious conscience and had only succeeded in rousing his fury.

Mr Willet, with true peasant frugality, scorns to put his precious land down to grass anywhere. The whole of this patch is dug over, with the narrowest of paths threaded here and there, and only where absolutely necessary. But he likes growing flowers as well as vegetables – unlike some of his neighbours – and his small front garden this evening was thick with velvety wallflowers of every colour, from palest yellow to deep blood red. Their scent was heady, and mingled with the clean, waxy smell of the small box edging which lined the brick path.

We found him bent double over the box edging, carefully parting the stubby branches with his gnarled hands. He was collecting snails, and dropping them, with a satisfying plop, into a pail full of salt water which stood on the path beside him.

'Kills 'em in a minute,' he told us, stirring the revolting frothy mixture with a stick. 'Snails loves a bit of box! Ten minutes' steady snailing along the box, saves a mort of damage in the garden. Come round the back, Miss Read, and see mother. She's doddlin' about there somewhere.'

We followed him to the back of the house, admiring his neat rows of vegetables as we went. A narrow strip bordering the path was devoted to flowers, and rosy double-daisies, grape hyacinths and early pansies flourished here.

'Look,' I said, 'your apple tree's breaking already!' The tight little knots of buds were beginning to show pink streaks, and it was plain that, if this warm weather lasted, Mr Willet would have his blossom within a week.

'Much too early,' said Willet, screwing up his eyes against the sun as he scrutinized this forward fellow. 'Don't like to see it! Plenty of frosts to come yet!'

He gave the grey, hoary trunk a reproving slap, and led us to the back door.

Mrs Willet was busy with her ironing, and her kitchen was filled with the comfortable smell of fresh linen.

'Take a seat, do, Miss Read,' she said, indicating two broad wooden chairs against the wall. She smiled at Amy, and I made introductions.

'I'll just finish off this shirt, and then we'll have a glass of wine,' said Mrs Willet, holding the iron to one side of her and spitting delicately upon it. A tiny ball of spittle sizzled across the surface and vanished for ever floorwards.

'Just right!' commented Mrs Willet with immense satisfaction, and plunged the iron into the depths of an armhole.

We talked while she worked, and I gave Mr Willet the message I had brought about small school repairs. Naturally, the topic of the proposed housing estate soon arose.

'I heard as 'twasn't just Hundred Acre they wanted, but a goodish bit of the downs behind,' said Mr Willet, as he leaned against the door-post. ''Tidn't right, you knows, to take farm land like that. They say old Miller's in a fair taking about it all!'

'Well, I don't know,' said Mrs Willet, hanging the shirt carefully over the clothes horse. 'You hears a lot about spoiling the view and that – but I knows one or two thinks it's a good idea!'

'And who might they be?' inquired Mr Willet, puffing out his moustache belligerently.

'Mrs Fowler, the Coggses –' began Mrs Willet.

'Faugh! That old Tylers' Row lot!' scoffed Mr Willet with scorn. 'I suppose they thinks there'll be some pickings for them out of it! Does Arthur Coggs reckon he'll get a jammy job there when they starts building? Plenty of overtime and skedaddle home when it starts to rain?'

'I suppose it would bring plenty of work,' said Amy.

'Not only work,' replied Mrs Willet, 'They reckons us'd get more buses through this way – probably some every day, not three times a week like we has it now.' Mr Willet snorted his disgust.

'Be everlasting traipsing to Caxley then, I s'pose, wasting time and money. I don't see no sense in it at all.'

'The Caxley shopkeepers might welcome the scheme,' I said doubtfully.

'They most certainly would!' said Amy with conviction. 'I was talking to Bob Lister at the ironmonger's and he reckons that a new housing estate would probably bring half as much trade again to that end of Caxley.'

'Not only Caxley,' pointed out Mrs Willet. 'They was saying down the baker's yesterday, that Tom Prince was thinking of getting another delivery van for the bread, if all these new people come. Bring trade to Fairacre and Beech Green, it would.'

'Miss Clare seemed to think that the young people in the village would welcome the buses to Caxley,' I observed. 'I know Miss Jackson hopes it will come. I must say it would give much more scope to the boys and girls who have just left school.'

'Well, I don't like to hear it even talked of,' said Mr Willet decidedly, 'I prays it won't come, and I'll back old Miller up, any day, in his fight. Why should the poor ol' feller give up his ground? He's farmed it well, ain't he, all his life? And his father before him? There's plenty of scruffy land between here and the atomic, fit for houses to be built on, without picking on as fine a bit of farming land as Hundred Acre!'

He shook his head, like a spaniel emerging from a stream.

'Ah well!' he continued, more mildly, as though this energetic shaking had rid him of all tiresome worries, 'What about that drop of wine, mother? Which d'you fancy, ladies? Cowslip or dandelion?'

'You know,' said Amy, when we were back at the schoolhouse, 'most people will agree with your Mr Willet. I can foresee a real battle about this wretched project. I know people in Caxley are furious about it, on the whole – particularly the *avant-garde* of the artistic group,' added Amy shrewdly.

'Are they all admirers of Dan Crockford?' I asked in some surprise.

'Dear me, no!' exclaimed Amy, 'but when you've gone to the expense of papering one wall different from the rest and buying a Degas to put on it, you're not going to see *any* artist's landscape defiled for the sake of a mere atomic power station. You see, they'll be firmly on Mr Willet's side.'

'It was the farming value of the land that weighed with Mr Willet,' I objected.

'It's the aesthetic value that will tell in the end,' forecast Amy, 'Just wait and see!'

'I hope you're right,' I said fervently.

Term started, and the children returned looking fit and brown, having been able to play outside during the fine sunny days of the holiday. I was sorry to see that three children – all from one family – had left the village and that our numbers were down to thirty-two, seventeen in my class and only fifteen in the infants' room.

'It's the smallest that the school has ever been,' I said to Miss Jackson, looking sadly at her little class. The children were drinking their bottles of milk, sucking steadily through their straws, and gazed owlishly over the top at us as we talked. 'There were over forty here when I first came.'

'People don't have so many children these days,' explained Miss Jackson kindly, as though I had been speaking of mid-Victorian times. 'They have fought for a higher standard of living, and intend to maintain it, which means that the family must be a more economic size. With the overthrow of the tyranny of church superstitions, and the setting-up of family-planning clinics –'

'All right! All right!' I broke in testily, 'there's no need to talk to me like some pink left-wing paper! And in any case, it isn't so much the size of the family, but the move to the towns that's depleting us here. This makes the third family within a year to leave Fairacre. They've all gone nearer the atomic station. Mr Roberts is still looking for a really reliable cow-man.'

'We shall get an influx when the new housing estate goes up,' observed Miss Jackson, 'or will they all go to Beech Green School?'

'I should think the children would go to either,' I said, shaking my head at a very naughty little boy who had decided to empty the dregs of his milk bottle into the ear of his neighbour. 'I wonder if we shall have to have any new buildings?'

'More likely to have a colossal new school on the estate,' hazarded Miss Jackson, rescuing the milk bottle.

I felt uncomfortably jolted.

'I never thought of that!' I answered slowly.

I drove over to the Annetts' house that evening for my weekly baby-sitting session.

Young Malcolm was having his jumping practice at the end of the cot, singing a tuneless and breathless accompaniment to this exercise. To his mother and to me, peeping through the crack of the bedroom door at this bundle of energy, it looked as though he would be at it for at least another hour.

The usual thousand-and-one last minute injunctions were given me by the departing mother, while her husband brought in coal and logs, for the evening was turning chilly, gave me the *Telegraph*, *The Times Educational Supplement*, *The Farmer's Weekly* and *Eagle* – the last, I suspected, confiscated from one of his pupils. I decided to read that first, whilst giving an ear to Isobel's directions.

'Let him jump until he falls asleep, and if you can get him into the right end of the bed, all the better. If not, tuck him up where he's asleep. If he stirs, you'll find the old shawl he takes to bed with him, somewhere among the covers, unless he's thrown it over the side. If he's wrinkled up his mackintosh sheet and you can possibly straighten it without waking him, it would be a help.

'I've left some boiled water in a blue jug on his bunny tray in the kitchen – not the white jug – that's got orange juice in it. And if he really seems hungry he can have some warm milk, preferably in his mug, but if he's really being frantically naughty put it into his bottle and he may drop asleep as he takes it that way. I'm trying to break him of the bottle, but he has it occasionally at bed time.'

I said I would remember all this, reaching for Dan Dare. Mr Annett called anxiously from the hall.

'It's past seven, Isobel!'

'Coming!' said she, throwing a scarf round her neck and grabbing her violin. 'Oh! And one last thing, take the bottle away as soon as he's asleep!'

I said that I would. Dan Dare appeared to be in a most awkward predicament, having been hoisted on a crane of some sort, by green-faced men with claws and legs like birds. I was dying to read about his adventures.

'You are a dear,' said Isobel giving me a hasty kiss, and knocking Dan Dare to the floor unnoticed. She rushed from the room and I heard the front door slam. I bent down to retrieve *Eagle* and heard the front door open again. Isobel's head appeared round the door. She looked extremely agitated.

'Of course, if he's *emptied* the bottle *before* he's asleep, take it away in any case, or he'll get the most *frightful* wind!'

She vanished before I could reply. The door slammed again, the car gave a distant and impatient hoot, and finally drove off towards Caxley.

I listened to my charge. He was still jumping rhythmically in the distance.

Sighing luxuriously, I leant back in my chair and put my feet up on a footstool. In ten minutes' time, I reckoned, I should insert my young god-child into the right end of his bed, put his comforting old shawl into his sleeping hand, and forget him.

Meanwhile, I turned my attention to Dan Dare, who, I was sorry to see, was in an even worse plight in the last picture than in the first with the green-faced crane operators.

Peace descended on Beech Green school-house as I read *Eagle* avidly from cover to cover, to the accompaniment of the distant squeakings of cot springs. Gradually, the squeakings grew less frequent, and finally stopped.

Heaving myself from the chair, and throwing Dan Dare aside, I made my way upstairs to attend to my duties.

6. Trouble and Love

MISS CLARE was busy putting the last minute touches to the supper table. It had been a lovely day, and she had been pleased when Miss Jackson had said, at tea-time, that she thought she would cycle into Caxley and call on a friend there.

'We might go to the pictures,' she had said, 'so don't wait supper for me if I'm a little late. It just depends how we feel.'

Miss Clare had been delighted to hear about the friend. She knew that she had met one or two young teachers in the town, but had feared that her lodger's unswerving devotion to Miss Crabbe, the psychology lecturer, might stand in the way of any warm friendship elsewhere. With great delicacy Miss Clare refrained from asking the sex of the Caxley friend, but hoped, for Miss Jackson's sake, that it was male, and that he was young, single and good looking. She was inclined to think, however, that the friend was much more likely to be female, and if it were that new gym mistress she, alas! was no more prepossessing than Miss Jackson herself, thought Miss Clare sadly.

By ten o'clock Miss Clare was beginning to think of bed, for she had risen at half past six as was her custom. She looked out of the window at the clear sky, and breathed in the fragrance from her garden. The lilac was in flower, and she could see the plumy pyramids of blossom outlined against the stars.

It was nearly eleven before Miss Jackson arrived. Miss Clare heard her calling goodbye, and a man's voice replying, in the distance. Then came the sound of Miss Jackson's bicycle thrown, with a clatter, into the shed. The back door burst open, and Miss Jackson with flushed face and shining eyes, stood before her. She looked very happy.

'Oh! You shouldn't have waited up,' she said reproachfully. 'I was later than I meant to be. We went to the pictures after all.'

Miss Clare enquired about the film. Yes, she was told, it was most awfully good, but rather a short programme. They had come out at a quarter to ten.

Miss Clare looked a little surprised, and Miss Jackson rattled on.

'We were so thirsty that we went into "The Bell" for a drink,' she explained, somewhat defiantly. 'Anything wrong with that?'

Miss Clare felt vaguely uncomfortable. It was obvious that Miss Jackson was very much on the defensive, and Miss Clare was beginning to wonder why. So far no name had been given to the friend, and whether it was male or female Miss Clare did not really know – but she was beginning to suspect that the friend was a man, and one that Miss Jackson felt she would not approve of.

'I don't know that "The Bell" is a very pleasant place for two girls to enter unescorted,' answered Miss Clare mildly, 'I see from *The Caxley Chronicle* that it is frequented by a number of Irish labourers who appear regularly before the magistrate.' She had chosen her words with some guile, and her manner was pleasant. Miss Jackson bolted her last mouthful of pie, and placed her knife and fork across her plate, with exaggerated deliberation.

'As it happens,' she said, raising her thick eyebrows, 'I was accompanied by a man.' Miss Clare congratulated herself privately upon eliciting this information. 'And what's more, he saw me home, so I was well looked after.'

'I'm glad to hear it,' said Miss Clare gently, pushing the cheese dish towards her lodger. 'Would you take some of my dark purple lilac to Miss Read in the morning?' she continued, skating gracefully away from thin ice. 'She has a lovely pale one, I know but no deep purple.'

'Of course I will,' said Miss Jackson heartily. She seemed relieved that the subject had been changed, and Miss Clare's misgivings grew. Who on earth could it be? She pondered the question as she made her way wearily up the little staircase.

Although it was late, it was some time before Miss Clare fell asleep. Her lodger had gone, singing, to bed. Miss Clare had waited for the two thumps which were the sign that Miss Jackson's shoes had been kicked off, for the click of the light switch, and the final creak as Miss Jackson clambered into the high feather bed.

Somewhere, in the velvety darkness, a nightingale throbbed out his song from a spray of blossom. He was urgent and languorous in turn, now brittle and staccato, now pouring forth a low, steady ripple of bubbling sound. Miss Clare lay in her shadowy room, listening to him, and thinking of the girl beyond the wall, so young, so very ignorant, and so pathetically sure of herself.

'She's really old enough to know what she's about,' Miss Clare told herself, 'And yet – how I wish her parents were here.'

She heard the church clock at Beech Green strike two before she fell asleep. And still the nightingale sang of love and trouble, trouble and love, as though his heart were full to overflowing.

It was Amy who first told me that Miss Jackson and the Franklyn man had been seen about together, on several occasions, in Caxley.

'They were in the cinema the other night,' said Amy, 'holding hands and with eyes only for each other. I wonder why courting couples pay good money to sit through films which must be a great interruption to them?'

'Nowhere else to go, I expect,' I said, trying to sound less concerned than I felt. 'But Amy, are you sure it was Franklyn?'

'How do I know?' said Amy reasonably enough, 'But Joy Miller was with me, and she said that she thought it was her uncle's gamekeeper from Springbourne. He was a biggish fellow with sandy hair and white eyelashes. Most unattractive I thought, but there – love is blind, they say.'

'It certainly sounds like him,' I observed. Amy and I had met one Saturday morning and were now having coffee together. We stirred our cups in silence.

'Isn't it the limit?' I said, after a bit.

'Jealous?' asked Amy slyly.

'No I'm blowed if I am!' I responded inelegantly, and with sudden warmth. 'The older I get, the more delighted I am that I'm single. Love seems a frightful nuisance.'

'Sure you're not having a reaction from Mr Mawne's perfidious attentions?' suggested Amy. 'Is this the brave front put on by an unfulfilled female of uncertain age?'

I looked at her acidly across the rickety oak table.

'If you're going to act the goat, and talk like that ghastly Crabbe woman Miss Jackson's always thrusting down my throat,' I said coldly, 'I shall leave you at once – and what's more, you can pay the bill!'

'Pax, pax!' said Amy hastily, crossing her fingers. 'Take back all I said! See my finger wet, see my finger dry, may I slit my throat, if –'

'All right, all right!' I broke in upon her gabbling, 'But talk sense for a moment. Do you really think Miss Jackson is serious about this man?'

'Looked like it,' said Amy.

'But he must be nearly forty – and his wife's only been dead a few months,' I objected.

'Just when he'd feel the need for a little sympathy and feminine company,' replied Amy, 'And dozens of men are at their most attractive at forty. What's against him? Do you think that his intentions are *not* matrimonial?'

'I don't think he'd marry Miss Jackson for a minute,' I said. 'And a very good thing too. It would be quite unsuitable. They've absolutely nothing in common. He's already got a daughter, he has a bad name in the village, and Miss Jackson's such an utter fool that she'd never see anything until she was in a complete mess, and then she'd be too pig-headed to ask for help. I don't like this business at all. If you ask me, he's a thoroughly bad lot!'

Mrs Pringle thought so too. I had wondered how soon the rumours would begin to fly, after Amy's disclosure over the coffee-cups. I had not long to wait.

Within three days Mrs Pringle broached the subject, obliquely, and with nauseating self-righteousness.

I was alone in the classroom after school. The children had gone home, and Miss Jackson had pedalled off towards Beech Green. Mrs Pringle, trudging through to the infants' room, with two brooms under one arm and a dust pan clutched across her stomach, stopped, ostensibly to pick a toffee paper from the floor, but in fact to impart and receive any news of Miss Jackson's affairs.

'Seems to have settled down nicely, she do,' said Mrs Pringle, in such dulcet tones that I was instantly on my guard. 'I like to see a girl happy.'

I made a non-committal noise and continued to look for a form which the office had told me (with some irritability) I had been asked to return three weeks ago. It did not appear to be in the drawer allotted – on the whole – to forms.

'A good day's work when Miss Jackson moved in with Miss Clare,' went on Mrs Pringle, raising her voice slightly. 'Not that she wasn't well looked after with you, I don't doubt,' she said, with the air of one telling a white lie, 'but she do look a bit more cheeful. Plumper too!' she added, with some malice, annoyed that I still turned over my papers busily.

'I didn't starve her, you know,' I observed mildly, opening the gummed paper drawer. The thing must be somewhere!

Mrs Pringle gave a high forced laugh.

'The very idea! We all knows that – but Miss Clare seems to suit her best, and of course, being young she's soon finding friends.'

'Naturally,' I said shortly, slamming in the gummed paper drawer, and opening the one with the log books and catalogues from educational publishers. It looked like being a hopeless search.

Mrs Pringle began to close in upon her subject.

'Not that I'm one to criticize. It's not my place, as I said to my husband when he repeated some gossip he'd heard about her down at "The Beetle" last night – but we've all got our own ideas, and say what you like, there's still such a thing as class.'

The form was not to be found in the log book drawer. I armed myself with a ruler, and set about getting into the drawer which holds envelopes full of cardboard money, packets of raffia needles, a set of archaic reading cards embellished with pictures of bearded men, ladies with bustles and little girls in preposterous hats and buttoned boots, and various other awkward objects known to all school teachers. By pulling the drawer open a crack, thrusting in the ruler upon the seething mass within, and bearing down heavily, it was just possible to jerk it open. (Every teacher who is not soullessly efficient has at least one drawer like this. I have several.)

Mrs Pringle warmed to her theme as I struggled.

'She's got all the world before her. A young girl like that, speaks nice, been to college, can read and write – why, she could have anyone! They do say there's someone interested. *Some-one*, I won't say a *gentleman*, because that he isn't, not by any manner of means! But we all hope that that young thing won't have her head turned, and by someone no better than he should be.'

I felt that it was time to speak.

'Mrs Pringle, do try and scotch any gossip about Miss Jackson. She's quite old enough to choose her own friends.'

'Ah! but do her parents know who she's going round with? Their only daughter, I understand.' Her tone grew lugubrious, and she assumed the pious look that the choir boys mimic behind her back.

'Their one tender chick,' she continued, with an affecting tremor in her voice. I thought of Miss Jackson's sturdy frame and attempted to keep my face straight. 'How would you like it, if she was your daughter? Think now, if she was!'

I did. But not for long.

'Look, Mrs Pringle,' I replied, 'I think you're all making far too much of Miss Jackson's innocent affairs. She is in Miss Clare's care – and mine, for that matter – and writes regularly to her parents, and frequently goes home to see them. There are far too many busy-bodies in this village!' I ended roundly, thrusting the last drawer back. Heaven alone knew where that form had vanished!

Mrs Pringle drew in a long, outraged breath. Hitching up her burdens, she continued her journey into the infants' room. Her leg, I noticed, was dragging badly.

Soon after this brush with Mrs Pringle, I was invited to tea at the vicarage.

The tea was set out on the verandah, sheltered from the wind and bathed in warm sunshine. Mrs Partridge had spread a very dashing cloth of red and white checks over the spindly iron table. This round table was painted white, and its legs were most intricately embellished with scrolls, fleur-de-lys and flourishes, with here and there a spot of red rust, for the table stood outside in all weathers.

A motley collection of chairs helped to furnish the verandah. Mrs Partridge, presiding over the tea-pot, sat in a creaking wicker chair which had once been cream in colour, but had weathered to grey. The vicar lay back in a chaise-longue, with his stomach skywards, until he was passed his cup of tea, when he straightened up, planted a leg on each side of his perch, and sat well forward, nearly split in half.

Mr and Mrs Mawne, who were also of the party, were more comfortably placed in canvas arm-chairs of a more upright nature. They sat very straight, to avoid knocking their cups off the narrow wooden arms, and looked remarkably careful and prim.

I think I was the worst off, for my seat was a basket chair, very close to the floor so that my legs could either be stretched straight ahead or pulled in with my knees just under my chin. No compromise seemed possible, and I feared that my best nylon stockings were taking a severe] tousling] from the wicker work which caught them maliciously from time to time.

Despite our discomforts, however, the tea was excellent, the sun shone and we chattered away cheerfully enough. Mr Mawne told the vicar about a whitethroat's nest he had discovered, built in a most extraordinary position; Mrs Mawne told me how the Women's Institute should be run, and Mrs Partridge, who is President of Fairacre W.I., listened unperturbed and poured tea for her critic, in the kindest manner.

It was Mr Mawne who first mentioned the proposed housing site.

'A scandal if that land is taken for building!' he said, chopping up a piece of chocolate cake viciously. 'More larks there to the square yard than anywhere else in England!'

'Have you heard any more?' asked Mrs Mawne, deflected momentarily from her account of the lost splendours of former W.I.s run by herself.

'I was on the telephone this morning,' said the vicar, 'to Miller – about an address I needed – and evidently things are moving.'

'Which way?' asked Mrs Mawne.

'As far as I could gather – and I must say he was so very – er – *cross* about the whole affair, that it was difficult to hear him clearly – it seems that he has had a letter pointing out that the land can be purchased compulsorily, if need be, and that the proposals are now in the hands of the County Council.'

'But we just *can't* have a great ugly housing estate on our doorsteps!' exclaimed Mrs Partridge, voicing the feelings of us all.

'Think what an enormous parish you'd have!' said Mr Mawne to the vicar, who had gently tipped back to his prone position, with his legs up.

'Think of the visiting!' said Mrs Partridge. There was a touch of horror in her tone.

'They might,' said the vicar, in a small voice, addressing the roof of the verandah, 'I say it is *just* possible that they *might* have a small church of their own.'

There was a shocked silence. It was broken by Mr Mawne, who shifted his canvas chair nearer to the vicar, with a horrible scraping noise on the tiles, and looked down upon him.

'You mean, it's going to be *that big*?' he enquired.

The vicar heaved himself upright again and straddled his leg-rest as though he were riding a horse.

'No one knows, but there's no doubt that five or six hundred workers are to be taken on. Then there are their families. They'll need a lot of houses, and I believe a row of shops is envisaged. Miller gave me to understand that the preliminary layout provided for a playing field as well.'

'Shall we have enough room at Fairacre School – and Beech Green – for all the children?' I asked.

The vicar turned his gentle gaze upon me. His face was troubled.

'It's possible,' he began slowly, 'that a school is planned for the estate as well.'

We looked at each other in silence. You could have heard a pin drop on the verandah.

'And my school,' I answered, equally slowly, 'is dwindling steadily in numbers –'

The vicar jumped to his feet, and smote me on the shoulder.

'It shall never close!' he declared militantly, his eyes flashing, 'Never! Never!'

PART TWO

The Storm Breaks

7. Miss Jackson's Errand

THE early summer months were bathed in sunshine, and Fairacre shimmered in the heat. The shining days followed, one after the other, like blue and white beads on a string, as every morning dawned clear.

The hay crop was phenomenal, and was carried with little of the usual anxiety at this time. Wild roses spangled the hedges, buttercups gilded the fields, and even in such raggle-taggle gardens as the Coggs' beauty still flowered, for the neglected elder bushes were already showing their creamy, aromatic blossoms.

The shabby thatch, which served the four cottages comprising Tyler's Row, was bleached to ash-blonde with age and the continued heat. In the garden of the second cottage Jimmy Waites, now nearly eight years old, was having the time of his life.

His mother, worn down at last by repeated entreaties, had allowed him to have the family zinc bath on the minute grass patch, and had let him put two inches of water in the bottom.

'But no more, mind!' she had said firmly. 'The well's getting that low, and us all shares it as you know. And don't tell your father as I let you have it – or there'll be no supper for you tonight!'

She spoke more sternly than she felt, for she was smarting from a guilty conscience not only about the use of precious water, but also of the bath itself. She was a good-natured mother, and had sympathized with her young son's craving for cool water on such a day. She watched him indulgently, through the kitchen window, as he splashed and capered in the bath, clad respectably in an old bathing suit of his sister's, that clung hideously to his brown legs.

To a gap in the hedge came the three eldest Coggs children, Joseph and his younger twin sisters. They watched enviously, their eyes and mouths like so many O's, as the bright drops glittered in the sunshine around the capering form of their lucky neighbour.

'Can us come?' growled Joseph, in his husky gipsy voice. The capering stopped. Jimmy advanced towards the trio, with delicious cool runnels of water trickling down his legs.

'Dunno. I'll ask my mum,' responded Jimmy.

Mrs Waites heard this exchange, and was torn between pity and exasperation. She had become very fond of Joseph whilst his mother had been away in hospital some time before, but did not care to encourage the family too much, for there was no denying the dirtiness and slap-dash ways which might undermine her own child's more respectable upbringing. She had, since Mrs Coggs' return, become a little more intimate with that dejected lady, lending her the weekly magazine which she took regularly, and occasionally handing over outgrown garments for Joseph. Arthur Coggs was notorious in Fairacre. 'A useless article,' was Mr Willet's summing-up of the head of the Coggs family, and Fairacre agreed.

Mrs Waites heard the padding of bare feet at the kitchen door, and opened it hastily. No need to have the clean brick floor all messed-up, she told herself, looking down into the upturned face of her youngest child. His blue eyes, bluer than the cloudless sky behind his fair head, melted her heart as usual.

'All right,' she said good-naturedly, 'let 'em come for a bit.'

With squeals of delight the three children squeezed through the ragged hedge, and hurled their battered sandals aside. Mrs Coggs hurried from her back door to see what caused this commotion and stood, nonplussed, at the sight that met her eyes. Mrs Waites hurried from her own cottage to reassure her. They stood, one each side of the hedge, and watched the four children jumping ecstatically up and down in the zinc bath.

'They likes a drop of water,' said Mrs Coggs indulgently. 'Pity there ain't no ponds much round here. The Caxley kids has the swimming bath, of course. They's lucky!' Her tone was envious.

'From what I hear,' said Mrs Waites, with some importance, 'Fairacre might get a swimming bath before long if that new estate comes along.'

Mrs Coggs looked suitably impressed.

'My! I hope it does then,' she said emphatically. 'That's what us wants for our kids, ain't it?'

Mrs Coggs's tacit assumption that she and Mrs Waites were united, jarred upon Mrs Waites considerably. She at once disassociated herself from such low company.

'Not that there won't be plenty against a new estate,' she said, as one explaining matters to a backward child. 'The high-ups is in a fine old fever already. And quite right too!' she added righteously. 'That's a real pretty view over there to Beech Green!' In a few sentences she had ranged herself on the side of those who Lead Affairs in Fairacre, and poor Mrs Coggs looked bewildered, and, once again, an outcast.

'But 'tis only a field!' she protested.

'It won't be if they builds houses all over it,' pointed out Mrs Waites.

'Well, I don't know, I'm sure,' said Mrs Coggs miserably, and faltered to a stop. It was obvious that she had put her foot in it somewhere, but just where and how, she could not determine. She made a fumbling attempt to get matters right again.

'Still, us might get a few more buses and that. 'Twould make it easier for shopping to be able to go to Caxley any day like.'

Mrs Waites agreed graciously. Somewhat emboldened, Mrs Coggs continued diffidently.

'Which reminds me! I wanted to slip up the shop for half a pound of broken biscuits. Would the kids be in your way?'

Mrs Waites, still in her role of great lady, was about to grant permission for Mrs Coggs' temporary absence, in suitably cool terms, when a cry from the zinc bath attracted her attention.

'Look at Jim!' crowed Joseph Coggs admiringly. Jimmy stood poised on his hands, in the water. His fair hair hung like a mop and his wet shining legs pointed towards the vivid sky.

'Ain't he *clever*!' squealed Joseph, beside himself. Touched by this tribute Mrs Waites' warm heart melted entirely. She cast a compassionate glance upon the bedraggled mother beside her.

Some life she had of it, poor toad, thought Mrs Waites. She

spoke gently, jettisoning the refined accent she had used during the conversation, and using her homely country burr.

'You be off, m'dear! Us'll be all right here. Yours can have a bite of tea with our Jimmy in the garden. You take your time!'

On an equally hot day, during the following week, Miss Clare and her lodger sat at tea in the cottage garden. A sycamore tree threw a welcome patch of shade across the sunny lawn and here the two sat eating bread and butter spread with lemon curd of Miss Clare's own making. A massive fruit cake, well stuffed with plums, stood on the table before them, and would have delighted the heart of Doctor Martin had he been there to see it.

A bumble bee fumbled about the flower border near by, and his droning added to the languor of the summer afternoon. Miss Clare, watching him, spoke slowly.

'I quite forgot to give you the jumble sale parcel this morning,' she said. 'Do you think the eldest Kelly boy is reliable enough to take it over to Springbourne?'

Miss Jackson appeared to give the matter some thought, and then replied quite excitedly.

'Would you like me to take it this evening? It is no distance on a bicycle, and I think it might be rather heavy for Tim Kelly.'

'But it's so hot, my dear,' protested Miss Clare, 'and quite a pull up through the wood. And then you don't know where Mrs Chard lives, do you? She's collecting the jumble at her house.'

Miss Jackson waved aside these little difficulties.

'You can easily tell me, and I'd really like to go out for a little while. I wanted to collect some twigs for the nature table, in any case, and the wood will be quite cool for doing that.'

Miss Clare was pleasantly surprised at her lodger's readiness to undertake this errand. The jumble sale was to take place on the following evening and she had promised Mrs Chard that her contribution would be delivered in good time.

'If you're sure –' she began diffidently.

'Quite sure!' replied Miss Jackson, putting her plate on the tray, and rising with unaccustomed animation. 'I'll just go and change into a cooler frock and then set off.'

She ran into the cottage, omitting to carry anything with her, noted Miss Clare sadly. She saw her head bobbing about in the bedroom window as she opened and shut drawers. Miss Clare stacked the tea things methodically on the tray. The magnificent cake remained uncut and Miss Clare, though still a trifle hungry, would not think of broaching it for herself alone. The shade of Doctor Martin seemed to approach and speak to her. 'Eat something else, Dolly!' it said authoritatively. Obeying her conscience, and smiling as she did so, Miss Clare meekly ate the last slice of bread and butter before gathering up her tray and returning, across the shimmering lawn, to the kitchen whose cool shadows fell like a benison around her.

She heard the girl above singing as she clattered about the ancient floorboards. Miss Clare washed the cups and saucers carefully in the silky rain water, and dried them lovingly with a linen cloth that was thin but snowy-white.

Miss Jackson burst in upon her as she was replacing the china on the kitchen dresser. Her lodger's face was shining, her hair carefully dressed, and she wore a becoming yellow cotton frock.

'How pretty you look!' cried Miss Clare. 'Don't spoil that lovely dress picking twigs.' She indicated the parcel which stood on the kitchen chair.

'Are you sure you can manage it?' she asked earnestly.

Miss Jackson swung it up easily and made for the door.

'Don't worry, I'll enjoy it! Just tell me where Mrs Chard lives, then I'll be off.'

The two of them walked together to the shed to collect the bicycle and then to the front gate. Miss Clare gave her directions clearly and slowly. Miss Jackson appeared impatient to be off.

At last she mounted the bicycle, waved erratically, and pushed steadily along the lane towards the rough track that led from the Fairacre road over the hill to the little valley where Springbourne lay.

It was only when Miss Clare had settled herself once again in the deck chair that something occurred to her.

The lonely track which Miss Jackson must traverse ran close beside the cottage belonging to John Franklyn.

Hilary Jackson, with the sun full upon her face, zigzagged laboriously up the chalky cart track. She had to keep carefully to the middle of the pathway for the ruts made by farm carts and tractors were deep and dangerous. Ahead she could see the welcome shade of the wood. Behind her rose a light cloud of chalky dust sent up by her bicycle wheels.

The path grew steeper, and some distance before it entered the wood the girl gave up pedalling and dismounted. It was very quiet. The fields sloped down to the Fairacre road which shimmered in the distance. The warm air was murmurous with the humming of myriad wings, and beside her, as she wandered with one hot hand on the handlebars, two blue butterflies skirmished together above the tall pollen-dusty grass.

Her head throbbed with exertion but also with excitement. Very soon she knew she would be approaching the cottage where John Franklyn, the gamekeeper, lived. His daughter Betty was now safely with the aunt in Caxley and he would be alone in the little house. She looked at her watch. It said twenty minutes past five. With any luck he would be at home, and perhaps he would speak to her. She quickened her pace, steadied Miss Clare's parcel which swayed across the bicycle basket, and entered the woods.

It was like stepping into an old, old church from a sunny field. The sudden chill raised gooseflesh on the girl's scorched arms, and the sudden quiet gloom, after the singing brightness of the chalky fields, created a feeling of awe. The companionable murmuring of insects had gone and silence engulfed her. The trees stood straight and tall, menacingly aloof, and to the girl, in her highly-strung state, they appeared like watchful sentinels who passed and repassed each other in the distance as she moved nervously between them.

On each side of the path festoons of small-leaved honeysuckle draped low branches of hazel bushes, and the cloying sweetness of its perfume blended with the moist fragrance compounded of damp earth, moss and the resinous breath of many close-packed trees. The path was damp beneath her feet and muffled the sound made by her sandals and the wheels of the bicycle. To give herself courage Miss Jackson looked at her watch again. Why, it was still really afternoon! Nothing to fear in a wood at five-thirty! If the watch had said midnight, now! She had a sudden terrifying picture of inky trees, a slimy path, and a furtive, leering, sickening moon sliding behind crooked branches. Owls would be abroad, screeching and cackling, and bats, deformed and misshapen, would leave their topsy-turvy slumbers and swoop out upon their horrid businesses. She took a deep, shuddering breath, pushed such fancies resolutely behind her, and, in two minutes had reached the bend of the lane which brought her within sight of the gamekeeper's cottage.

It stood quite close to the path, tucked into the side of a steep slope which rose sharply behind it. The garden was narrow, and lay to the side of the house bordering the track through the woods. The currant bushes were heavy with fruit, and the acrid smell of blackcurrants was wafted to the girl as she dawdled past. She noticed the tidy rows of vegetables, the two apple trees, sprucely pruned, and already bearing a crop of small green apples. A rough shed, painted with tar to protect it from the dripping of the surrounding trees, stood at the far end of the garden. Hilary could see that the door was shut and the padlock fastened as she passed by it.

She looked at the cottage hopefully but her heart sank as she noticed the closed windows and door. She could see no movement anywhere. The windows were dirty and the curtains looked grubby. Clearly the mistress of the house was here no more, and the neglected dwelling place contrasted strongly with the trim garden in which it stood.

Disappointment flooded the girl's heart, but relief too, for she half-realized that she felt fear as well as infatuation for this odd soft-spoken man who had noticed her. She was now past the house, rising steadily, until in a few moments she could stop and look down upon its tiled roof, stained with lichens and bird-droppings and streaked with murky tears shed by the trees overhead. In a dappled patch of sunlight at the side of the house she could now see a small tabby kitten rolling luxuriously in some dry earth beneath a jutting window sill. It looked up, startled, as she chirruped to it, and fled helter-skelter out of sight.

At the top of the hill Hilary Jackson paused for breath and looked down upon the hamlet of Springbourne scattered below in the valley. Ah, there was Mrs Chard's white house, with the pine tree at its gate, just as Miss Clare had said.

She smoothed her yellow frock, adjusted the parcel once more, and clambered up into the saddle. The wind rushed past her, cooling her flushed face and quieting her restless heart. Within five minutes she was pushing open Mrs Chard's green gate and approaching the open door.

8. The Gamekeeper's Cottage

WHILE Hilary Jackson sat in Mrs Chard's cool green and white drawing-room sipping a glass of lemon squash and listening to her hostess's ecstatic comments as she unpacked the parcel of jumble, the vicar of Fairacre was talking to Mr Mawne.

The two men lay back in deck chairs in the shade of a fine copper beech tree which John Parr's great-grandfather had planted. Upon Mr Mawne's chest were lodged his binoculars. which he frequently clapped to his eyes the better to observe some distant bird on the far side of the garden. Upon the vicar's chest lay his folded hands, pink and damp with the heat, and above them his mild old face looked aloft worriedly.

'And Philpotts should know,' he was saying. 'He is one of the chaps on the rural district council, and a most reliable fellow.'

'Sh! Sh!' hissed his companion, adjusting his binoculars, and making his deck chair emit noises far more violent than his friend's gentle voice. The vicar was obediently quiet until the binoculars were lowered again.

'And it means,' continued the vicar in a gusty whisper, 'that the rural district council have seen the plans, and there's no doubt about it that a school will be needed on the site.' He sighed heavily, and a blackbird rattled from a hawthorn tree, scolding and squawking madly. The vicar looked penitent.

'I'm so sorry, my dear Mawne! Another bird that I've scared, I'm afraid.'

'That's nothing,' said Mr Mawne indulgently. 'Carry on. So what's worrying you?'

'Why! My school!' said the vicar sitting suddenly bolt upright and turning his wide-opened eyes upon his friend. 'Don't you see, it may mean that our children are taken by bus to this new school, and Fairacre school may close!'

'I don't believe it!' said Mr Mawne with conviction. 'Fairacre school won't be closed as long as the parents want it to stay open.'

'I hope you're right. Indeed, I hope you're right,' said Mr Partridge, in a troubled voice, 'but the numbers have dwindled to almost thirty – and I don't know – ' His voice trailed away unhappily. Silence fell between the two men. Far away a cow lowed, and a tiny stealthy sound from the hawthorn tree made Mr Mawne raise his binoculars again and scrutinize it for some minutes. Finally he lowered them, pulled the strap over his head and replaced them in the leather case which lay on the grass at his feet. He spoke with decision.

'I think you're worrying yourself unnecessarily, but to put your mind at rest why don't you go and see someone at the county council offices, and see what the plans are for your school and Beech Green's?'

'It's an idea,' responded the vicar slowly.

'The local authority will have the job of providing the new school,' went on Mr Mawne, snapping the clasp on his binoculars, 'and they'll know what's happening to the existing schools if this business goes through.'

He looked at his old friend and clapped him on the shoulder. 'Cheer up!' he said, struggling from his deck chair. 'Come and have a glass of sherry. These gnats are getting me.'

He held out his hand to the vicar and hauled him to his feet.

'You've given me new heart,' confessed the vicar, as they

made their way into the house. 'I'll do that.' A sudden jangling of church bells broke out in the distance.

'Bless my soul!' exclaimed the vicar. 'Half past six already! The bellringers have started practising promptly tonight.'

He sank back into an armchair and accepted the glass of sherry, which his friend carried over to him, with great care.

'You're a good fellow, Mawne,' he said. 'You've comforted me with words, and now with wine.' He raised his glass to his host before he sipped.

The sound of the bells ringing floated across the warm evening air to Hilary Jackson as she made her return journey. The slope up from the Springbourne valley was shorter but steeper than that from the Fairacre road and the girl was obliged to go on foot, wheeling her dusty bicycle. Her thoughts raced ahead of her slow feet. Would he be back yet? Should she knock at his door? She was torn between a wild strange excitement which drove her on, and nagging doubts, half-fearful, which held her back. Hilary Jackson was in love for the first time.

For a girl of twenty-odd she had very little experience of men. An only child, educated at a girls' school and going from thence straight on to a women's training college, where the redoubtable Miss Crabbe had engaged her affections and admiration, she had had little occasion to mix with the opposite sex. John Franklyn's casual attentions had lit a greater fire than he would ever guess in the foolish heart of this girl. Despite the rumours which rumbled round Fairacre, and which were causing Miss Clare and Miss Read such heart-burning, the meetings of the two had been by chance, except on the occasion of the visit to the cinema. John Franklyn had been pleasantly surprised by the ardour with which his casual invitation had been accepted. He flirted, as a matter of course, with any woman, but with young Miss Jackson he had tempered his usual bonhomie with a certain amount of reserve due, he felt, to the teacher of his daughter. He had not bargained for the response which he had received and, truth to tell, was half-embarrassed by it. Like all countrymen he wished to avoid trouble, and he disliked the sly teasings which he feared might get to the ears of his sister in Caxley who was giving a home to his child. It would 'look bad' to have this girl tagging after him, he told himself, but at the same time his vanity was flattered. He had loved his wife, and he missed her sorely; and though he had no intention of asking Hilary Jackson to become his second, he was in need of comfort and tempted to accept it, at the moment, from any source.

As Hilary Jackson approached the cottage she became conscious of the homely smell of frying onions. The door of the tarred shed now stood open and the little cat was lapping at a saucer of milk set out on the brick path near the back door. The girl stood irresolute and called softly to the cat. At that moment John Franklyn emerged, with an armful of sticks, from the shed. Hilary called out joyfully.

'Hello! Your supper smells good!'

'Want some?' replied the man, half jocularly.

Constructing this as an invitation to the house, Hilary propped her bicycle against the fence, and entered the garden. John Franklyn watched her with mingled dismay and pleasure. She was an awkward great lump of a girl, he told himself, his eyes on her thick ankles and broad flat sandals, but her feelings seemed warm enough. He motioned her to enter the kitchen and followed her in.

'What have you been up to?' he asked, dumping the sticks on the top of an old copper which stood in the corner. His tone was bantering. Hilary told him breathlessly of her errand, her eyes roaming round the little room.

Sizzling on a primus stove stood a gargantuan frying-pan full of onions. On a white enamel plate nearby lay two freshly-cooked rashers, the biggest and thickest that the girl had ever seen. A three-pronged small fork and a pointed knife with a horn handle flanked the plate, and a bottle of sauce and a bottle of beer stood before it.

'Take a seat,' said John Franklyn, nodding towards a kitchen chair by the table. It was obviously little used for it was thick with dust. Too flustered to bother about its effect on her yellow frock the girl settled herself and watched the man turning the onions over and over with the small fork.

The room, after the brilliant sunshine outside, was murky, but as her eyes became accustomed to the gloom Hilary noticed that the dust was general. The window sill was thickly coated, and a dead geranium, whose leaves crackled under her touch, was a silent sad memorial to the dead mistress of the house. The window looked out upon a damp wall made of flints, which acted as a barrier against the shifting soil of the steep slope of the wood against which the cottage had been built so snugly. The wall was so close that even short-sighted Hilary could see the holes in the ancient flints quite clearly. All her senses seemed acutely sharpened. She noticed, as she had never done before, that the chalky covering of each grey flint caused a milky edge round the transverse section, and that many of the jagged holes in the flints were filled with a glistening granulated substance that looked like thick honey.

Tiny ferns grew in the crevices and some small mauve flowers, unknown to the girl, cascaded down the damp surface. A little movement attracted her notice. Close beside a ribbed hartstongue fern, which lolled from the mouth of a miniature cavern, squatted a toad. She saw his coppery eyes gleaming above the pulsing throat. Shivering, the girl turned again to the domestic scene before her. John Franklyn was now lifting the onions from the pan, and a second plate lay beside the first.

'Oh please!' begged Hilary, 'I don't really want any of your supper! I thought you were joking!'

'Plenty here,' said the man, ladling it out carefully.

'I couldn't, honestly!' protested the girl. Her eye lit on the bottle. 'But I'd love something to drink.'

'Beer do?' he asked, pausing in his operations. She nodded. He put down the frying pan and made his way out of the kitchen along a corridor to the front parlour. The girl could hear him opening and shutting doors and moving furniture. At last he returned bearing a florid china mug with a picture of King Edward VII and Queen Alexandra on the side.

He set it before her and filled it, then poured the rest of the bottle into his own battered enamel mug.

Hilary felt better after the first draught. She watched the man tackle his supper heartily, and though the noise which he made in eating would have revolted her had it been anyone else, so besotted was she that his hungry gulpings perturbed her not a whit. He finished the plateful, scraped his knife carefully across the surface, then between the prongs of his fork, ate the last morsel, wiped his mouth on the back of his hand, and leant back in his chair. He looked at the girl from beneath his sandy eyelashes and smiled.

'Ah, that's better! A chap gets sharp set out in the air all day.'

'I expect so,' said Hilary, gazing at him fondly through her thick glasses. Half-remembered descriptions of strong earthy men from the works of D. H. Lawrence and Mary Webb floated bemusedly through her head. She sipped her beer again.

'Haven't seen much of you lately,' continued John Franklyn, raising his own drink. 'What's up?'

'Why, nothing,' said Hilary. 'I just haven't been to Caxley lately.' She set her mug very carefully on the table, unable to meet his eyes, and John Franklyn putting his hand over hers bent across the table. Even the smell of onions could not quell the uproar in Miss Jackson's romantic heart.

'You enjoyed our last evening there?' asked John Franklyn softly.

'Very much,' faltered Hilary. The room seemed darker and hotter than ever. She lifted her mug with her free hand and drank deeply.

'What about next Wednesday?' said the man. His face seemed amazingly close and very pink. 'Good film on at the same place.' He gripped Hilary's hand in a hot and rather painful grasp. Muzzy with unaccustomed beer and bliss she leaned gently towards him.

'Hi!' said a shrill voice from the doorway, 'What yer want done with this lot?'

A small boy, with a roll of wire netting lodged across his shoulder, gazed interestedly upon them. Miss Jackson recognized him, with instant dismay, as one of Miss Read's pupils although she did not know his name. She leapt to her feet and smoothed her dress nervously.

Without any trace of embarrassment John Franklyn rose slowly from his chair and came to the door.

'I'll give you a hand with it to the shed, son,' he said, mildly. 'Tell your dad I'll settle up with him when I see him.'

The child stared at Hilary unblinkingly, his mouth slightly open. He lowered the wire netting and between them he and the man carried it down the garden path. Hilary, trying to overcome her discomfiture, emerged into the sunlight as they returned.

'You don't have to go yet,' muttered John Franklyn urgently. The child gazed from one to the other. The girl spoke primly and rather loudly.

'I really must. Thank you very much for giving me a drink.'

John Franklyn looked quizzically at her. The sun was getting low now and his light sandy hair was turned to a fox-like tawny red by its rays. She knew that he was amused by her clumsy acting for the benefit of the child who gaped beside her, and this upset her. Even more upsetting was the breaking of that charmed spell, now shattered beyond hope of regaining. For one dreadful moment, the girl felt tears rise behind her thick glasses, and prayed that they should not fall. John Franklyn saw all and pressed home his advantage.

'You're welcome to the drink,' he said with loud heartiness. He turned to the boy. 'Time you got back, Jim. Off you go!'

The child, still staring, edged slowly towards the gate, and Hilary, shaken with love and hurt pride, went with him. The man ambled slowly behind them and leant over the gate as he watched the girl lift her bicycle from the fence where it rested. He spoke very low and with his face averted from the laggard boy.

'Wednesday then? You'll come?' The girl could only trust herself to nod, her eyes downcast.

'Same time, same place?' His voice gained a new urgency which was music to her. 'You'll come?'

'I'll come!' replied Hilary.

The boy, who had come over the hill from Springbourne, walked backwards up the slope from the gamekeeper's cottage with slow thoughtful steps, his eyes fixed on the fast-moving figure of one of his school teachers. A light cloud of chalk dust rose from behind her skimming wheels as she swooped down to the distant Fairacre road.

He remembered the scene in the murky cottage kitchen and his eye brightened.

'Coo-er!' he said rapturously, aloud. For in matters of the heart, despite his tender years, he was not 'as green as he was cabbage-looking', as his mother would have said.

As for Hilary Jackson, careering headlong towards Miss Clare's cottage with her slightly dizzy head awhirl with dancing anticipation, what a pity it was that she had not taken heed of the moral to be found in the story that she had been reading to her infants that very afternoon! It was the tale of that foolish creature Jemima Puddleduck, who was so easily – so easily – beguiled by a certain foxy gentleman.

9. The Vicar Does His Duty

RUMOURS about the proposed housing estate continued to fly about Fairacre, Beech Green and the busy streets of Caxley. To begin with, opinions had been almost equally divided. Many of the Caxley shopkeepers, seeing a considerable source of income in the scheme, approved the idea. A number of the inhabitants of Beech Green and Fairacre agreed with Mrs Coggs that a more frequent bus service to Caxley, which must inevitably result from a greatly increased village population, would be of great advantage to them.

The opponents of the scheme included those who disliked change of any sort – and certainly the change brought about by hundreds more people in their own secluded corner of the country – those who were shocked at any desecration of

Dan Crockford's landscape, and those who had the foresight to see that a great number of urban dwellers set down suddenly in a small rural community could cause more commotion than just the despoiling of a much-loved scene.

But when the rumour of the new school and possibly the closure of Fairacre's own village school began to be bruited abroad, the opponents of the scheme found their number swelling.

'Been up our school all my schooldays and my father afore me! Catch me sending our two little 'uns all that way – bus or no bus!' was the sort of comment one heard, delivered in a robust burr, by staunch Fairacre worthies. One such remark particularly amused me. Mrs Partridge overheard two parents discussing the project heatedly, and retailed it to me.

'Well,' said one, with decision, 'our Miss Read ain't much to look at, poor toad, but her learns 'em fair enough. And I will say this for her – she don't bring 'em up in the weals old Hope did us, do she now?' With which modest tribute I was well content.

The vicar had pondered Mr Mawne's advice about getting some official light on the matter of the school's closing. He was very much perplexed over the way he should go about it. Should he ignore the rumours and wait until an official declaration was made, as it must be, if there were any truth at all in the proposal? Should he call a meeting of the school managers to discuss things? Or should he say nothing, but approach someone in the Education Office at the County Hall, and feel the way?

After much earnest thought he had decided that he would go privately to his county town, seek an interview with the Director of Education, and let his fears either be put to rest or confirmed, before meeting his managers.

Accordingly, one overcast morning, the vicar set off in his shabby car, along the shady lanes, to his appointment. He drove alone, for not even his wife knew his business that morning, and he pondered many things as he rolled sedately along, hooting gently when he approached any bend, crossroad or, more frequently, any newly-fledged bird which sat, fearless and innocent, on the hard highroad. Apart from his conjectures about the forthcoming interview, he was also sorely perplexed about a more personal matter.

He had in his wallet a book token for one guinea, treasured from a recent birthday. Should he be extravagant and add yet another guinea to it and buy the new volume on the subject of George Herbert, the parson-poet, for whom he had such a high regard? He feared that it might be an indulgence. His stipend was very small and a guinea's expenditure was not to be undertaken lightly. His wife, he knew, would not hesitate to encourage him to buy it, selfless soul that she was; yet only that morning she had told him that saucepans would have to be replaced and that yet another sheet had been ripped from top to bottom by his own careless big toe. The vicar sighed heavily, discovered that he was now in a built-up area, dropped the speed of his car from 35 miles an hour to 25, and cautiously approached the Education office.

His appointment was at eleven o'clock and at five minutes to the hour the vicar was ushered into a waiting-room by a pretty young typist.

'If you'll wait,' she said, turning such a dazzling smile upon the vicar, that he felt quite young again, 'I'll tell Mr Temple that you're here.'

The room was oppressively quiet when she had gone. Mr Partridge, crossing to a table which held an imposing spread of magazines and newspapers, was conscious of the noise that his black shoes made on the bare linoleum. He felt acutely nervous and looked, with lack-lustre eye, at the literary fare set out for his refreshment. *The Teachers' World*, *The Times Educational Supplement*, *The Schoolmaster*, *The Journal of Education* he supposed were the right and proper things to find here, but his eye brightened as it fell upon the local paper.

The first thing he saw, when he opened it, was a photograph of a fellow parson who was noted for his outspoken dicta on subjects of which he had the scantiest knowledge.

'Dear, oh dear!' said the vicar aloud, folding back the paper. 'And how has poor old Potts put his foot in it this time?'

Completely engrossed, his own troubles for the moment forgotten, Mr Partridge was unconscious of the Town Hall clock which boomed eleven times and was the signal for hundreds of coffee cups to appear on desks all over the county town.

The pretty girl reappeared.

'Mr Temple can see you now,' she said. The vicar dropped the paper, and his head awhirl with poor Potts, inadequate book tokens, sheets, saucepans and the plight of his adored village school, followed her to the door of the Director's office.

Meanwhile, the vicar's wife was paying a call at Fairacre School. The Flower Show was imminent and she had come to see how the children were progressing with their dancing.

The infants only were taking part in this particular activity, and I had given Miss Jackson a free hand in choosing some simple song and dance to amuse the onlookers. Somewhat to my dismay, she had unearthed a quite dreadful thing, called 'The Song of the Roses', whose inane words echoed and re-echoed through our two classrooms as the interminable practising went on. The words had been printed up on a black-board, for the past month, in the infants' room.

> We are little rosebuds gay,
> Nidding, nodding through the day.
> Some are pink, and some are white,
> Some are clad in scarlet bright.
> See us scatter petals sweet,
> Like confetti, at your feet.

After this had been chanted with various halts, cries of despair from Miss Jackson, false starts, and so on, the floorboards would begin to quake to the ensuing dance, as the roses wove their way, thunderously, between each othr. A light dust would rise from between the ancient cracks, and my class would groan heavily next door.

This morning, however, Miss Jackson was taking a rehearsal in the playground.

'I want someone to take a message to Miss Jackson,' I said. Mrs Partridge and I watched the effect of this innocent remark on the posture of all the children in my room. Shoulders were pulled back, chests thrust out, and eyes of every hue raised to mine with looks of mingled pleading and responsibility.

Patrick was chosen to ask Miss Jackson if we might all watch the rehearsal, and as he skipped joyfully doorwards the rest of the class relaxed their fierce posture and breathed again quite naturally.

While we waited for Patrick's return Mrs Partridge told me of a further complication in the dancing programme planned for the Flower Show.

'Mrs Waites has asked if Cathy can do her scarf dance again,' she said in a worried voice. 'It really is difficult.'

'What's the problem?' I asked. Cathy Waites had performed her scarf dance at more village functions than I cared to remember and I wondered what the objection could be to her repeating it yet again.

'Well, dear,' said Mrs Partridge, in a very low voice, carefully turning her back to the class to foil any astute lip readers, 'the last time Cathy did it was two years ago, and even then Gerald – and a great many other people too – felt that her costume was – well – *inadequate*, shall we say? And Mrs Waites showed me the new one, and really – !' Mrs Partridge's normally rosy face took on a deeper hue.

'Nothing, my dear, but a few wisps of chiffon,' she continued gravely, 'and poor quality chiffon at that. And yet she's so keen, and a good church-goer! It does make things difficult!'

Patrick returned as Mrs Patridge sighed, and we all trooped out into the playground where the twenty or so infants stood about in positions of acute self-consciousness. At Miss Jackson's command they shuffled into a faint resemblance of a crescent. Miss Jackson raised a plump arm, fingers daintily extended, and fixing her eyes upon her inattentive class she sang very loudly: 'Ready? We are little –'

A ragged bashful chorus took up the ditty in true country burr:

> 'We are li'l rawse buds gy-ee
> Nidd'n, noddn' all the dy-ee.'

Here the children shook their heads stolidly, their expressions wooden. A few fierce nudges and shovings resulted in five or six unhappy little girls stepping forward to say:

'Some are pink – ' Here they stepped back, with disastrous results, among their fellows, whilst a few more were projected forward to recite:

'And some are whoite.'

A group of bigger boys then took their place, shouting cheerfully:

'Some are clad in scawlet broit.'

After this there was a short embarrassed silence, until Miss Jackson, throwing herself forward and up again in an unlovely way, reminded them of the final couplet. Wielding their arms as though they were pitching bricks into a well, and panting with their exertions, the infants gasped out their last two lines:

> 'See us sca'er pe'als swee'
> Like confe'i a' your fee'.'

We all clapped heartily at this performance, whilst I made a mental note to speak to Miss Jackson about curing the glottal stops which our children much prefer to the sound 't'.

'Absolutely splendid!' said Mrs Partridge enthusiastically. The children preened themselves and exchanged smug smiles.

'It's only just over a week to the Flower Show,' she continued, 'and I'm sure everyone will enjoy the dancing.'

Miss Jackson smiled graciously at this kind remark, but had a gleam in her eye which dismayed me.

'It is for the *children's* benefit primarily,' she began. 'It is a wonderful release from the rigid type of exercise which they were accustomed to, and gives them freedom for true imaginative expression.' She had just drawn a deep breath, preparatory to embarking – as I knew from bitter experience – on a tedious rehash of Miss Crabbe's half-baked psychology notes, when St Patrick's clock saved us by striking twelve.

The children broke into cries of pleasure, Mrs Partridge remembered that she had cutlets to egg-and-bread-crumb, the 'Dinner Lady' approached the schoolroom door, and Miss Jackson's monologue mercifully remained unsaid.

The vicar had returned much relieved in his mind, and sitting on the verandah with a comforting pipe in his mouth, he had confessed the main purpose of his trip to his wife.

'A most pleasant fellow,' commented Mr Partridge on the Director of Education, 'an uncommonly pleasant fellow – sympathetic, intelligent – and gave me a very good cup of coffee too!' In the vicar's gentle eulogy there sounded a faint note of bewilderment as though he had expected Directors of Education to have small horns and cloven hooves and a whiff of sulphurous fumes emanating from them.

'He has heard indirectly of the housing scheme and says he feels sure that our Parish Council will know more about it before long.'

'But what about the school?' asked his wife anxiously. 'Is it likely to close?'

The vicar leant across and patted her knee comfortingly.

'Evidently not, my dear. But if a new school were to be built on the site it's quite likely that Fairacre School would take infants only, and the juniors would go by bus to the new building.'

Mrs Partridge put down a hideous straw hat she was embroidering with fearsome raffia flowers for the fancy stall of the Flower Show, and gazed thoughtfully across the garden. 'It's a relief of course,' she said slowly, 'to know that much. But the village won't like the idea. Anything touching the children rouses the village at once. I wish we knew more about this wretched business!'

The villagers of Fairacre and Beech Green had not long to wait before more was known about 'the wretched business'.

Caxley Rural District Council having been notified of the proposed scheme decided that here was a matter which might well prove contentious.

'Best let the Fairacre and Beech Green Parish Council know of this,' said burly Tom Coates, the retired estate agent. 'Let's hear what the feeling is out there before we send word back to the planning committee.'

It was agreed, and within two days Mr Roberts the farmer, one of the Parish Councillors, was propping up on his kitchen mantelpiece the notice of the meeting to be held in the near future in Fairacre School.

'And that should set 'em all talking!' he observed to his wife. 'If the fur don't fly from Mrs Bradley I'll eat my hat!'

His gigantic laugh rustled the paper spills on the shelf before him. The formidable and ancient Mrs Bradley was a fellow councillor. They together represented their Parish Council on the Caxley Rural District Council, and if parley were to be made Mr Roberts could ask for no better ally than Mrs Bradley beside him.

'Bless my soul!' he continued, slapping his breeches with a hand like a ham, 'that'll be a meeting worth going to!' His eye was bright at the thought, for Mr Roberts dearly loved a scrap, and it looked as though plenty of trouble were brewing somewhere.

His wife observed his relish with misgiving.

'Now don't go saying anything you'll regret,' she cautioned. 'You remember that business over collecting the pig-swill! You're too hasty by far!'

'I shall speak the truth and shame the devil!' declared Mr Roberts roundly. 'And 'tis the truth that old Miller should keep what's his own! And 'tis the truth, too, that that's some of the finest growing land in the county and should never be built on!'

'Well, speak *quietly* then,' implored his wife, as her husband's voice shook the bunches of herbs which hung from the kitchen ceiling.

'I shall speak as mild as milk!' roared her husband, his hair bristling. 'I shall coo at 'em, like a turtle dove, but I'll coo the truth!'

He thrust his arms into his jacket, shrugged his massive shoulders into it, and made towards the door. His wife watched him go with a quizzical look. From across the yard she heard his voice raised in cheerful song. He was singing:

'Onward Christian soldiers, marching as to war,' with all the zest in the world.

10. The Flower Show

THE day of the Flower Show dawned with a brilliance which enchanted most of Fairacre, but which caused the weatherwise minority to shake its head.

'Don't like the look of it,' said Mr Willet, mallet in hand. He was putting the final touches to the stakes which supported the ropes of the bowling-for-the-pig site. Mr Roberts was busy building a sturdy wall of straw bales near him.

'Keep your fingers crossed, Alf,' he answered. 'If the wind turns a bit by noon we may miss the squall.'

Mrs Partridge and a bevy of helpers were pinning bunting round the produce and sweet stalls, and Miss Jackson, Miss Clare and I were straining our thumbs by pinning notices at various vantage points to some of the hardest wood I had ever encountered.

'Come out of Sir Edmund's old stable roofs,' said Mr Willet, when I commented on our difficulties, 'and weathered to iron almost. When this lot's over, I'm having a few of these beauties to make a little old gate. I'm looking forward to working with a bit of good wood.'

And a fine job he would make of it, I knew, looking at those sinewy old hands that gripped the mallet. They were probably the most skilled and useful hands in the village, I thought, cursing my own inadequate pair which had just capsized the tin full of drawing pins into the long grass. I had seen Mr Willet's hands at work daily on wood, stone, iron, earth and tender plants. They were thick and knobbly, with stained and ribby nails edged with black, but I never ceased to marvel at their deftness and precision as they tackled the scores of different jobs, from lashing down a flailing tarpaulin in a howling gale to pricking out an inch-high seedling in fine soil.

The great marquee which dominated the vicar's garden was full of hustle and bustle, as people carried in their entries for the Flower Show, and walked round to admire – and sometimes to envy – the other exhibits.

Mrs Pringle had left the smaller tea tent, conveniently placed near the vicarage so that boiling water was available from the kitchen, and had come to look at her son John's entries. She gazed with pride upon the six great bronze balls of onions, each with its top neatly trimmed and laid to the side at exactly the same angle. His carrots, placed with military precision upon their tray, glowed with fresh-scrubbed beauty, and a plate of white currants gleamed like heaped pearls. Mrs Pringle's heart swelled with maternal pride, until her eye fell upon Mr Willet's entries which lay beside her son's. There was little to choose between the size, quality, and colour of both displays, but Mr Willet had covered his tray with a piece of black velvet, a remnant from an old cloak of his mother's, and against this dramatic background his exhibits looked extremely handsome.

'Black velvet indeed!' exclaimed Mrs Pringle scornfully to her neighbour. 'Funeral bake-meats, I suppose. About all them poor things are fit for!'

Huffily she made her way back to the tea tent, with her limp much in evidence.

By half past twelve all the preparations were completed. Mr Willet's mallet had tapped every stake and the stalls fluttered their bunting above sweets, jam, bottled fruit, raffia hats, wool-embroidered egg-cosies and all the other paraphernalia of village money-raising. In the marquee the air was languorous and heady with the perfume from sweet peas, roses and carnations, and in the tea tent rows and rows of cups and saucers awaited the crowd which would surely come.

The sun still shone, but fitfully now as the clouds passed lazily across it. Mr Willet surveyed the weathercock on the spire of St Patrick's church with a reproachful eye.

'Git on and turn you round a bit!' he admonished the distant bird, shaking his mallet at it, and making Miss Clare laugh at his mock ferocity.

She and Miss Jackson came back to lunch at the school house with me, and within ten minutes Miss Jackson was setting the table and Miss Clare grating cheese whilst I whipped up eggs for three omelettes.

'Though I says it as shouldn't,' I shouted above the din, 'I can cook a good omelette.'

'And I can't!' confessed Miss Clare sadly. 'I think I must get the pan too hot.' She watched my preparations intently, as I buttered the frying pan and finally swirled the mixture in.

'You're probably too gentle,' I told her. 'You must be bloody, bold and resolute when dealing with eggs. Master them, or they'll master you.' Luckily, my demonstration of egg-management was thrice successful and we sat down to a cheerful lunch party.

Our conversation turned, naturally enough, to the Flower Show. Miss Jackson was anxious that the infants' dancing display should go without mishap. Miss Clare, as so often before, was going to play the accompaniment to the rose song-and-dance, which I so heartily detested, on the vicarage piano. My two guests discussed the intricacies of timing and the best position for Miss Jackson to take up on the lawn so that both the children and their accompanist could see her.

'Who's turning the music for you?' I asked. 'Shall I ask Ernest to help you? He's a sensible boy.'

'Betty Franklyn is doing it,' answered Miss Clare. On hearing the name Miss Jackson dropped her fork with a clatter. It rebounded from the edge of her plate and fell to the floor. Muttering apologies, Miss Jackson dived headlong after it. Her face remained hidden from view as she grovelled. Miss Clare continued calmly.

'I met the child with her aunt in Caxley last market day. They said they were coming out to the Flower Show and I asked her then. She seemed a bit disappointed because she wouldn't be dancing with her old friends, of course, and I thought that turning the pages might be some comfort.'

By this time Hilary Jackson had emerged from under the table with a very red face. Miss Clare, observing her discomfiture with one swift glance, turned the subject to the matter of the new housing estate.

'Of course those two men must have been surveyors, I suppose,' she said, 'and what a long time ago it seems since I saw them walking up and down poor old Miller's field! I hear that it's going to be a really big affair.'

'With a site for a school already planned,' I observed. I began to serve the raspberries which I had picked early in the morning, but I felt Miss Clare's wise gaze upon me.

'And Fairacre's plans?' she queried softly. There was the very faintest tremor in her voice, and I remembered with a sudden pang the forty-odd years which Miss Clare had spent under that steep-pitched roof and of the scores of Fairacre men and women who had learnt their letters, their manners and their courage from this devoted schoolmistress.

'The vicar tells me that it won't close,' I assured her. Her sigh of relief was music to hear. 'But it may become "infants only".' I passed her the sugar and cream, and set about filling Miss Jackson's bowl.

'And your own plans?' she continued gently. For a moment I was at a loss to know what to answer, for my own plans, in face of this project, had been perturbing me more than I had cared to admit.

'I should like to stay,' I said slowly, 'but I haven't had much experience with infants. The managers may prefer to get some-one who is better qualified to teach young children.'

'What utter rubbish!' declared Miss Clare roundly. 'Fair-acre will never let you go! Never!'

And with these few stout words my long-sore heart was comforted.

When we had washed up Miss Jackson vanished across to the school to collect music and other odds and ends for the dancing display. Miss Clare and I sat in the garden, resting before the fray.

'Of course,' I said, turning back to Miss Clare's own prob-lems, 'this housing estate will be bang next door to your cottage. Will it make much difference, do you think?'

'I can't believe that it will ever happen,' replied Miss Clare, 'and even if the plans go through I imagine it will be some time before building actually begins. I doubt if I should live to see it.'

These last few words were uttered in such a matter-of-fact tone that at first I could hardly take in their importance.

'But surely,' I said shocked, 'you are stronger now! You look much better than when you were teaching. I sincerely hope that you'll flourish for at least another thirty years.' It was my turn to be comforter now, but Miss Clare brushed aside my words, with a shake of her white head that had never had a shred of self-pity in it.

'I've had a good life, and a useful one too, I hope. And I've loved every minute of it,' she continued soberly. 'But, to tell you the truth, my dear, I'm getting tired now, and I shall be happy and ready to step aside whenever the time comes. I like to think of someone else teaching the children here, someone else picking my roses and sitting under the apple tree I watched my father plant. I've had my party, said my party piece, and I shall be glad to give my thanks and go quietly home.'

St Patrick's clock chimed a quarter past two. Miss Clare patted my knee and said briskly:

'But the party's still on, you know! It's time we went across to the vicarage and took our place in the revels!'

We took the short cut through the churchyard. Across the silent tombs and cypresses came the sound of a dance tune played through the loudspeaker.

Hardly daring to look to left and right, I hurried with Miss Clare towards the gaiety and safety of the Flower Show, as though ghosts were at my heels – as, in very truth, they were.

In the vicarage garden the scene was colourful and gay. Despite the overcast sky and a threatening line of black clouds which advanced from the south-west, the women and children were in their prettiest summer frocks and the men in open-necked shirts. Mrs Finch-Edwards, who had once taught with me at Fairacre School, was one of the most beautifully dressed women there, in a lilac creation of her own making, and her daughter Althea, now at the toddling stage, was in a froth of white frills. She was to present the bouquet to the opener of the Flower Show, who was a friend of Mrs Bradley's, and a famous gardener, and Mrs Finch-Edwards was having some difficulty in preventing her daughter from squatting down on the ground the better to eat worm-casts.

'Althea, please!' implored the distracted mother, dusting down the dozen frills tossing around the child's hind parts. She had grown into a chubby attractive child, with dimpled arms, and a mop of auburn curls like her mother's. The bouquet of roses was being secreted under a near-by stall, guarded by Joseph Coggs, and Mrs Finch-Edwards hoped that Lady Sybilla would soon make a start on her speech, that the speech would be very, very brief, and that her daughter would do her credit, and neither hurl the bouquet from her en route to the dais nor stop to pick it to pieces.

'I'd rather work a fortnight at the shop!' she confessed to me. 'This is agony!' But she looked very gratified, despite her agitation, at this honour done to the family.

I inquired after the shop in Caxley, which she and Mrs Moffat had recently opened and was not surprised to hear that they had already enough orders for clothes to keep them occupied until late autumn.

At this moment Lady Sybilla was led to the microphone and introduced. She was a large, vague, charming old lady, wearing a black cartwheel hat which gave her some trouble. One white-gloved hand rested upon its crown, and in the other she held her notes. A nasty little wind fluttered her silk draperies as she leant forward to speak into the microphone.

'It is indeed a pleasure – ' she began, in a sweet light voice, when a mumble of thunder sounded overhead, there was a crackling from the microphone and we heard no more. Quite unaware that four-fifths of her audience were unable to hear a word Lady Sybilla continued with her speech, and the people of Fairacre watched this dumb show with docility. Mrs Finch-Edwards was terrified that she might not know when the speech was over, but all was well. With a charming smile and much nodding of the cartwheel hat to left and right, Lady Sybilla stepped back from her non-cooperative microphone, and Althea Finch-Edwards was propelled forward, bearing the bouquet which was nearly as big as herself. She acquitted herself well, handed over the bouquet, and turned to rush back to her mother, but remembering, in time, her curtsey, turned back, some yards away from the dais, to make a wobbly bob.

The crowd dispersed to the various stalls. The Bryant boys, dour-visaged and clad, despite the warmth, in Sunday black, made straight for the bowling-for-the-pig where they would stay for the remainder of the Flower Show. It was a foregone conclusion that either Amos, Malachi, Ezekiel or Gideon Bryant would bear away the prize.

Inside the giant marquee the judges, among them Lady Sybilla, walked thoughtfully about with their notebooks in their hands, and their brows furrowed. They pinched gooseberries, smelt roses, tasted jelly and cut cheeses, giving to every case that concentration of wisdom and experience which they knew was expected at Fairacre Flower Show. Many an anxious eye was cast upon them when at last they emerged, having left the tickets 1st, 2nd and 3rd, which would cause such joy or despondency to the exhibitors.

The rumbling of thunder became more ominous as the black cloud arched over Fairacre. It was decided to put forward the dancing display which was to be held on the lawn, in case the rain came, and the vicar announced through the badly-crackling microphone, that Miss Cathy Waites would open the proceedings, followed by Miss Jackson's children.

There was desultory clapping as Cathy came skipping from behind the vicar's laurel bushes, and one lone wolf whistle from a rude Beech Green boy.

Cathy, her dark hair blowing in the breeze, was clad in the flimsiest of garments as Mrs Partridge had feared. Luckily, she appeared to be wearing her High School knickers of a commendable staunchness and a brief but adequate brassiere, but over these basic necessities floated a yard or two of green chiffon of the most diaphanous nature.

In her hands Cathy held a long strip of the same material which she tossed from side to side as she bent and capered gracefully between the cedar tree and the produce stall. Occasionally, she fell on to one knee, cupping her ear as if listening to the horns of Elfland. In actual fact, the voice of one of the Bryant brothers who had just missed two skittles whilst bowling for the pig, was deplorably audible, whilst Miss Waites remained, wide-eyed and expectant, in her listening attitude, and the words used must have given a more innocent nymph considerable revulsion.

'That girl would do better with more clothes to her back,' observed Mr Willet to his neighbour, in a carrying whisper.

'Flaunting herself in next to nothing,' boomed Mrs Pringle from the door of the tea-tent. 'Catch me looking like that at her age!' She wobbled her three chins aggressively, but remained to goggle as the scarf dance wound its airy way to its end.

I hurried round the edge of the crowd to the shrubbery where Miss Jackson and the children awaited their entry. Roses of every hue, the children were in a fine twitter of excitement.

'Why can't us wear our shoes? I've been and stood on a prickle!'

'Can I be excused? I can't wait.'

'I can't remember the words.'

'I feel sick.'

'My knicker elastic's busted.'

With such ominous phrases well known to teachers in all school crises, the children greeted me. Miss Jackson, flushed and heated, was doing her best to calm her flock.

'Would you remind Miss Clare that we'll have the first part twice?' she implored me, and I made my way to the drawing-room where Miss Clare was visible sitting at the piano by the open french windows.

As I threaded through the edge of the crowd I noticed a man, with a woman and a little girl, also approaching the french windows. Betty Franklyn was arriving at her page-turning appointment with her father and the aunt from Caxley. We greeted each other and I made enquiries about Betty's new school in Caxley. The aunt was a pleasant, fresh-faced person, who chattered away about her little niece, but John Franklyn stood slightly apart, eyeing the crowd and looking self-conscious.

'You run along to Miss Clare now,' said the aunt, pointing to the piano, and as the child stepped over the threshold the woman turned to me as though she were about to speak, but stopped short.

From among the crowd a large young woman, in a bright yellow beach frock which matched her brassy hair, stepped purposefully towards John Franklyn who watched her approach with obvious amusement.

'Fancy seeing you, Johnny,' said the plump beauty, looking at him sidelong from under well-plastered lashes. She edged a little nearer.

'And what are you doing anyway at Fairacre?' he responded jocularly.

'I've got an auntie lives this way. At Tylers' Row. Mrs Fowler she is.'

I remembered suddenly that Mrs Fowler had a niece who was barmaid at 'The Bell' in Caxley. This must be the girl. The two began to stroll slowly away towards the shrubbery where the Fairacre children still waited for Cathy to finish fluttering her draperies on the lawn.

Betty was listening to Miss Clare's directions by the piano, and the aunt turned to me in some agitation.

'John was a good husband to my sister – but there, he's like all of 'em, needs company. Sometimes, I think – ' But here her voice faltered to a stop.

Her eyes were fixed on a little scene near the shrubbery, and my gaze followed hers.

Hilary Jackson had come running out, presumably to give Miss Clare another last-minute direction, and had encountered John Franklyn and his brazen companion face to face. She grew as red as a poppy, and stopped short, her mouth open.

John Franklyn, with all the assurance in the world, inclined his head politely as he passed by her.

'Got a nice crowd here today,' he commented, without pausing in his leisurely progress.

Speechless, Hilary Jackson rushed past them, and past Betty's aunt and me, stumbling towards Miss Clare. Her face was suffused and her eyes were full of tears. Once she was well inside the aunt put an appealing hand on my arm, and spoke in a low urgent whisper.

'He's a bad lot with women. If you don't tell her, Miss Read, then I shall!'

After this unnerving incident I watched the rose dance with even more detachment than usual. Miss Jackson was visibly upset, but luckily the children remembered their steps and the words perfectly, and encouraged by the applause of the onlookers, excelled themselves.

As they made their way from the lawn, bobbing breathlessly along with a fine disregard for Miss Clare's accompaniment, a wicked tongue of lightning flickered across the black sky, followed by an ear-splitting crash of thunder. Within a minute huge drops began to fall, the rain drumming down upon the baked lawn and bouncing dizzily from its surface like a myriad spinning silver coins.

Covers were hasily thrown over the stalls, and the crowd ran for shelter, either to the marquee or the tea tent. I found myself wedged by the table bearing a score of entries for 'Annuals in a Soup Plate' and remembered that spring evening when I humbly suggested this class. First prize I noticed had gone to Mrs Willet who had massed nasturtiums in a deep plate with green dragons on it.

In the corner behind the vegetable stall I caught a glimpse of John Franklyn and his companion. They seemed quite engrossed in each other and as I was contemplating the outcome of this affair, a voice spoke behind me.

It belonged to Mr Willet, and the innocent words, delivered in his slow country voice, seemed pregnant with meaning to me.

'Been stewing up a long time this 'ere storm,' commented Mr Willet.

11. Parish Council Affairs

THE Fairacre Parish Council meeting was held in the village school. Mr Roberts had seated himself on a long ancient desk which stood at the side of the room. His tall, burly frame was too big to cram itself into juvenile desks, but Mrs Bradley, small, alert and ready for battle, looked quite at home in the front desk usually occupied by Joseph Coggs.

Two members from Beech Green sat nearby, for although that village was larger than Fairacre it came in the latter's parish. Mr Annett had unashamedly rummaged in his desk, abstracted Ernest's arithmetic book and was studying his work with a censorious eye. Beside him sat the Beech Green butcher's wife, a large, florid lady, looking as succulent as her husband's joints.

Mr Lamb, from Fairacre Post Office, who was Clerk to the Council, had set out his papers on the teacher's desk and was now roaming round the classroom looking at the children's pictures which decorated the walls.

'Too much paint slopped on this one,' he remarked to anyone who cared to listen. 'Shocking waste of material! And never had these durn great lumps of paper when I was here! Half a sheet of small white, just big enough for a sprig of privet, and then shade the lot in careful!'

At this point the vicar bustled in, breathless and full of apologies, and took his seat as chairman. Mr Lamb sank on to the chair beside him, and applied himself to his papers.

'Apologies from Colonel Wesley, laid up with lumbago, I'm sorry to say,' began the vicar. At once remedies were suggested by all present.

'Nothing like old-fashioned brown paper ironed on!' asserted Mr Lamb.

'Nothing but heat and rest does any good!' vowed Mrs Bradley.

'Plenty of exercise and forget about it!' said Mr Roberts, at the same moment. He had never suffered an ache or pain in his life.

The vicar raised his voice slightly.

'And from Mrs Pratt who can't leave her poor old father, I fear. He's at his most trying as the moon waxes.'

There were murmurs of sympathy. Mr Annett, stuffing away Ernest's arithmetic book, looked sceptical.

'And now to the main business,' said the vicar, opening out a very long typewritten document, which had so many pages that even the stoutest heart among the parish councillors quailed a little as thoughts of supper grew sharper. 'I'd better read this straight through. The letter attached is from the Clerk to the Rural District Council who says that he encloses the proposed plan for an estate to house workers at the atomic establishment and he would be glad of our comments.'

'Unprintable!' said Mrs Bradley vehemently.

'Please, please,' begged the vicar, 'let us keep an open mind until we have studied this document.'

'Poor Mr Miller,' sighed the butcher's wife, 'he came into our shop last week, and he looked proper broken up!'

'We don't know, officially, that Mr Miller is involved in any way,' said the vicar patiently. No one appeared to hear him.

'Talk about Russia!' commented Mr Roberts with a snort.

'Taking first-class farmland for a pack of townees to ruin!' exclaimed Mr Annett warmly. 'And five times too many children swarming into my school!'

'And what's to happen to our own kiddies?' asked Mr Lamb, thumping the desk to emphasize his point.

The vicar thumped beside him, and the parish council looked with surprise and some disfavour at this display of officiousness on the part of its chairman.

'Ladies and gentlemen, please!' protested the vicar, his mild old face quite pink with effort. 'You are all jumping to conclusions! I must beg of you to listen to the proposals here set out, and we will discuss them – impartially, I hope – after we have heard them!'

The councillors settled themselves more comfortably in their cramped quarters, and turned attentive faces to the vicar. He began to read in his beautifully sonorous voice and his audience listened intently. Outside, the swifts screamed past the Gothic windows and, now and again, the lowing of Samson, Mr Roberts' house cow, was heard. From the windowsill the scent of honeysuckle wafted down, from a fine bunch which had been stuffed by a child's hand into a Virol jar.

The wall clock, whose measured tick had acted as a background to the vicar's monologue, stood at ten to eight when at last he put the papers down on the desk, removed his reading glasses, and gazed speculatively at his thoughtful companions.

'Well?' he asked. Mr Roberts shifted his long legs.

'Can't say I took it all in,' he confessed.

'Nor me,' admitted Mr Lamb sadly. Mr Annett caught his chairman's eye and spoke in his brisk, light, schoolmaster's voice.

'It seems to me that it all boils down to this. Perhaps you'll correct me if I'm wrong?' He turned to the vicar questioningly and received a gentle nod.

'The atomic energy authority proposes to purchase – compulsorily, if necessary, and it looks as though it will be – a site between our two villages comprising about a hundred and fifty odd acres. This will take in Miller's Hundred Acre Field with about half the slope of the downs behind. Provision is made for a school, playing fields for the community, and a row of shops. In other words this township would be a self-contained unit.'

'There is no church,' put in the vicar. His tone held a mild rebuke.

'No. No church,' agreed Mr Annett. 'But presumably there would be room for more people in Fairacre or our own church.' The vicar nodded his agreement rather sadly.

'Plenty of room!' he admitted. 'Yes, my dear fellow, plenty of room!'

'Water and sewage is also proposed, and these services would probably be extended to include Fairacre and Beech Green. As I see it this means that although the atomic energy authority pays a considerable part our local authority will also have to pay, which means that our rates will go up again.'

'Impossible!' said Mrs Bradley. 'There's not a soul will stand for it!'

'And anyway,' pointed out Mr Roberts, 'who wants to pay for something he doesn't want?'

'Exactly,' said Mrs Bradley vehemently, turning her back on the meeting and settling herself face to face with the farmer for a really downright argument. The vicar thumped the desk again.

'Thank you, my dear Annett, for summing-up so neatly. Now, ladies and gentlemen, your opinions, please!'

'Not a brick to be laid on Dan Crockford's landscape!' snapped Mrs Bradley.

'I think poor Mr Miller should keep what's his own!' asserted the butcher's wife.

'I'm not sure that the people themselves won't be a confounded nuisance,' said Mr Annett decidedly. 'I can see them making trouble about shocking rural schools –'

'But they'll have their own!' protested Mr Roberts.

'Not for years, if I know anything about school-building,' replied Mr Annett feelingly, 'and I'll have a procession of outraged urbanite parents inspecting my school's sanitary arrangements, and telling me that my teaching methods are archaic.'

'I don't know that that water idea isn't attractive though,' said Mr Roberts meditatively. 'Getting water up to the sheep on those downs has always been a problem.'

'What's the matter with the dew-pond?' demanded Mrs Bradley. 'One of Dan Crockford's best pictures that was, "The Ancient Dew Pond".'

'My husband had it on his trade almanack one year,' began the butcher's wife conversationally. 'He said those sheep drinking were as fine a flock of Southdowns as he'd ever seen, and would've ate beautiful!'

'Nothing to touch a good saddle of mutton!' agreed Mr Lamb.

'With onion sauce,' added Mr Annett.

The vicar seeing his meeting getting out of hand again, coughed gently.

'The business, my dear people! The planning committee asks for our observations. Can I have firm proposals, please?'

Mr Roberts suddenly stood up, partly because he was getting cramped and partly because he felt that the time had come for a decision. His great figure dominated the room.

'I propose that we have an open village meeting here in Fairacre and tell the people just what we've heard tonight, and get their reactions.'

'Stout man!' ejaculated Mr Annett, 'I'll second that proposal.' Mr Lamb scribbled busily in his minute book.

'Agreed?' asked the vicar. Everyone raised a hand.

'The only thing to do,' said Mrs Bradley, gathering her

belongings together fussily, 'There's much too much at stake for just the parish council to dispose of. Let's make it soon.'

'Next Monday?' suggested the vicar.

'No good for me,' said Mr Roberts.

'Friday?' said someone.

'Choir practice,' said Mr Annett.

At last, after various village engagements had been sorted out, the following Thursday was chosen, and Mr Lamb guaranteed that he would put up notices in Fairacre, and Mr Annett offered to put up more in Beech Green and let his pupils copy a notice each to take home to the parents, as well.

St Patrick's clock chimed eight-thirty as the members of the Parish Council emerged into the playground. From a near-by lime tree came the fragrance of a thousand pale flowers, hanging creamy and moth-like beneath the leaves.

'Smells good!' said Mr Lamb, sniffing noisily, 'but I'd sooner it was my supper!'

He spoke for all of them.

It was on the following day that Miss Jackson burst into school in a state of great excitement. I was glad to see her so happy, for ever since the day of the Flower Show she had gone about her affairs in an unnaturally subdued manner and I had felt extremely sorry for the girl. I was also much perturbed in my own mind about speaking of her infatuation for John Franklyn until I had learnt more from Miss Clare, and as that lady was looking so frail I felt diffident about worrying her unduly. As I have a horror of stirring up emotional upsets and very much dislike receiving confidences from overwrought individuals who will doubtless regret their own disclosures as soon as they have come to their senses, I had so far kept silent on this matter, but it had given me many uneasy moments and I wished to goodness that either Miss Jackson's affections could be engaged elsewhere or that John Franklyn could find employment at a distance, preferably in another hemisphere.

'I've had such a wonderful letter from Miss Crabbe,' exclaimed Miss Jackson ecstatically. 'She wants to come and spend next weekend here. Isn't it lovely?'

I said that that would be very pleasant indeed for them both, and where was she going to stay?

'Of course, Miss Clare can't manage it,' said Miss Jackson. 'I wondered if "The Beetle and Wedge" would put her up? Or "The Oak" at Beech Green?'

I suggested that she should go down to 'The Beetle' during the dinner hour and see what could be done. It was already nine o'clock, the children were milling about the classroom talking at the tops of their voices, someone had knocked over an ink-well, and from the infants' room a young finger was picking out 'The Teddy Bears' Picnic' on the piano with excruciating inaccuracy.

After we had dispatched cold pork and salad and a very sticky date pudding which the children greeted with cries of joy, Miss Jackson set off for 'The Beetle'. But within ten minutes she had returned with a glum face.

'No good,' she announced, sinking on to the front desk. 'They've got a friend coming for the fishing that weekend.'

'Try "The Oak",' I said. 'Go and ring up now, if you like, then you'll feel more settled.'

She went across the playground to my house, and at once a new child burst into the room to tell me.

'That other one,' she said accusingly, 'has busted into your place.' She was a plump red-haired infant, obviously a sensationalist, and dying for me to take instant recriminatory action. She watched my motionless figure with growing annoyance.

'Ain't you going to do *nothing*?' she demanded shrilly.

'No,' I said equably. 'I said she could go in.' The child looked suddenly deflated.

'Oh well!' she said, shrugging her shoulders, as if dismissing the whole incomprehensible affair, 'if you *said*!' She vanished round the door and a minute later Miss Jackson reappeared.

'Hopeless! Don't take in people. Now what's the next move? Caxley, I suppose?'

I pointed out that she and Miss Crabbe would waste a lot of time in trying to meet. Miss Jackson grew even more melancholy.

'I suppose I could ask Miss Clare if I could use the sofa in the sitting-room and Miss Crabbe could have my bedroom,' she sighed.

'It means that Miss Clare would have more work to do,' I said as kindly as I could.

'Oh, I'd help!' responded Miss Jackson vaguely. A horrid thought had entered my head. My spare room stood ready for just such an emergency, but my heart sank at the idea of having the redoubtable Miss Crabbe at such close quarters. I knew only too well that if Miss Clare were appealed to she would readily agree to have Miss Jackson's guests and undertake bed-making, extra cooking and shopping without a tremor. Steeling myself I took the plunge.

'Would Miss Crabbe care to stay in my house?' I suggested. I could almost feel the draught from my guardian angel's quill as he eagerly scribbled down this rare good point in my record. Miss Jackson's dazzling smile would have been ample reward for a better-natured woman. Although I was pleased to cheer the girl after her recent misery, I was beginning to feel that the price might prove too much for me.

'It would be perfect,' she said. 'We won't be in your way, I promise you. I know Miss Crabbe wants to go for a long tramp across the downs on Saturday, and of course she'll have to go back on Sunday.'

'Then that's settled,' I said. 'Tell her that I am looking forward to meeting her.' And in a way, I commented to myself, that is true, for my curiosity about Miss Jackson's paragon had frequently been whetted by my assistant's eulogies.

Further discussion was cut off by the entry of a mob of children surrounding a very large, shaggy, smelly dog which had obviously been rolling in something extremely unpleasant.

'Miss, he's lost!' exclaimed Ernest, flinging his arms round the creature, which stood wagging its tail at the sensation it was causing. Another child proffered a piece of biscuit and two infants patted its matted flanks with loving hands. The din was as appalling as the odour.

'Take that animal out!' I directed, in a carrying voice. Casting sorrowful, shocked looks over their shoulders the children and their noisome friend departed. I opened the Gothic windows to their fullest extent.

'Mean old cat!' floated up a low voice, from outside. 'She wouldn't give a home to no one, I bet!'

Oh, wouldn't she! I thought, as the memory of my noble, but rash, invitation came home to me once more.

12. *Miss Crabbe Descends upon Faircare*

MRS PRINGLE came, as she said, 'to straighten me out', after school on Thursday, in readiness for Miss Crabbe's visit.

'These sheets will soon need sides to middling,' she observed dourly, as we made the spare bed together. 'Pity you didn't buy better quality while you was about it. Always pays in the end!' I let this comment on my parsimony go by me.

'And this 'ere white paint everywhere,' continued my helper morosely, 'shows every speck of dust, don't it! Now, when Mrs Hope lived here – and she was what I'd call a really CLEAN woman – it was all done out a nice chocolate brown that never showed a mark. But there, Mrs Hope had a FEELING for housework and dusted regular after breakfast and after tea, day in and day out.'

I remarked, a little shortly, that Mrs Hope didn't teach all day, and then felt sorry that I had risen so easily to Mrs Pringle's bait.

We heaved the blankets up together.

'Fair strains me back!' groaned the old misery, laying one plump hand there.

'If this is too much for you, Mrs Pringle,' I said firmly, 'you must let me do it all alone. I don't want you laid up on my account.'

Mrs Pringle's mouth took on the downward curves I know so well.

'I can manage!' she said, with a brave, martyred sigh. 'Always was a one for giving of my best cheerful!'

We worked together in silence for a little and then Mrs

Pringle, changing the subject tactfully, asked me if I had heard the news about Minnie, her niece. Minnie Pringle lives at Springbourne and is the young and inconsequent mother of three small children. She has no husband.

'She's getting married,' volunteered Mrs Pringle, with pride.

'Good heavens!' I said, startled. 'Who to?' It seemed odd to me that Minnie, having got along for all this time without the encumbrance of wedlock, should suddenly decide to regularize her position.

'You wouldn't know him,' said Mrs Pringle complacently. 'He's a widower chap, very steady, getting on a bit, but can still enjoy a pipe and a read.' This conjured up a picture of a doddering individual on the brink of the grave, and I was at a loss to think how the lively young Minnie had been attracted to him. Further disclosures enlightened me.

'He's got five children of his own, so with Min's three, it'll make a nice little family to be going on with,' said Mrs Pringle. 'And Min's mother has been that awkward with her lately, it'll be best for all parties if our Min has a place of her own.'

'Does she seem fond of him?' I felt impelled to ask. Mrs Pringle's answer held a wealth of worldly philosophy.

'He's got a nice bit put by, and he's getting on. Min'll do right by him for the few years she has to, I don't doubt, then there's plenty of children to look after her later.'

It certainly sounded reasonable enough, I thought, if not wildly passionate. I smoothed the counterpane while Mrs Pringle puffed about the room with a duster.

'D'you want this great chest of drawers heaved out?' she asked. There was a menacing streak in her voice which I chose to ignore.

'Yes, please,' I said. Mrs Pringle leant gloomily against the piece of furniture, which glided easily away before such an onslaught.

'One thing *does* worry me,' confessed Mrs Pringle as she flicked her duster. 'I've been invited to the wedding and I think I must put my hand in my pocket for a new hat.'

'What about the one with the cherries?' I suggested. The

hat with the cherries is an old and valued friend of Fairacre's, and I felt a pang at the thought of it being put from sight for ever.

'Just that bit past it!' announced Mrs Pringle. 'It's been a good hat, bought up in London first by Miss Parr, and given to the Primitive Jumble Sale for the Welcome Home Fund after the war. It's done me well, I must say, but I fancy a navy myself. Navy with white – say a duck's wing like, or a white lily laid acrost – always looks smart.'

I said that it sounded just the thing.

'It's to be a fairly dressy wedding,' went on Mrs Pringle. 'Min was all for a long white frock and having the children as attendants, but her mum made her see reason, so she's got a pale-blue that looks quite a treat.'

I agreed that it would be more suitable for Minnie.

'And I'm giving an eye to Min's three at the back of the church while my sister sees to his five,' continued Mrs Pringle. 'Should go off very nicely. I always enjoy a wedding.'

She stood motionless in the middle of my spare bedroom, duster in hand, and a faraway look in her eye, as she gazed across the playground. A rare and maudlin smile played across her normally grim visage.

'Ah, Love!' she sighed gustily. 'It rules the world, Miss Read, it rules the world!'

It transpired that Miss Crabbe was coming by car and would arrive at Fairacre in the early evening, so that I prepared a cold supper for Miss Jackson, our guest and myself, and went upstairs to make quite sure that fresh rainwater filled Miss Crabbe's ewer, that her bed was turned down, and everything in readiness in the spare room.

I had put a vase of my choicest roses on the bedside table, and spent some time in deciding on a variety of books. After much thought I had selected *Country Things* by Alison Utley, *The Diary of a Provincial Lady* by E. M. Delafield, *Winnie the Pooh* by A. A. Milne, an anthology of modern verse, and one of Basil Bradley's novels bearing a reclining Regency beauty on its dust jacket.

'And if she can't find something there to enjoy, she must be very hard to please,' I told myself.

At seven o'clock Miss Jackson arrived looking very spruce in a new pink linen suit. She was happy and excited, the wretched John Franklyn forgotten for once.

It crossed my mind that Miss Crabbe might be able to help in discouraging this affair, but it remained to be seen what manner of woman she was before approaching her.

'She's always terribly punctual,' said Miss Jackson ardently. 'She said half past seven in her letter, so she won't be long.'

She followed me down the stairs and I noticed her searching scrutiny of the supper table. All must be perfect for the approaching goddess. She appeared satisfied with what she saw, and we walked out into the school-house garden which was still warm in the July sunshine.

Before long St Patrick's struck the half hour and Miss Jackson began to look anxious. But within ten minutes we heard a car approaching. There was a tooting which sent Miss Jackson flying from my side to the gate, and I followed her more slowly, wondering if my mental portrait of the unknown psychology lecturer would bear any resemblance to my newly-arrived guest.

During supper, whilst Miss Crabbe and Miss Jackson exchanged news of college friends and I cut innumerable slices of bread for my visitor's side plate which seemed constantly empty, I thought how wrong I had been about Miss Crabbe's looks.

I had imagined a massive woman about six feet in height, with flashing eyes, a resonant voice and an overpowering presence. In fact Miss Crabbe was a wispy five-foot-three with thin faded hair dragged back into a skimpy bun, and her most noticeable feature was a long thin nose with a pink flexible end which always appeared in need of attention. Her voice was slightly nasal and whining, but very soft. It was, however, never silent, I was beginning to discover. It flowed ruthlessly on, brooking no interruption, and appeared to function whether she were in the process of eating or not.

With considerable forethought for my own catering arrangements over the weekend I had cooked a piece of gammon and one of Mrs Pringle's chickens. These cut cold, with salad, or with new potatoes and peas from the garden, I had proposed to rely on for the main meals. Miss Crabbe, with one devastating sentence, knocked all my plans askew as soon as I picked up the carving knife to attack the cold bacon.

'I'm not a flesh eater,' she said in a low voice, as though discussing something of an intimate nature. I felt at once that to be a flesh eater was to be put on a par with all the less pleasant carnivores of the animal world, and I wondered which of them, the vulture, the wolf or the carrion crow, I most resembled.

'Let me cook you an egg,' I offered. 'Or I've plenty of cheese.'

Miss Crabbe smiled in a resigned fashion.

'A little of this delicious salad,' she said, 'is all that I shall need.' But I very soon found that it wasn't. Miss Crabbe's consumption of bread was alarming, and I began to fear that I should not have enough left for breakfast. Fresh fruit followed, and when Miss Crabbe had demolished a banana, some grapes, a Beauty of Bath apple and a generous helping of raspberries from the garden, she and Miss Jackson agreed to my suggestion that coffee in the sitting-room would be pleasant. They both rose from the table, still talking, and with never a backward look at the mound of dirty crockery, left me to it.

I set the coffee on the stove and cleared the table as it heated.

'This is going to be lively, Tibby,' I said to the cat. We exchanged morose glances.

Miss Jackson was listening entranced to Miss Crabbe's monologue when I took in the coffee.

Its theme, I gathered, as I set about pouring out was the regrettable manifestations of cruelty among children and how best to avoid them.

'It must be something lacking in our own approach as teachers,' asserted Miss Crabbe.

Miss Jackson nodded owlishly.

'Black or white?' I asked, for the second time. Miss Crabbe continued, brushing aside this interruption.

'Fundamentally, the Good should predominate in the normal child. Certain maladjustments do occur, of course, but with the right kind of environment –'

'Black or white?' I said loudly.

'Black, please,' muttered Miss Jackson. Miss Crabbe droned on.

'Which we should be able to make for them if we, as teachers, are appropriately adjusted, they should be non-existent. It is, to a large extent, a question of Aura. Now, I personally have an Ambience which, I am told by my professional friends, suffuses a room and creates an atmosphere conducive to a ready flow between the children and myself –'

'Black or white, Miss Crabbe?' I repeated fortissimo, handing Miss Jackson hers. Miss Crabbe looked at me coldly.

'White, please,' she said, speaking more in sorrow than in anger. Now that she had noticed my presence in the room she seemed to feel that some conversational sop should be thrown to me. Speaking with maddening condescension she continued with her face turned towards me.

'We were discussing the little outbursts of spite which one still comes across in the classroom. Petty pinchings and so on. The children, of course, are the victims of their own dominating impulses, and Hilary and I were trying to find a solution to this problem. It calls for very great delicacy in approach, I feel – an application of psychological knowledge which helps the child who has had this emotional outburst without upsetting its ego. What do you do in these cases?'

'Smack!' I said briefly, and at last passed the coffee.

The evening wore on. By a quarter past eleven Miss Crabbe had told us about her recent lecture tour in the northern counties, her argument with a colleague about comprehensive schools and their influence on future political developments, the reactions of the press to her recently-published thesis on 'Play Behaviour in the Under-Fives', and her suggestions for the complete reorganization of Fairacre school. Overcome as I was with mingled amusement, irritation and fatigue, I could not help admiring the lady's amazing command of the English language. She flowed on remorselessly, her voice soft and faintly nasal. She paused neither for breath nor thought, but let her monologue stream forth like some smooth, never-ceasing, steady river which washed impassively about Miss Jackson and me as we sat helpless in our seats.

'Loungin' around and sufferin'!' I thought, echoing Uncle Remus. Finally, I rose to collect the coffee things, and suggested to Miss Jackson that she should set out on her cycle ride to Miss Clare's. She went with the greatest reluctance, after making complicated plans about the morrow's arrangements, and I conducted Miss Crabbe to her bedroom.

I showed her how to work the switch of the bedside lamp and indicated the books. She studied them briefly, with a sad smile.

'Juvenilia!' she said, dismissing my darlings in one word. 'In any case, I like to spend an hour jotting down notes on my reactions to the day's affairs. I find that people take so much out of me – one gives and gives and gives! My little hour before I sleep restores my spiritual resources, then I am refreshed enough to face the next day's demands on me.'

I hoped privately that my own depleted ration of sleep would refresh me enough to remain civil to my exhausting guest during the next day. Aloud I wished her goodnight, closed the door gently upon her, and tottered thankfully to my own bed.

The week-end slowly crawled by. Luckily, Saturday was a fine day and the two friends set off for their walk along the downs bearing packets of sandwiches – carefully non-flesh in Miss Crabbe's case – and flasks. Miss Clare had invited them to tea and so I was able to get through the usual week-end jobs undisturbed.

Miss Crabbe's unceasing conversation continued unabated for the rest of the time. She had changed her plans and decided to depart during Monday morning instead of on the Sunday evening as first arranged. After tea on the Sunday, she and Miss Jackson set off again for a walk. The sky looked threatening.

'I am unduly sensitive to weather conditions,' announced Miss Crabbe, 'and it certainly won't rain.'

It gave me some satisfaction to see the heavens open an hour or so after their departure, but I sincerely hoped that they would find shelter, for the shower was heavy, and lasted a good half-hour.

They reappeared at about eight and I was careful to avoid any reference to the weather. Miss Crabbe volunteered the information that they had sheltered in a cottage in the woods and so had missed getting wet, but I did not press for further details. It was apparent, however, that something was amiss between the two. Miss Crabbe's aura was anything but benign as we sat down to supper and Miss Jackson was visibly upset. Somewhat to my relief she made her farewells considerably earlier than on the previous nights, and seemed anxious to get away.

Miss Crabbe too seemed unduly thoughtful, and though she more than held her own in our civil exchanges there was an occasional pause when the silence fell heavily about us.

As half past ten struck from St Patrick's Miss Crabbe ascended the stairs. On the landing she paused and confronted me.

'What is between this Franklyn man and Hilary?' she demanded. Her neck had flushed an ugly red, and I was quite relieved to see that the impregnable Miss Crabbe could feel emotion as sharply as her neighbours.

Before I could reply she continued. Her voice was shriller than usual, and by the glint in her eye I guessed that Miss Crabbe, behind that impassive veneer, had a very nasty temper.

'Hilary knocked there for shelter, and it didn't take me two minutes to sum up that situation! The little fool's in love with him, and he's willing too!'

Could it be jealousy that had brought an angry tear to this furious woman's eye, I wondered? I was soon to know.

'I won't stand for it, I tell you!' she almost screamed, and flounced into the bedroom, slamming the door behind her.

13. Fairacre Speaks its Mind

THE Thursday of the parish meeting was also the last day of term. The children were excited, chattering like starlings, and bustling between their desks and the wastepaper basket as they put all in order.

The cupboards gaped open as Ernest and Eric packed away the books for their seven weeks' rest. Linda Moffat was removing pictures from the partition between the two rooms, Patrick was cleaning out the fish tank outside, at the stone sink in the lobby, and holding a noisy conversation with Joseph Coggs who was washing inkwells in the playground. Miss Jackson's infants were equally busy and vociferous and we were only too thankful when playtime came and we could refresh ourselves with a cup of tea.

Miss Jackson had been in a black mood ever since Miss Crabbe's visit. The friends had parted civilly enough on the Monday morning, and my guest's outburst had not been mentioned again. I had received a thank-you letter in which, I was relieved to find, there was no reference to Miss Jackson. That young lady was going about her affairs with a stony face and, I suspected, an equally stony heart. She was in a pitiable plight, and I was glad to hear of her holiday plans.

'My parents have taken a house by the sea for a month,' she told me. 'I didn't know quite what I should be doing, but I've decided to go there. They always like me with them,' she added, with the breath-taking assumption of the young that their parents find them indispensable.

I remembered that a holiday with Miss Crabbe, in Brittany, had been mooted earlier in the term, but obviously this had fallen through. The month by the sea, I thought, should give poor Miss Jackson time to sort out her tangled emotions, but I felt very sorry for her parents.

The vicar called in to take the final day's prayers and to wish everyone a happy holiday.

'And the same to you, sir!' bellowed Fairacre School in a

combined roar. Their faces beamed and their eyes shone so brightly that an outsider might suppose that their school hours normally consisted of back-breaking labour and physical tortures devised by their two sadistic teachers, so obvious was their relief at having a holiday.

Clutching their possessions to them they scrambled headlong to the door and out into the sunny playground. The vicar smiled benignly as their excited cries floated back to us.

'Good children!' he commented. 'All *good* children! Shall I see you at the meeting, Miss Read?'

The meeting to discuss the proposed housing site was held in the village hall, an unlovely corrugated iron building which had faded from a hideous beetroot red to a colour resembling weak cocoa.

There was an unusually large number of Fairacre people in the hall when I arrived. On most occasions a village meeting consists of a dozen or so, but this evening there were about four times that number, and seats were getting scarce.

Mr Willet seemed to be in charge of the seating arrangements and led me towards the front where Mr and Mrs Mawne were already seated. One chair stood vacant, beside Mr Mawne, at the end of a row. We greeted each other, and Mr Willet politely held my chair while I sat down.

'Between two fires!' commented Mr Willet, with misplaced gallantry, to Mr Mawne, who smiled vaguely. Mrs Mawne, however, turned a frosty glance upon Mr Willet and another, hardly less cold, upon her innocent husband and me. I remarked feebly that the evening was dark, and was not answered.

At this moment there was a stir by the door and the vicar and his wife entered. He made his way briskly to the chairman's seat, followed by Mr Lamb bearing a sheaf of papers.

'Lor!' said someone at the back of the room, in an awed voice, 'I hopes us ain't got to sit through that lot!'

The vicar rose to his feet.

'Could we have the lights on?' he asked. Several people crowded round the switches by the door, and frantic clickings began. Sometimes one of the four hanging bulbs lit up, but never the one nearest to the chairman's table.

'Do seem to be a bit awkward-like tonight, sir,' admitted one of the operators. 'Wants a new bulb, or summat o' that.'

'A power cut, I expect,' boomed Mrs Pringle gloomily. Several people started to explain to her, in a fine confusion, that this could not be the case. Mrs Pringle, arms folded across her massive bosom, remained unconvinced.

'Never mind, never mind!' said the vicar benignly. 'We may be able to get through our business before it gets too dark. Mr Lamb, would you care to read the letter from the Rural District Council.'

Mr Lamb arose and read, first, the letter, and then, at a nod from the vicar, the proposals of the United Kingdom Atomic Energy Authority. His voice sawed steadily up and down, and though many an eye glanced at watches, the people of Fairacre listened in attentive silence. The vicar came round from his chair, when Mr Lamb had finished, and sat on the front of his table instead. He had ruffled his fine white hair as he had listened, and his lined, kindly face wore a look of perplexity. He appeared at that moment, particularly vulnerable and endearing to his parishioners.

'You see why the Parish Council has invited you to hear about this proposal. We are asked if we have any observations to make, and I do earnestly beg you to consider just what these proposals will mean.

'We shall have, between our two villages, a third new one, larger by far than either Fairacre or Beech Green. The people living there will have come, in the main, from towns. They may take some time to adapt themselves to our ways. They may, in some cases, never become adapted.

'Hundred Acre Field and a considerable area beyond that will be built over.

'We are told, in the proposals, that new roads will have to be built, that provision has been made for street lighting, sewage, a school, playing fields and shops. These plans are only in rough, as it were, and may be modified.

'There is no doubt that our two villages would benefit by

the electricity and sewage schemes and by more frequent bus services between here and Caxley and the atomic station. But it remains for you to say what you feel about this project.'

At the end of this very fair and unbiased account the vicar walked round the table again and resumed his seat. Mr Willet was the first to take the floor.

'Mr Chairman,' he began, 'I'm a plain man and don't pretend to have understood all the rigmarole the Parish Clerk has just read us. But this I do say. I for one don't want to see Fairacre swamped by another young town—'

'Here, here!' muttered several of his neighbours.

'And I don't see paying out good money in rates and that for a lot of street lights and waterworks what we've done without long enough. I'm a plain man, and I reckons it's best to speak out plain.'

Mr Willet, puffing out his stained moustache, reseated himself heavily.

Beside me Mr Mawne shifted uncomfortably.

'If that fellow keeps saying that he's a plain man,' he whispered to me, 'I fear that someone will shortly get up and agree with him.' I was having some difficulty in controlling my enjoyment of this dry statement, when I caught Mrs Mawne's eye, and sobered up immediately.

Mrs Bradley, a diminutive figure in black, hoisted herself upright by prodigious clawing at her neighbour's shoulder, and added her views.

'I feel that someone should point out to the meeting that the land scheduled for building purposes is a particularly valuable local heritage.'

'Jest ol' fields, ain't it?' breathed someone in the row behind me, in a bewildered whisper.

'Our great local artist, Dan Crockford—'

'Ah now! He were a one for the girls!' commented the voice behind appreciatively.

'— immortalized that part of the country, which will be ruined,' went on Mrs Bradley.

'Two-penny halfpenny dauber!' muttered Mrs Mawne viciously to her husband.

'I should like to protest, most strongly, against the idea of houses being built on one of the most beautiful parts of our country. A part which has proved an inspiration to generations of our countrymen, and to the great Dan Crockford in particular.'

Applause greeted this robust statement and Mrs Bradley resumed her seat, flushed with success.

'And what about this school?' boomed Mrs Pringle before the clapping had died away. 'Am I to be out of a job at Fairacre school if the kids goes to the new one? Or are that lot all to come tramping over my floors making double the work?'

'There appears to be no doubt that the school here would remain open,' said the vicar hastily, 'only its status might be altered.'

'*Meaning?*' queried Mrs Pringle, in a menacing crescendo.

'It might take just the very young children,' admitted the vicar, 'and the juniors would perhaps attend the proposed new school. But, of course, nothing is definite –'

A hubbub arose in the hall.

'What? Send our Bert off in a bus?'

'And who'll take the little 'uns to school if their brothers and sisters goes elsewhere?'

'And have a headmaster, like as not, caning 'em cruel.'

'Ah! Us had enough o' that ourselves, with old Hope, way back.'

'And do Miss Read stop on? Or do she get the push? Like Miss Davis?'

''Tis proper upsetting for the children.'

The meeting, until then, had been quiet, but this murmur of change affecting the children roused it amazingly. The vicar thumped on his table.

'Please, please! I think the time has come when a few proposers and seconders are needed, so that Mr Lamb can get down his points in order. Mrs Bradley, would you care to put your motion?'

Mrs Bradley climbed precariously to her feet again.

'I propose that this meeting protests strongly against the

taking of a noted local beauty spot – the subject of many of Dan Crockford's pictures – for building purposes.'

'I second it!' said Mr Mawne beside me. His wife cast up her eyes significantly.

'And I propose us protests on the grounds of expense – rates and that,' put in Mr Willet.

'Voting first, please, on Mrs Bradley's proposal,' said the vicar gently. All hands were raised.

'Now, Mr Willet?' Mr Willet put his proposal, in rather better terms this time. Mrs Pringle seconded it, and it was passed unanimously.

Mrs Moffat, chic in a coral-coloured coat, rose to frame her protest against the possible alteration in status of Fairacre School and its effect on the pupils and village life in general. It was seconded, surprisingly enough, by Joseph Coggs' father. Mr Lamb scribbled busily at the table, his tongue slightly out and writhing as he wrote.

'And tell 'em,' shouted an unknown stalwart from Beech Green, who appeared to be under the impression that Mr Lamb was taking down a letter direct to the authority involved and was hurrying to catch the post, 'tell 'em we're all right as we are and don't want the place mucked up with a lot of toffee-nosed types from town!'

'Could that be put a little more formally?' suggested the chairman.

After a certain amount of murmuring a proposal was put forward in more orthodox terms and it was seconded and carried. At that moment there was a disturbance by the door, and in stumped the figure of old Mr Miller, the owner of the land under discussion.

'Sorry to be late,' he barked. 'How far are we, chairman?'

'We are putting down our protests,' the vicar told him. Mr Miller took a deep breath, and his eyes flashed fire.

'Then here's the biggest one,' he roared. 'That's been my farm, and my family's farm, for generations. I do more than protest against good farm land being put under buildings! I'll see them damned first!'

There were one or two indrawn breaths from those ladies of

refinement, including Mrs Pringle, who objected to such strong language. Mr Miller, red in the face and brandishing his arms, was about to continue his diatribe, when the vicar broke in gently.

'Perhaps you would put that in the form of a proposal?' he suggested.

Mr Miller was attacked by a paroxysm of coughing and someone helped him to a chair.

'You do it!' he gasped to Mr Roberts who approached him.

And so it was a fellow farmer who added Mr Miller's heartfelt protest to the list which lengthened under Mr Lamb's hand, while the irascible originator lay back in his chair and nodded his shaky head vehemently as he listened.

'Poor old chap!' whispered one woman to another. ''Tis too bad he got this to put up with at his age! Right's right, after all, and he should keep what's his!'

The meeting drew briskly to its close, and I had never seen Fairacre so stirred. The people, normally so docile and mono-syllabic, were unusually heated, and spoke up bravely. Slow to kindle, once their hearts were fired they blazed strongly. The vicar spoke again.

'If there are no further comments I think we will ask Mr Lamb to send our protests to the Rural District Council, and close the meeting. I do so hope that we have been guided aright, and I thank every one of you who has come here tonight to put his wisdom and experience at the disposal of his neighbours. May the hand of the Lord guide our path!'

'Amen!' said a number of people fervently, and the vicar stepped down from the platform.

Soberly the villagers made their way out into the summer twilight.

The vicar had hurried directly to Mr Miller after the meeting and was insisting that he rested at the vicarage before returning to his home. We watched the two white-haired men, one so fiery and the other so mild, make their slow progress arm-in-arm towards the haven of the vicarage drawing-room.

'I shall go home and make a nice cup of tea,' announced a

woman to her neighbour. 'I feel fair twizzled up inside after all that!'

The first day of the holidays dawned bright and fair. I made up my mind to spend it alone, savouring to the full the exquisite pleasure of being free.

To those who have never had to undergo regular employment with set hours of work, the glory of not being clockbound cannot be truly appreciated. I looked gleefully at my kitchen clock as I took a leisurely breakfast at nine o'clock, and thought to myself, 'Ah! Yesterday at this time I was marking the register!'

I wandered round the dewy garden, admiring the velvety dark phlox just coming into flower, and getting an added fillip from the thought that normally I would be setting about an arithmetic lesson at the stern behest of the timetable on the wall. It is heady stuff, freedom – this cocking-a-snook at clocks, bells, whistles, timetables, syllabuses and all the other strait-jackets curbing the gay flow of time.

I sauntered through the village, swinging my basket, as St Patrick's clock struck eleven o'clock. ('Time to bring them in from play!' warned my teacher-shadow. 'And rats to that!' chortled my exuberant holiday-self.) What bliss it was to be at large in Fairacre on a Friday morning, instead of cooped up in a dark school!

It was fun to see the difference in the village at this time of the morning. The sun slanted from a different angle, winking on the brass knocker of Mr Lamb's door, a beautiful lion's head with a ring in its mouth, which I had not noticed before when the sun had slipped further round. In a cottage window stood a cactus plant which I had noticed before, but now, with the sun shining full upon it, two vivid orange flowers gaped like young birds' beaks in its warm benison.

On the other side of the village street a topiary hedge, finely clipped into towers and battlements, cast its black shadow upon the sun-drenched road, and a young thrush with jewelled eyes sheltered in the cool shade there.

Other Fairacre folk were still about their everyday business.

From the Post Office came the irregular thumping of Mr Lambs' date-stamp as he hastened to get the mail ready for the van. The clinking of brass weights came from the grocer's and the whirring of the coffee-grinder, accompanied by the most seductive of all food smells.

Dusters flapped from upstairs windows as the bedrooms received their morning toilet. Here a woman bent in her vegetable garden cutting a lettuce or pulling spring onions for the midday meal. A baby lay kicking in its pram, eyes squirrel-bright as it crowed at the fluttering leaves above it.

From the bakehouse at the rear of the grocer's shop wafted the homely fragrance of new bread. In there, I knew, the great tables had been scrubbed clean and the white-overalled baker, with his shirt sleeves rolled up, would be waiting to rap the top of his loaves to see if the batch were done. And at the far end of the village, near Tyler's Row, I caught a glimpse of Mr Rogers, the blacksmith, in dusky contrast to his equally hot bakehouse neighbour, standing at the door of his forge to get a breath of fresh air.

Nothing can beat a village, I thought, for living in! A small village, a remote village, a village basking, as smug and snug as a cat, in morning sunlight! I continued my lover's progress, besotted with my village's charms. Just look at that weeping willow, plumed like a fountain, that lime tree murmurous with bees, that scarlet pimpernel blazing in a dusty verge, the curve of that hooded porch, the jasmine – in fact, look at every petal, twig, brick, beam, thatch, wall, pond, man, woman and child that make up this enchanting place! My blessing showered upon it all.

It was the first day of the holidays.

14. A Day of Catastrophe

I WAS to look back with longing upon that first halcyon day, in the week that followed, for the clouds gathered with alarming speed.

On that Friday evening, I had driven to see Miss Clare and was shocked by the change in her. She looked suddenly old. Her hands shook uncontrollably as she poured out a glass of her home-made parsnip wine for me, and she seemed to move more slowly about her little cottage.

'It's just a touch of rheumatism,' she said, dismissing my anxious enquiries. 'And I haven't slept well lately.'

'Is it that wretched girl?' I asked.

'Hilary? No, not really. She hasn't mentioned that Franklyn fellow again, but I think that little tiff with Miss Crabbe upset her more than she'll admit. I don't know what it was all about, and didn't enquire.'

I did not enlighten Miss Clare either, but a vision of Miss Crabbe's distorted and furious countenance flashed into my mind uncomfortably.

'Anyway,' continued Miss Clare, 'the child went off very happily this afternoon to her home. And the family go off to the sea for a month on Monday. I believe it will do her good.'

I pressed her to come and stay with me for a few days and have a rest. I had a clear week at Fairacre before I went away for my own holiday, and I knew I should go more happily if Miss Clare were less frail. But she would have none of it.

'No, no, my dear, though it's sweet of you to offer to have me. Now that I'm alone, and can get up a little later and not bother with quite as much cooking and shopping, I shall soon pick up.'

She agreed to come to tea during the following week and I had to be content with this. But I drove back to Fairacre far from easy in my mind about my old friend's health and happiness.

I woke the next morning still worried about Miss Clare, and within an hour or two had yet another disturbing incident to perturb me.

Mr and Mrs Mawne were in the butcher's shop when I went there to buy my weekend joint. Amy was coming over from Bent to have lunch with me and I was out early to do my shopping.

Mrs Mawne, never particularly affable to me, was even less amiable than usual. Mr Mawne, to my surprise, was in a bantering mood, quite unlike his normal vague daze, and I could sense that the couple were on edge with each other. Mrs Mawne prodded a piece of beef with a disdainful finger as Mr Mawne greeted me with unnaturally high spirits.

'Well, well, well, Miss Read! What a morning, eh? Just right for a trip to the sea!'

Mrs Mawne sniffed and I said guardedly that it was indeed a fine morning.

'Another trip to Barrisford would be just the thing!' said Mr Mawne with one eye on his wife. I disliked this teasing very much, particularly as he was using me to annoy his wife. The butcher looked at me as though I were Jezebel.

'We had a most enjoyable trip together last year,' continued Mr Mawne, addressing his wife. 'I really believe Miss Read would come again if I asked her nicely!' Mrs Mawne grew red and her mouth tightened. I was no more pleased than she was and looked steadily at her facetious little husband.

'I fear that you flatter yourself, Mr Mawne,' I said, and then felt a brute as his face fell under this pin-prick to his self-esteem.

'I'll call later,' I said to the butcher, and left the shop and the Mawnes as quickly as I could.

Amy was in one of her what-a-pity-you-aren't-married moods when she arrived for lunch, particularly irritating after Mr Mawne's earlier exhibition of male conceit.

'Now James,' she told me, attacking the beef with gusto, 'is absolutely devoted and seems to get fonder of me as the years go by.' With a heroic effort I desisted from reminding her of several unhappy occasions when she had endured James's lapses from strict fidelity. 'Sour grapes' is the phrase that readily trips from the lips of married ladies when reminded by their single friends about male frailty, and behind this two-word shield many a married man or woman has evaded a spinster's straight aim.

'You see what a waste of talent all this is,' continued Amy, as

I bore in a plum pie, a little later. 'You're quite a good cook, really and a man would appreciate it.'

'I appreciate it too,' I said, cutting the crust.

'But with two of you,' persisted Amy, bent on furthering the cause of matrimony, 'you would enjoy it all far more.'

'I should have to do twice as much cooking,' I pointed out, 'and that might pall.'

'Really!' said Amy exasperatedly, 'you are the most trying, awkward, maddening, *unfeminine* woman I've met, and thoroughly deserve to be single!'

'Have some cream,' I suggested consolingly. 'It covers the nerve endings.'

'Tchah!' exclaimed Amy, and took a generous helping with a smile.

The shock came as we were washing up. Amy wandered to and fro in the kitchen drying up for me and occasionally returning a piece of china for a second wash. Amy's standards are much higher than mine and she scrutinized each article with an eagle eye.

'I know two adorable sisters,' I told her as she flung back a spoon into the washing-up bowl, 'who work on the principle that one wets the things and the other wipes. And a very nice cooperative job they make of washing-up with never a harsh word between them!'

Amy was not impressed.

'I don't wonder Mrs Pringle ticks you off. Look at this smear of mustard! Must be ages old! It's a wonder you don't pop off with typhus!'

I surveyed the plate which she held out to me with interest.

'That,' I said, with pardonable smugness, 'happens to be gilding.'

Amy had the grace to laugh, and returned it to the dresser. As she lodged it she said:

'And when is Hilary Jackson going away?'

'She's gone,' I answered, busily scouring the sink.

'Well, I saw her last night, with that dreadful Franklyn fellow. They were just going into "The Bell"!'

I felt as though I had been hit. Could that foolish young woman really be in the neighbourhood? Was she really so infatuated with Franklyn that she could deceive Miss Clare and her parents and also hope to evade the all-seeing eye of Fairacre and its environs? Or could Amy have been mistaken? I clung, for one endless second, to this forlorn hope, but in my heart I knew immediately that Amy was far too sharp-eyed to be deceived. And I knew too, with a sudden sickness, that Hilary Jackson was quite silly enough to imperil her good name, the happiness of her friends and her teaching career, at the promptings of this ill-fated infatuation.

In a flash I decided that Amy must not know of my doubts. There was still a chance that I might be able to get in touch with the girl and get her to see sense before the tongues started wagging in the neighbourhood.

'She must have gone off this morning then,' I said, trying to sound casual.

Luckily, Tibby created a most welcome diversion by bringing in a squeaking shrew. In the following few frantic minutes, whilst Amy and I tried to rescue it from the outraged cat, Miss Jackson and her affairs were shelved.

At two o'clock Amy drove off. I had found the time from her disclosure until her departure agonisingly long, and could only hope that my anxiety was not too apparent.

I waved goodbye with relief, and before the car was round the bend of the lane I had fled up the stairs, two at a time, to get myself ready for my visit to the cottage in the woods, where I hoped to find Miss Jackson.

It seemed best to go on my bicycle, for the steep track would tax my ancient car's asthmatic powers, and would be more readily noticed. A bicycle, leaning against John Franklyn's fence, could be anybody's, but the car could belong to me alone.

The day was close and sticky. Clouds of minute thunderflies wafted about in the warm air, tormenting and tickling sensitive places like one's neck and eyes. I was seriously perturbed, as I pushed along, about the best way to handle this uncomfortable interview. It might be easier, though perhaps more painful for Hilary Jackson, if Franklyn were there, for I had no doubt that the craven fellow would be only too pleased to back out of an awkward situation, and would side with me in persuading the girl to return. No gallant hero, this Franklyn, I suspected, but the sort of man who would let a girl break her heart rather than endanger his own skin.

Hilary alone might be a different proposition, full of fervid and misplaced loyalties and seeing herself as the Passionate Woman Who Dared All for Love. A middle-aged headmistress, plain, and untouched by romance, stood a small chance of succeeding against such formidable odds, I told myself.

The track grew steeper and dustier and I dismounted. So far I had not met a soul. I stood on the slope of the downs and looked back to the peaceful valley. The still heat was all-enveloping and shimmered on the road so far below. In the dry fine grass, which whispered at my bicycle wheel, a cricket chirruped tirelessly, and away above, a speck against the dark clouds which gathered ominously above the wood, a lark trickled out his clear song, like sparkling drops from a fountain. With that awareness which comes from a state of heightened emotion I could hear each separate liquid note, and smell the aromatic tang of the small thyme bruised under my feet. From a tall dock plant near by hung a dying scarlet leaf, a neat and elegant triangle, fluttering like a pennant from a mast. It was as though these small lovely things held out their beauty for the comfort of my sad heart. How easy to succumb, to sit upon this thymy bank and to lose oneself in the company of these old and ever-faithful friends! What business was it of mine to meddle with Hilary Jackson's affairs, whispered a small siren's voice?

Sighing, I resumed my uphill pushing, and with a throbbing head and heavy heart approached the cottage in the woods.

Hilary Jackson was alone. She had answered my knock at the kitchen door, her face flushed and her eyes bright but wary. She had invited me into the dim interior, cool after the heat of the climb, and we sat now, one each side of the grubby kitchen table and surveyed each other.

'John,' said the girl, throwing the Christian name across at me like a challenge, 'John has gone to Caxley and should be back for tea. Perhaps you'll stop?' Her air was studiedly insolent and she was more nervous than she cared to admit. I decided that a plain approach would be best.

'Miss Clare is under the impression that you returned home yesterday. Only by chance I heard that you had been seen in Caxley yesterday evening.'

'And what have my affairs to do with Miss Clare? Or anyone else, for that matter?' demanded the girl, tossing her head.

'Only this – that the way you behave is noticed by everybody in a small community. By consorting with John Franklyn, whose affairs have been watched for many years, I may say, you are giving yourself a bad name. As a teacher you should be doubly careful of the example you set and by flaunting the conventions – which are, after all, only the commonly accepted modes of decent living – you are not only making a fool of yourself but jeopardizing your whole career. One silly slip now may mean much future unhappiness.'

Hilary's face had darkened as my homily unwound.

'I don't care a row of pins for what people think of me – back-biting, narrow-minded, evil-thinking country bumpkins, as stodgy as you are yourself! John Franklyn is a fine man and I'm proud to be seen with him. I suppose a withered old spinster like you thinks that love doesn't matter! Well, it does – and for me everything else must take second place!'

Her eyes flashed behind her thick spectacles and she thumped vehemently upon the kitchen table. I answered her quietly.

'The world is never "well lost for love" in my opinion. And this is not even love, I'm afraid, but a foolish infatuation on your part which I am positive John Franklyn does not share.'

'You'd never dare to say that to his face!' she flared.

'Indeed I would, and I hoped that he would be here when I called. I think that you might have seen him in his true colours.'

There was a pause in the heat of the battle. Through the open door came soft woodland scents that cooled my warm blood. I tried again.

'Look, Hilary. Please come back to the school-house with me for the night. I'll take you to the station early tomorrow and you can get home with no one knowing any more about this business. I shall say nothing to Miss Clare, or anyone else, and we can scotch any rumours started by people yesterday.'

The girl rounded on me furiously.

'Do you think I'm ashamed to be seen with him? Why, I'm *glad* that people saw us together yesterday! I suppose your beastly mind thinks that we spent the night here. Well, it's wrong! I stayed at John's sister's in Caxley, and she thinks I've gone home today!' Her voice was strident and triumphant, and her eyes glittered with dangerous excitement. She thrust her face close to mine. 'And where I spend tonight is my own business! I'm old enough to look after myself!'

'Old enough,' I said sadly, rising to my feet, 'but not wise enough. I can see you're in no mood to see reason. Someone will have to make you – but I can't obviously.'

I drew the door further back and made my way unhappily into the green and gold glory of the wooded garden.

Hilary Jackson stood in the doorway, pink and panting from the tussle, and exalted with her own fine, but foolish, outpourings. She looked so young and silly that I remembered Jemima Puddleduck who was so cruelly deceived by another foxy-whiskered gentleman.

'I'll be in Fairacre if you want me,' I called back, lifting my bicycle from the fence. 'Don't be too proud to ask for help if you need it. And *please do* think over what I've said!'

'*Amor omnia vincit!*' quoted Miss Jackson, loudly and soulfully. And, distressed as I was, I noted that my assistant's pronunciation of Latin was execrable.

It was hotter and more oppressive than ever as I rode back down the steep slope to the Fairacre road. I must get in touch with her parents at once, I told myself, my head throbbing and eyes half-closed against the myriad flies that bombarded my face.

I did not know the Jacksons' address and nothing would make me worry Miss Clare for it, ill as she was. Luckily, by the time I was pedalling along the road towards the spire of St Patrick's, I remembered the name of Hilary's home town in the Midlands, and also that her father's Christian name was Oliver.

Black clouds were gathering swiftly overhead and there were ominous rumblings from the Caxley direction as I entered the school-house and made straight for the telephone.

'Inquiries, please,' I said to the girl and sat down thankfully, cradling the receiver. The line crackled as the thunder grew nearer. There was a rushing sound outside as the wind which precedes a storm lifted the branches of the elm trees that stand at the corner of the playground. A fierce eddy twirled a few dead leaves and dust round and round, in a miniature whirlwind, outside the window.

The girl was a long time in tracking down the Jacksons' telephone number from the few poor clues that I could supply. As I waited I was torn with anxiety. Supposing that they had already gone to the house by the sea and that there was no one at home? This was Saturday, and people generally took over a holiday house on that day of the week. And if I did get through – how on earth could I word the dreadful news which I must transmit? Confound the wretched girl, I thought wrathfully, ruining my own and her parents' holidays!

A jagged orange streak split the black sky behind St Patrick's, and a crash like a ton of coals let down upon the school-house roof, rocked the room. A faint voice spoke through the hubbub.

'You're through!' it said.

Mr Jackson listened to my somewhat incoherent remarks with commendable patience.

'I'll come straight away,' he said decisively. 'I can be there in two hours and I'll bring her back with me. Don't worry, and many thanks!'

I said I was so relieved to find them at home.

'My wife had an attack of migraine,' he answered, 'so we postponed the journey until tomorrow.'

Another fearful crash shattered the air around me, and must have penetrated to the telephone.

'Are you all right?' said Mr Jackson. He sounded alarmed. I

explained that we were in the midst of a violent thunderstorm.

'Oh!' said he, 'that all? For a moment I thought you'd fainted! I'll ring off now, and be on my way!'

Through the teeming rain which now lashed against the window I saw the church clock. The hands stood at half past four. On trembling legs I made my way to the kitchen and filled the kettle.

I spent the next few hours making plum jam, with a quarter of my mind on the operation and the other three-quarters imagining the happenings at the game-keeper's cottage. Would Hilary refuse to go? Would there be any violence? Would the cottage have been struck by lightning and the sorrowing vengeful father arrive only to find two charred bodies among the smoking embers? I did my best to curb these morbid fancies and to concentrate on the jam, but it was uphill work.

The storm still raged and muttered, following the line of the downs. At times it died away in intensity, but returned again periodically with renewed vigour. The playground streamed with water and I guessed that the skylight would be letting through a regular steady trickle into my classroom.

At nine o'clock the telephone rang. It was Mr Jackson's comfortable deep voice at the other end.

'All's well! A few tears on the way, and now the girl's in bed. I thought you might be worrying. We'll write from the other house. Meanwhile, all our thanks.'

What a day, I thought, as I climbed the stairs to bed two hours later. The gutters still gurgled and the thunder still growled in the distance. I looked out upon Fairacre's glistening church and a few streaming roofs among the tossing trees.

This was the halcyon village I had mooned over so sentimentally early in the holidays, I thought grimly. Where now was the tranquil sunshine, the serenity, the innocent-hearted populace going about its honest business?

I thought of the misplaced passion of Hilary Jackson, the cupidity of John Franklyn, the evil gossiping of neighbours, the sad injustice of Miss Clare's ill-health, the misery of the

Coggs family at the mercy of their drunken father under the broken dripping thatch of Tylers' Row, of the chained unhappy dogs in back gardens, bedraggled hens cooped all too closely in bare rank runs, and, over all, the tension engendered by the housing scheme and the ugly passions it aroused.

A flash of lightning illuminated the landscape in quivering mauve and yellow lights, distorting its normal lovely colouring to something livid and sinister.

Sick at heart, with the noise of the storm still raging round me, I sought in vain for the comfort of sleep.

PART THREE

Thunder and Lightning

15. Dr Martin is Busy

ON the hottest day of the year Dr Martin drove on his rounds along the winding lanes of Fairacre. Heat throbbed from the dusty road, the cows were gathered into any patch of shade that they could find, and the distant downs shimmered under a burning sky.

He had just paid a visit to old Mr Miller who had not fully recovered from his paroxysm at the parish meeting. He had aged considerably since this infernal business about the housing estate had blown up, thought Dr Martin. In a long life Mr Miller had had many troubles, but usually he had had his own way. The possession of his farm and his beloved acres, inherited from his family and in trust for the next generation, had given him confidence and joy. With that threatened he was a lost man, and though he fought bravely and his spirit burnt as fiercely as ever, his ageing body paid the price. He no longer slept the deep dreamless slumber of the healthily tired man who has spent the day working in the open air. His appetite had dwindled, and his sturdy compact little figure now had a pathetic droop. Dr Martin knew well that his medicines could do little against this spiritual canker. He doubted very much if they were taken at all, and though he had prescribed sleeping tablets for his crusty patient, he had been told by poor tearful Mrs Miller that her husband would not countenance them. Ah, it was a wretched threat that hung over them all! And until the thing was settled, one way or the other, Dr Martin supposed that he and his country neighbours would have to continue from day to day feeling as though a weight lay upon their chests.

He drew his car into the side of the lane, switched off the engine and filled his pipe meditatively. Through a wide gap in the hazel hedge beside him he had a clear view of Hundred Acre Field and the threatened landscape, which lay now with a heart-lifting serenity before him. How long those lovely lines had endured, thought the doctor, blowing out a fragrant blue cloud of tobacco smoke!

How many troubled and heavy-hearted men before him, clad in homespun, silks and lace, doublet and hose . . . ay, and rough furs too . . . had looked, as he did now, at those immemorial downs and had there found comfort? 'I will lift up mine eyes unto the hills, from whence cometh my help,' the psalmist had said, in plain, sober, simple words, as lovely and as refreshing as clear water. And as vital too, the doctor mused, his mind now running on his patients. In these last few months he had had far more cases suffering from nervous strain than ever before. His advice was generally, 'Get out into the fresh air. Look at the life about you. Look out and not in. Nature can cure you where I can't. I can only give her a hand.'

Doctor Martin was a wise man and took his own advice. His observant eye watched now a bee pushing its way busily in and out among the velvety toadflax flowers that flared beneath the hedge in the hot sunlight. Along the edge of the open window crawled a ladybird, so recently alighted that its underwings were untidily folded under their red enamelled case, and protruded gauzy black snippets. It was moments like these, precious, quiet, contemplative breaks in the doctor's busy day that revived him, and gave him the happiness and power to inspire his patients.

'Did me good just to see him,' people said. 'Always got time to listen to you. That chap at Caxley, as is always buzzing about like a blue-bottle, fair puts you in a tizzy when he comes tearing into the room, and don't appear to listen to half you says. Now our Doctor Martin he can speak sharp if need be, but you knows it's for your own good and he intends to get you well again. He's a real gentleman!'

The doctor took a last refreshing look at the view through the gap. In the distance he could see the humped thatch of Miss Clare's cottage, his next calling place. He'd better get along, he supposed, switching on the engine. Do the job before him and not linger too much on the misty future.

The engine came to life, but before moving off the doctor rested his hot sticky hands on the wheel and gazed unseeingly before him. He was drowsier than usual, in this heat, and say what you like this housing estate was deuced unsettling for a man of his age. What would become of him and his wife and all his great family of patients? He looked forward to retiring very soon, to spending more time with his much-loved wife, to tending his roses which were among the finest in the country, to pottering about in Fairacre – but the Fairacre he loved and worked in for so many years, not some raw new suburb of Caxley, smearing his beloved hills. It might be better to move if this came about. But why on earth should he? Lord, it was little enough to ask after a long life, surely? Just a few years' rest in the same place, with the same friends, the same pastimes and hobbies – and the same, please God, the same downs!

The doctor blinked rapidly and let in the clutch.

'Let's see if Dolly Clare can give me a cup of tea,' said he to the ladybird. 'If I go on like this I shall be in bed with poor old Miller!'

Miss Clare, in Dr Martin's opinion, had gone back in health during the past few weeks and he knew, as well as the rest of Fairacre knew, just why. The indiscretions of her lodger had not passed completely unnoticed, though no one quite knew how far the affair had gone. Miss Clare had been blaming herself needlessly for not warning the girl against the Franklyn fellow, whose name was a byword. Could she have helped her more? The question remained unanswered in the days that followed Hilary Jackson's adventure, and sadly troubled Miss Clare.

Mr and Mrs Annett had evolved a plan of which Dr Martin thoroughly approved.

'We're taking a little house for three weeks in August, by the sea, near Barrisford,' George Annett had said to the doctor when he had called in with young Malcolm's tonic.

'Though why he needs a tonic, I really don't know,' observed the doctor, eyeing his young patient, who was bouncing energetically up and down in his pram to the detriment of its springs.

'But you ordered it!' protested Mrs Annett, wide-eyed. She looked up from buckling her exuberant son into his harness.

'Should have been bromide,' returned the doctor, smiling.

'Push him into the garden and then come and tell me all about the holiday plans.'

It appeared that the Annetts were as perturbed as the doctor himself was about Miss Clare's frail health, and had invited her to spend the three weeks with them by the sea, but she had gently declined.

'There's a spare bedroom,' went on Mrs Annett earnestly, 'and we truthfully would love her to be with us, and I'm sure the air would do her a world of good –'

'But she feels she may be in the way; that she would be an added expense, that you three young things should be together alone, and so on, and so on. I know. You don't have to tell me what's in Dolly Clare's mind. She's a living saint and as obstinate as a mule,' responded Dr Martin.

'Can you do anything to help?' asked Mr Annett.

'I should think I might try,' said the doctor, his eye taking on that gleam which meant that he was up to his tricks. 'I shall tell her that you two could get out together if she weren't such a selfish old woman as to refuse to do an hour or two's sitting-in –'

'*Please*,' begged Mrs Annett, horrified, 'don't say anything so wicked!'

'And then I could tell her that I am having sleepless nights because she is such an obstinate patient and won't do as she's told, and my health is suffering,' he continued warming to his theme. 'And finally, I could threaten her with Sister Ada who has offered, somewhat grudgingly, to have her there if need be. That should settle it nicely,' said this incorrigible meddler in the affairs of others, with a satisfied smile.

The Annetts gazed at him aghast. George was the first to find his breath.

'I don't really think there's any need for such wholesale lying,' he began in a schoolmasterish voice, but he was cut short.

'There's no need at all,' agreed the doctor with a disarming smile, making his way to the door, 'but I enjoy a thundering good lie if it makes my patients see reason. Remember your Kipling?'

He stood in the doorway, his white hair standing out like an aureole, and his eyes twinkling.

> 'Not a little place at Tooting –
> But a country house with shooting,
> And a ring-fence, deer-park lie!'

he quoted triumphantly, and vanished into the sunshine.

The door of Miss Clare's cottage stood ajar on that throbbing hot afternoon. Dr Martin put his head round, but there was no one to be seen.

He stepped down into the brick-floored living room. It was cool in here, under the sheltering thatch, and a fine bouquet of mixed roses caught his eye. Their reflection gleamed in the polished table on which they stood.

He looked around him, noting the freshness of the curtains, the gleam of copper on the mantelpiece and the crystal clearness of Miss Clare's leaded panes. These silent objects stood as proof of their mistress's zeal and devotion to them. They might be older than, and as frail as, their owner, but they were as full of grace.

'An hour's less polishing, and one more hour in bed,' thought Dr Martin, 'would be ideal, but I'll never get her to do that, I fear.'

A small noise above attracted his attention. He went to the door of the box staircase, opened it by its latch, and called aloft.

'Anybody there?'

There was a creaking of a bed and Miss Clare's voice answered.

'I'll be down in just one moment, doctor. I was having a rest.'

'You stay there then. I'll be up,' said the doctor, stooping for his black bag.

'But I'm in my petticoat –' began Miss Clare.

'All the better,' responded Dr Martin, mounting the narrow stairs sturdily, 'I want to listen to your chest, anyway.'

He entered the bedroom to find his patient propped up

against two fat feather pillows, with the eiderdown over her legs. Miss Clare's top half was decorously clad in a pale-grey lock-knit petticoat with a modestly high neckline. A novel lay, face downward, upon the bed.

'It was too hot for anything round my shoulders,' she said.

'Well, you won't shock me, my dear, I can assure you. That petticoat's a sight more decent than Minnie Pringle's sun top she was flaunting in the lane just now.'

He fetched a cane-bottomed chair, set it by the bedside, and adjusted his stethoscope. It was very quiet in the cottage bedroom. Outside a faint rustling came from the jasmine at the window, and a sparrow, who lived in the thatch above, glanced in, upside down, with a beady eye and, with a frightened chirrup, flew away.

'Humph!' said the doctor grimly, folding up his instrument and stuffing it in the black bag. 'You're not doing as well as you should.'

'I'm sorry,' said Miss Clare contritely, and patted the doctor's hand, as though it were he, and not she, who needed reassurance. Dr Martin saw his opening.

'I must admit it worries me. Here I am doing all I can for you – and I do honestly believe you are eating more and resting more often – but you don't quite get on as I'd like. I don't mind telling you, Dolly, I'm begining to wonder if I'm past my job.' He shook his white head slowly. For such a burly fellow he really had a very nice line in pathos. Miss Clare watched him quizzically.

'You can't be expected to replace worn-out hearts,' she said gently. Dr Martin continued to look sad.

'I wonder if you ought to join forces with your sister Ada,' he said, with such sweet, spontaneous reasonableness, that even he was surprised to hear his own voice.

'Never!' said Miss Clare firmly. 'Not even for your comfort, doctor!'

Dr Martin now rose and paced restlessly about the diminutive bedroom, his head narrowly missing the beam that ran across the whitewashed ceiling. He had thrust his hands into his pockets, and with shoulders hunched he prowled thoughtfully, wearing an expression of extreme perplexity. Miss Clare watched him affectionately.

'If only you could get away somewhere – have a change of air, preferably by the sea – say, for two or three weeks, I believe it would set you up completely.'

'Would it?' said Miss Clare, with suspicious meekness.

'Indeed it would. Otherwise, I must see about a nursing home or something of that nature for you, for a spell before the winter.'

There was a slightly threatening note in this last sentence, which did not elude Miss Clare.

'And what about my lodger?'

'Your lodger,' burst out the good doctor, standing stock-still and glaring at his patient over the bedrail, 'could do with a dam' good spanking, and I hope her father's given her one by this time!'

'She's only young and silly –' Miss Clare began to protest; but she was cut short.

'I won't waste my breath on such a fool, but she's responsible for your set-back, and that I cannot forgive.'

'I shall get better now that the holidays are here. Don't worry about me.'

'You won't unless you get away. Everything here reminds you of her, and in your present low state it will take more than half an hour under the eiderdown to cure you, my girl.' There was a pause, and doctor and patient looked steadily at each other across the quiet room. The doctor broke the silence first.

'Dolly, I shan't feel at ease until you have a holiday. What about it?'

Miss Clare gave him a slow, lovely smile, but her eyes were mischievous.

'You've been talking to the Annetts,' she said.

Dr Martin threw his head back in a gusty laugh.

'Well, what of it?' he protested. 'I did just have a word –'

'And planned all this after that word!' smiled Miss Clare. 'And how well you do it too! I was beginning to feel quite anxious about your failing powers!'

'But, Dolly,' said the doctor, suddenly grave. 'Will you go?

It isn't all humbug, you know. I'd like you to be well again. This offer means health for you, and a chance for those two young people to get out on their own without that baby, if you'd feel up to coping with it occasionally.'

This aspect of it, as the wily doctor had foreseen, touched Miss Clare at once.

'If I really can be of help,' she said slowly, 'then I will go with the greatest pleasure.'

'You will!' shouted Dr Martin, with delight. 'That's the best news I've heard today. Now mind you keep your word!'

'Of course I shall,' said Miss Clare indignantly. 'And now, if you'll wait downstairs I'll get dressed and we'll make a pot of tea.'

'Put your legs straight back under the eiderdown,' ordered her medical adviser, 'and *I'll* make the tea and bring it up here.'

Whistling discordantly, the doctor clattered cheerfully downstairs.

His last call of the day was at Fairacre school-house where he found a most interesting operation going on.

Mrs Pringle had for many months deplored, loudly and bitterly, the condition of the spare-room feather bed.

'One heave,' she had said to me, 'and the room's thick with feathers! As soon as we gets a fine still day I'll tip the lot into a new ticking I'll run up for you.'

She had been as good as her word, and the new striped mattress cover, with its inside seams carefully sealed with a dampened piece of that yellow bar soap which was Mrs Pringle's household standby, lay spread on the lawn awaiting its contents.

Mrs Pringle and I had spread an enormous sheet on the grass and together had emptied out a mountain of feathers, white, speckled and coppery brown, upon it. Mr Willet, who had come to clip the hedges, had abandoned his job and joined us on the lawn. He greeted the doctor boisterously.

'Us only wants the tar, doctor, then us be all ready for you!'

'Not in this heat, Willet. Have pity, man,' said Dr Martin,

settling himself in the shade. He looked at Mrs Pringle who was busy turning the feathers over and over, 'to get a bit of clean air into the poor things,' as she so tactfully told me.

'That leg any better?' he enquired.

'Torture!' said that lady implacably. 'Simple torture. Flaring, burning, twitching, jumping, itching, throbbing –'

'No better then, I take it,' said the doctor calmly. He lay back upon the grass and closed his eyes. Mrs Pringle cast a disgusted glance at his peaceful figure.

'What if a wind come up?' asked Mr Willet suddenly.

'Come wind, come rain, come fair, come foul,' announced Mts Pringle majestically, 'my leg's still torture to me.'

'Wasn't speaking of your leg, gal, but the feathers,' responded Mr Willet without gallantry. 'You wants to thank the Lord you're not worse. Remember last Sunday's psalm?'

'I know as well as you do,' answered Mrs Pringle sourly, 'and I remember some pretty botched-up singing too, in that new chant.'

Mr Willet was stung.

'There wasn't one of us in that choir could sing that agrarian chant,' he said wrathfully. 'I don't say Annett don't know his job at teaching, but for a choir-master he's got pretty rum ideas. Too popish by half, if you ask me! Might just as well go to St Peter's over the other side of Caxley!'

'And what, pray,' began Mrs Pringle loftily, 'is wrong with St Peter's? I went there a time or two when I was courting and we had some real beautiful services.'

'I been there,' said Mr Willet heavily, 'but the once. Never again, I said, never again! Pictures all round the walls, curtains hanging up, candles blazing away all over the place, people bobbing up and down – I tell you! ' Mr Willet's sturdy Calvinistic frame shook at the very remembrance of the place.

Dr Martin rolled over on to his front, giving me a slow wink on his course.

'And that minister of theirs,' continued Mr Willet warmly, 'a beardless boy, young enough to be me son, told me to call him father when I spoke to him! I tell you it's against nature – and so's that agrarian chanting, to my mind; no proper tune at all!'

'Maybe you just don't know real music when you hears it,' suggested Mrs Pringle sarcastically. She bent over the feathers, corsets creaking, and began to stuff handfuls into the new mattress cover. I knelt down beside her, and Mr Willet and Dr Martin set to with us.

The sun beat on our heads and the white sheet reflected the light blindingly. Despite the heat and energetic thrusting of feathers Mr Willet rose to the challenge.

'I heard the *Messiah* at the Corn Exchange last year,' puffed Mr Willet, 'and that's what I call real music. Good, plain, God-fearing, English-sounding music that you can sing out hearty! It done you good! Plenty of up and down, and soft and loud, and everyone having a rattlin' good time of it!'

'Takes some beating,' agreed the doctor, sneezing some feathers from his nose. 'Here, why don't we lift the lot up in the sheet and ram it all in?'

This sensible suggestion was welcomed. Mrs Pringle and I folded the sheet carefully, imprisoning the rest of the ubiquitous feathers some of which had floated far and wide in the summer garden, while the two men held open the gaping mouth of the ticking.

Coughing and spluttering we finally made the transfer. The sheet still bore a mass of fluff and the lawn looked as though a snowstorm had passed over.

'Fiddlin' stuff!' observed Mr Willet, 'but it give us all a nice set-down and a chat. I'll be back to my hedges.'

He stumped off, swinging the shears and humming to himself. Mrs Pringle watched him go.

'What that chap lacks,' said she slowly, 'is soul!'

Dr Martin refused all refreshment, picked himself a rosebud and returned to his car.

'Nearly forgot,' he said. 'I called to tell you that Miss Clare is going to have a break with the Annetts, by the sea.'

'That's absolutely wonderful!' I cried. 'How did they manage to persuade her?'

'They didn't,' answered Dr Martin smugly. 'I did!' The car moved slowly forward.

'And what farrago of arguments did you concoct this time?' I shouted, after the departing car.

Two derisive hoots were my answer, and I returned, smiling, to my feathered garden.

16. Miss Crabbe Reappears

THE heat continued. A few days after Dr Martin's visit I went to Devonshire to spend three weeks with two sisters, friends of mine since childhood, who owned a cottage by the sea. Sunshine, sea, bathing, boating, walking and the cheerful companionship of old friends dispelled my Fairacre worries about Miss Clare, the future of the school, the housing estate and the problem of Hilary Jackson's affairs of the heart.

The holiday was almost at an end and I was spending an hour doing a little leisurely shopping for gifts to take back with me, when I decided that the blazing sunshine reflected from the tiny market-square's cobbles, called for an ice.

I turned into a small café and on opening the door came face to face with Miss Crabbe. Our mouths dropped open in surprise.

'On holiday?' I inquired weakly. Miss Crabbe assured me that she was combining business with pleasure, attending a summer course at a nearby manor house recently taken over for this purpose.

I persuaded her to return to her table and eat another ice while she told me all about it. My invitation was not completely altruistic, as I welcomed this opportunity of finding out how matters stood between this lady and my unfortunate assistant.

'The course is most imaginatively conceived,' began Miss Crabbe, and I felt that dreadful ennui overtaking me as she got into her stride. 'It deals with every possible means of self-expression, and we have tackled pottery-making, miming, finger-painting and stick printing. Some of us have attempted some really worth while work in music, making our own instruments first, as a matter of course, and I have made a set of most satisfying bamboo pipes.'

The voice droned on whilst I demolished my ice. As I had noticed during Miss Crabbe's visit to my house she had the ability to eat and talk at the same time, and even quite large portions of strawberry ice seemed to glide down, whilst an endless flow of words streamed up, from the same orifice. I was fascinated.

No mention was made of Miss Jackson and I determined to broach the subject myself. There was no doubt about it, Miss Jackson might well be influenced by the woman who now sat with me, and it was worth asking for her help. Hilary's reckless behaviour with this undesirable man had dated from her clash over him with Miss Crabbe, for before that time, as far as I knew, she had been a little more circumspect. What Miss Crabbe thought really mattered to the girl, and I suspected that their estrangement was a secret source of grief to both of them, but that neither would give way.

Miss Crabbe's countenance flushed an unlovely pink when I spoke of Hilary Jackson.

'I have had no word from her since we met at Fairacre,' she said stiffly.'We had made tentative plans for visiting Brittany, but as I heard nothing, I applied to come on this course at the last minute. She seems to have become a very silly girl since she left college. We all had great hopes of her there.' The last two sentences were spoken so primly that she could only infer that Hilary's shocking state of silliness was due to the influence of those foolish people whom she had met since leaving college! I did not rise to this bait.

'To be frank,' I said, 'I think Hilary Jackson has always been a silly girl, but she has two great qualities, warm-hearted affection, and loyalty to her friends. In this affair with Franklyn it is these two qualities which have led her astray.'

I paused for a moment, wondering whether I dared to go on. Miss Crabbe's mouth, now mercifully free from food, was set in a stubborn line. I decided that I might as well hang for a sheep as a lamb and continued.

'If only she could have continued to direct this affection and loyalty to you, I think all would have blown over between Hilary and this fellow, but when she saw that you – er – felt so strongly about it she was forced to take sides. Unfortunately, she took the wrong side, and because she was so thoroughly miserable she flung herself at this man.'

'Then she's only herself to blame,' remarked Miss Crabbe decidedly, but to my watchful eye she appeared slightly mollified.

'Loyalty to him,' I went on, 'won't allow her to get in touch with you as she knows that you don't approve; but, believe me, she has been desperately unhappy about this break, and I know she'd give the world to make things up if only you'd give her a sign.'

Miss Crabbe began drawing geometrical patterns on the tablecloth with the handle of her spoon. Her face was set and thoughtful. She too, I guessed, had suffered considerably from the withdrawal of her young friend's adulation. Jealousy of John Franklyn was merely the outcome of her own overweening pride.

'It would be so much easier for you to make the first move,' I went on. 'You are an older, wiser woman, and if you left John Franklyn's name out of it for a bit I'm positive that the whole wretched affair would die a natural death. The man does not want it, I feel convinced. Meanwhile Hilary makes herself unhappy, and Miss Clare and her parents, and all her friends.'

'She does indeed,' said Miss Crabbe slowly and softly. She looked up from her drawing and took a deep breath.

'I'll think it over. It might be a good thing for the girl,' she said.

'It would be a great service to everyone,' I responded. Particularly to Miss Crabbe herself, I surmised privately. 'I should be very grateful indeed, She is at the start of a very promising career. A word from the right person now means such a lot.'

Miss Crabbe inclined her head graciously.

I looked at my watch.

'Would you like to come and meet my friends?' I asked. 'They have a little house in Fore Street, just round the corner.'

But Miss Crabbe excused herself, saying that she must get back to a percussion band class after tea.

We parted amicably in the hot sunshine.

'I'm glad we met,' I said truthfully, 'and do please help if you feel that you can!'

'I shall sleep on it,' Miss Crabbe assured me solemnly, 'but I think I may say, here and now, that I shall extend the olive branch to that poor misguided child.'

And so we parted, she to her percussion band class and I to my friends' cottage, where I celebrated this minor victory with scones, strawberry jam and a large dish of clotted Devonshire cream.

The countryside, as I approached Fairacre on the return drive, slept peacefully in the heat. Things were getting their shabby end-of-August look. The trees were heavy and dusty, the grassy banks parched by the prolonged sunshine, and already the farmers were busy harvesting. In the fields of one or two of the smaller farms the stooks of corn waited in neat rows for the farm carts which would take them to the ricks, but on Mr Miller's Hundred Acre Field, a combine-harvester crawled busily along, an enormous red monster that poured the grain from its gaping mouth into a truck that drove slowly beside it collecting the rich harvest. This was the crop that Miss Clare had watched growing beside her garden, throughout the year, and the one which two strangers had studied on that Spring morning, so long, it seemed, ago.

The school-house at Beech Green was shuttered, I noticed, as I drove by, and Miss Clare's little house too. They would all be returning at the week-end, for school began on Tuesday morning. I sincerely hoped that Miss Clare's health would have benefited from the sea air and sunshine.

My own house greeted me with a wonderful aroma of furniture polish. Mrs Pringle had been left in charge of my household matters, the cat Tibby being the most important of her duties. This disdainful animal came down the stairs as I entered and greeted my own effusive cries with a glassy stare, never pausing in his progress to the garden.

A bottle of milk stood on the kitchen table and under it lay a note in Mrs Pringle's hand. It said:

Dear Miss Read

Hope you have had a good time. Milk here six eggs in safe lettuce and tomattos in basket and bread in the bin. Young Prince had not no holemeal but only this coberg (white).

Cat have et like a horse.

Mrs Pringle.

I boiled one of the eggs for my tea, for I had made an early start and was hungry, and carried my tray into the sunny garden. How lovely it was to be back, I thought! The garden was drooping sadly in the drought, the lawn was scorched and the garden beds were baked hard, but it still smelt fragrant and lapped me in peace, and the air from the high downs blew softly upon it all. Tibby, seeing food, approached me lovingly and gave me, at last, a belated wlcome.

I was still sitting in the garden, reading back numbers of *The Times Educational Supplement* which had piled up in my absence, when Mrs Partridge called bearing the Parish Magazine.

'Well, well, my dear!' she greeted me affectionately. 'It is so nice to see you back again.'

'Tell me all the news,' I begged, pushing a deck chair towards her. She settled herself in it gingerly.

'I never quite trust them,' she confessed. 'As a child I caught my finger in one once, and the nail went quite black and had to be taken off at the hospital –'

'Please don't tell me,' I pleaded hastily, 'I'm a squeamish woman, and anything like that makes my back open and shut like Mrs Pringle's!'

Mrs Partridge smiled kindly.

'Then I won't tell you, my dear, for the sequel was perfectly horrid.' She licked her lips ghoulishly, and took a breath.

'It went septic –' she began, but I cut her short.

'DON'T!' I protested, putting my hands over my ears.

Mrs Partridge opened her eyes very wide, and I saw her lips moving. Very cautiously I took my hands away.

'So of course I won't mention it again,' she was saying. Breathing a sigh of relief I put my hands back in my lap.

'What's happened in Fairacre?' I pursued. 'Any births, deaths or marriages?'

'No. No, I don't think so,' said the vicar's wife in a slow, considering voice. Then her eyes brightened.

'But Mrs Pringle tells me that Minnie is expecting her fourth in the New Year.'

'Make a nice change to have one born in wedlock,' I said comfortably, closing my eyes against the sun's lowering rays. Mrs Partridge agreed.

'And the estate?' I ventured.

'Not a word more directly. We've heard that the Planning Committee of the County Council object to the idea. It doesn't fit in with their ideas for that area any more than it does with ours. So we're all unanimous on that point. But that's not to say there isn't plenty of strong feeling in Caxley and elsewhere. I suppose that the County Planning people will register their objections and then we all wait to see what happens.'

'All most unsettling!' I said.

'Don't let it worry you,' said Mrs Partridge gently. She leant forward and patted my knee. 'Fairacre School will always be here, and you with it, I hope, for many, many years.'

She departed very soon after this, leaving me to relish my much-loved little house and garden, the sight of the village school awaiting the new term's activities, while her comforting words rang in my head.

17. Joseph Coggs Leaves Home

JOSEPH COGGS was locked out. The shabby wooden door of Number 2 Tyler's Row, from which the faded paint was flaking fast, was firmly shut against him, and the little house was empty.

Mrs Coggs and the two youngest children had gone to Caxley

to buy shoes for the winter, and she had forgotten, in the last minute helter-skelter rush for the bus, to put the door key in its usual hiding place.

Joseph had pelted home from school through pouring rain, had flung open the rickety gate and heaved up the old pail which served as a dustbin by the door, to find the key. It was not there. He tried the door, found it locked, shrugged his wet shoulders philosophically, and wandered down the garden path to seek shelter in the shed.

This was not the first time that Joseph had found himself locked out. His mother, poor, feckless, overworked creature, all too often forgot to put the key out in 'the secret hiding-place', and Joseph prepared now to wait for almost an hour, when he knew the bus from Caxley was due back.

The shed was a flimsy construction of corrugated iron sheeting, and the rain drummed relentlessly and deafeningly upon it. Joseph upturned a bucket, usually used for mixing the chickens' mash and heavily encrusted with the remains of long-past meals, and sat himself down with his elbows on his knees and his chin cupped in his cold hands.

He wondered idly where his little sisters had got to. They had set off from school a few minutes before him, but he had run past them in the lane where they were blissfully paddling in a long, deep puddle with sticks in their hands with which they stirred the murky depths, quite oblivious of the rain which soaked their flimsy clothes.

'Come on 'ome!' Joseph had directed hoarsely. 'Mum won't half go on at you! Look at your shoes!'

The twins had scarcely spared a glance either for their brother or for their canvas-topped plimsolls which were almost hidden by water. They had answered him boldly:

'Don't care! Tell her then! Don't care!' they had said tauntingly.

> 'Don't care was made to care,
> Don't care was hung!
> Don't care was put in a pot
> And boiled till he was done!'

shouted their brother threateningly; but seeing that they took no notice he had sped away home.

Apart from the drumming of the rain above his head and the trickling of a little stream that ran in the ditch which separated the Tyler's Row gardens from the field beyond them, Joseph found the shed very peaceful. It was a dirty place, but that did not worry Joseph unduly, for he was well acquainted with dirt. The floor was of hard earth and upon it lay an assortment of objects, poor enough in themselves, but of great service to the Coggs family. A treacle tin, with a loop of wire for a handle, stood half full of creosote. Arthur Coggs had purloined this in order to 'do the fowl house sometime', but so far that time had not come.

Strips of boxwood, which had once housed oranges and margarine, lay in a heap ready for kindling wood, beside a heavy bar of iron which had once been part of Mr Roberts's harrow but had 'been found' by Arthur Coggs who had prudently put it by for future use. Joseph idly turned this over and watched innumerable woodlice scurry for shelter.

He picked one up, a scaly, grey little creature, with its myriad legs thrashing wildly. Gently, he turned it over on his palm, fascinated to see it roll itself up into a tight ball no bigger than a goose grass seed. It was like a minute football, with its even lines round and round it. Joseph tipped his grimy palm this way and that, watching his treasure roll.

At last it rolled between his fingers to the ground. The legs reappeared as if by magic and away the wood louse scuttled to find its own again. It vanished beneath a sack containing dusty straw, a sack which gave forth a strong odour of dog-biscuits and stale corn which reminded Joseph of his own empty stomach.

He rose and pulled out an ear or two from the musty wheat straw, and began to roll the grains between his palms. Four hard grains rewarded his labours and he chewed them contentedly enough, his old posture with elbows on knees resumed, and his gaze fixed upon the chicken run which he could see through the open door.

The bare earth there was a slimy mass of mud, starred with the marks of chickens' claws. The unhappy birds stood hunched beside their rickety house, a converted tea chest. They were in an advanced state of moult, several without tail feathers, and most showing areas of pink pimply flesh here and there.

They were sadly bedraggled and half starved, but Joseph loved them. It grieved him to see them now, almost shelterless, without food, enduring the pitiless rain upon their bare backs with such humility and hopelessness. Tears sprang to his dark eyes as he looked upon these pathetic prisoners. It wasn't fair, thought young Joseph passionately, that some birds should be able to fly wherever they liked and have all the food that they could eat and be warmly wrapped in thick feathers, while others had come out of the eggs only to find a naked hungry world awaiting them!

It did not occur to Joseph that he himself could be compared with his own unhappy hens, the victim of poverty, neglect and callous indifference, equally hungry, cold and without shelter.

He sat there as hunched as the hens, beneath his glistening ragged clothing, comforting himself by squelching his bare wet toes up and down inside his soaking canvas shoes, and watching the small bubbles bursting from their sides.

Four miles away the bus from Caxley crept slowly towards Fairacre through the puddles that swirled around its wheels.

Term was now several weeks old. An unusually silent and subdued Miss Jackson reigned in the infants' room and relations between us were strained, which was not surprising. I did not blame her for resenting my intrusion into her private affairs, and I had no knowledge of her father's handling of this delicate matter, after he had summarily removed her from Franklyn's cottage.

I had received a letter from Mr Jackson at the beginning of term thanking me for my care of his daughter and asking me, in effect, to keep an eye on her movements. This letter gave me some uneasy moments and I really wished that Mr Jackson could have quelled his very natural parental anxieties and not placed me in the dubious position of 'policeman'.

I disliked the feeling of conspiring with her father behind Hilary's back, but, after some thought, I decided to say nothing to her about the letter, and contented myself with a brief reply to the effect that Hilary seemed more settled.

The girl vouchsafed nothing about either Franklyn or Miss Crabbe, and I began to wonder whether that lady had ever written to Hilary, as she had said she would. I told Hilary of our encounter in Devon, of the heat and the ices, but nothing, naturally, of our conversation. The girl's response was off-hand, and if indeed Miss Crabbe had proffered the olive branch I began to wonder if it had been spurned.

Altogether it was being a most uncomfortable term. The heat wave had given way to a long dreary spell of rainy weather, which meant that the children lacked fresh air and proper exercise, and were nearly as crotchety as their much-tired teachers.

The one bright spot was the return to good health of Miss Clare. The three weeks' rest by the sea in glorious weather had restored her considerably and she returned with a most becoming tan that showed off her white hair beautifully. Her lodger's low spirits had not gone unnoticed, but I gathered from her comments on them that the girl was genuinely more cheerful at Miss Clare's than she was in my damping presence at school.

'I think her father has written a pretty straight note to Franklyn,' she said to me, 'and forbidden Hilary to see him.' She paused, and shook her head sadly.

'But whether she does or not, I really don't know. She goes into Caxley quite often, but I can't bring myself to cross-question the child about her comings and goings. It's really not my affair at all, and I'm sure the girl has learnt her lesson now.'

'I hope so,' I answered. 'But I can't help feeling that a teaching post well away from this part of the world would be the best thing for everybody. She's a capable girl, but she needs young company. As one of a large mixed staff she'd get her corners rubbed off, and a lot of fun into the bargain!'

Our conversation was interrupted by some peremptory thudding at the door. On opening it I discovered Miss Clare's imperious cat, who deigned to enter only when I had held the door aside for a full two minutes. After this, rather naturally our conversation turned to happier things.

But very soon afterwards an incident occurred which gave me food for thought. I had taken the car into Caxley to be overhauled after school one day, had stayed there for my tea and caught the six o'clock bus, in driving rain.

I sat in the front of the bus watching the raindrops course down the window in front of me. We made various stops, the driver good-naturedly drawing up near roadside cottages where he knew certain of his passengers lived. The bell tinged as we approached the long, lonely track up to John Franklyn's house and the bus pulled up in a sheet of water, milky with the chalk which it had collected in its journey down the side of the downs.

A man stepped off first and turned to help his companion over the puddles. It was John Franklyn, and I recognized the woman whose arm he tucked so protectively under his own. She was the same person who had accompanied him to the Flower Show – the barmaid from 'The Bell' at Caxley.

It was on this same wet day that Joseph Coggs had taken shelter in the shed. His sojourn there, surveying the wretched hens before him, had been a prelude to unsuspected drama.

Mrs Coggs had returned from Caxley wet and cross. The shoes had cost far more than she had ever imagined, and she found that a mere six shillings and a few coppers remained in her shabby purse to last her until the following Saturday night when Arthur Coggs would hand over a grudging three pounds for housekeeping.

The sight of her three older children, waiting by the rickety gate and drenched to the skin, did nothing to mitigate her despair. More firing needed to dry that lot of dripping clothes by morning, she thought bitterly, as she fished at the bottom of her basket for the key.

A reek of paraffin oil met her nostrils as she grated the door back over the grubby brick floor. It overwhelmed the usual aroma of the Coggs' household which was compounded of stale food, damp walls and unwashed clothing. The oil lamp, overturned by the cat, lay across the table, its glass chimney shattered and its precious oil seeping steadily into half a loaf of bread which had been left beside it.

Another woman, facing this final blow after so many, might have sat down and wept. Not so Mrs Coggs, who gave one piercing hysterical shriek, dropped her basket to the floor, and set about cuffing her children out of the way to relieve her feelings.

'Git on upstairs out of it, you little 'uns,' she screamed. 'Out o' this mess till we've cleared up! Git a cloth, Jo, you great ninny standing gawping!' She gave him a resounding box on the ears which sent him reeling into the diminutive scullery where the floor cloth lay. He returned with it to the dusky room, his eyes full of tears. It wasn't that he minded the box on the ears, although it had been a particularly vicious one, but he hated to see his mother in a mood like this. His father's blusterings and heavy blows he could endure equably, for he expected him to behave in that way; but that his mother should shout, and banish the youngest ones for no fault of their own, hurt Joseph.

He retrieved the bread from the floor whilst his mother set about mopping up the oil, scolding and railing all the time. The baby, a smelly bundle still wrapped in its shawl, had been thrust into a sagging armchair, and now began to wail pathetically. It was more than tender-hearted Jo could bear. He picked a piece of bread from that part of the loaf which was still free from oil, stepped across his mother's swirling floor cloth and handed it to the baby. He himself was now faint with hunger and hoped, under cover of the darkness which was gathering quickly, to break himself a piece too. But his luck was out.

Whether he stood accidentally on his mother's hand, or whether she jerked her arm and overturned him, Joseph never knew; but he heard a scream of rage and found himself falling towards the chair. He hit his head with a crack, while behind him his mother, beside herself by this time, let fall a torrent of yelling abuse.

For Joseph, as for his poor tormented mother, this was the breaking point. Confused images of the unhappy innocent hens, of his equally innocent and helpless young brothers and sisters floated before him. Not fair, not fair! rang in his dizzy head. His mother might be cold, might be hungry, might be sad. Weren't they all? Weren't they all as wretched, sunk in the same deep pit? And more than that, he and the little 'uns and the hens were small, weak, and had to do as they were bid. They couldn't even answer back like the grown-ups could!

He struggled to his feet. He felt as though he were battered by his mother's shouting, the baby's wailing, the snufflings of his frightened sisters, and his own intense hunger and dizziness. He lurched unsteadily towards the door.

'Don't you go out!' warned his mother. 'There's plenty for you to do here, and you've ruined enough clothes for today!' Her voice grew shriller as she saw the child wrench the door open.

'Where you going?' she screamed.

'I'm clearing out of here!' growled Joseph, and ran out thankfully into the pitiless rain.

18. The Public Inquiry

FAIRACRE tongues wagged busily one Monday morning early in October. Three notices had appeared in the village. One was fastened to the wire grille in Mr Lamb's Post Office, another was displayed by the bus stop, and the third was fixed to the notice board outside the village hall.

The notice had been issued by the Caxley Rural District Council and it announced that the Ministry of Housing and Local Government had fixed a date for a public inquiry into the proposed plans for a housing estate to be built in that area, following the objections already received to the said scheme, as put forward by the County Council.

'I'll bet Mrs Bradley's got summat to do with this,' said Mr Willet sagely to me. 'There's been talk down at "The Beetle" –

and more in Caxley – about her harrying the Planning Committee with tales of Dan Crockford. And some other chap's got a bee in his bonnet about them downs.'

He knitted his brows in an effort to remember and tossed a small screwdriver thoughtfully from one horny hand to the other.

'Lor'! I'll forget me own name next!' said Mr Willet, exasperated with his own shortcomings. 'But he comes from some lot that keeps all on worrying about beauty spots and old monuments and that. Begins with a C.'

I looked blankly at him.

'Not C. of E.,' he explained, throwing the screwdriver even faster, 'but that sort of thing.'

'C.P.R.E. ?' I hazarded. 'Council for the Preservation of Rural England ?'

'Ah! That's it!' said Mr Willet triumphantly. 'I'll bet he's there, and old Miller, of course, and someone from the Office about the schools.' He checked suddenly, and put the screwdriver in his pocket. His expression grew embarrassed.

'If this did come, God forbid,' said he more slowly, 'would you feel like staying on, Miss Read ?'

I looked from the massive brass and mahogany inkstand to the wheeling rooks that I could see through the Gothic window.

'I'd feel like staying on,' I answered.

The same notice appeared next morning in *The Caxley Chronicle*. The inquiry was to be held on the Thursday of the following week in the premises of the Caxley Rural District Council.

'And some very uncomfortable chairs they've got there,' said the vicar sadly to Mr Mawne, who was taking coffee with him that morning. 'And we're bound to take a long time.'

'Everything official takes a long time,' said Mr Mawne, shamelessly fishing out his lump of sugar and eating it with the greatest relish. 'Dash it all, all this began last spring. The R.D.C. saw the plans last June, we had our village meeting way back in July, and here we are in October, just putting the whole boiling before the Inspector from the Ministry of Whatsit! Heavens alone knows when we get the Minister's ruling!'

He helped himself to two more sugar lumps, the vicar obligingly pushing the bowl to his elbow.

'Have you any idea,' asked the vicar, 'how long we shall have to wait?'

'Might be a couple of years,' said his friend airily.

'No!' exclaimed the vicar. 'Surely not as long as that!'

'Well – might be three months,' admitted Mr Mawne grudgingly, 'but we'd be lucky! I bet the Inspector's report will find a resting place in many a tray and pigeon-hole before any decision is made.' He paused, and peered into the sugar bowl.

'I say,' he said anxiously, 'I seem to have finished the sugar!'

'No matter, my dear fellow,' answered the vicar genially, 'I don't believe it is rationed now.'

The chairs in the offices of Caxley Rural District Council were indeed uncomfortable, as the vicar had said, but that had not deterred a large number of local people from attending.

The room in which the inquiry was to be held had first been the principal bedroom of a hard-riding, wealthy merchant who had built this solid Georgian house in 1730. Three long, handsome windows, looking over Caxley High Street, let in a watery sun that flickered over wide oak floor boards, highly polished in the merchant's day by a posse of mob-capped maids, but now dull and scuffed by many feet, and grudgingly swept by one overworked old man.

At one end of the room the Inspector from the Ministry of Housing and Local Government sat, with his secretary beside him, at a big table. He was a large man, with a pendulous dewlap and heavily lidded eyes, which gave him a deceptively sleepy appearance. His manner was ponderously formal, but an astute and lively mind lay hidden behind his slow movements.

The chairs were arranged in arc-shaped rows before the table, and supported, in varying degrees of discomfort, according to the clothing and natural padding of their occupants, about sixty people.

At one side, in the front, sat various people who would be called to put forward the case for the United Kingdom Atomic Energy Authority, and on the other side were a number of people, including old Mr Miller and his solicitor, who would be called as witnesses to support the objections which had caused this public inquiry. About a dozen Fairacre folk, including the vicar, Mr Mawne, Mr Roberts and his wife, and Mrs Bradley were also present.

There was an air of expectancy in the room. The smoke from pipes and cigarettes spiralled in the sloping rays of sunshine. People spoke urgently to each other. The months of waiting, the many heart-searchings, arguments, wild rumours and distressing suspense had now reached a climax. Here, in this once-lovely room which had witnessed so much history, so many 'old unhappy, far-off things', yet another battle would be fought. It would be fought politely, with decorous words read from innocent slips of paper held in unbloodied hands, and the account of that battle would be jotted down in neat shorthand by the Inspector's imperturbable secretary and, in the fullness of time, would reach headquarters.

But a battle it would be, as everyone present sensed, and the Minister could be likened to a General in those headquarters, who would read the communiqué, sum up the situation and give his decision on the issues at stake.

The Inspector opened the proceedings and invited the representatives of the Atomic Energy Authority to put forward their case.

Mr Devon-Forbes, Q.C., counsel for the authority, was a tall, cadaverous individual with sardonic dark eyebrows that rose to a sharp point in the middle, like a circumflex accent. In a deep, resonant voice that rang round the room he put forward the desirability of this site for the housing of the authority's workers. He spoke feelingly of the exhaustive survey carried out as a preliminary measure to find an area which would not only prove suitable for the scheme, but would give the absolute minimum of disturbance to the local inhabitants and their environs. The scheme, if carried through, he added, his voice taking on a note as soft and seductive as black velvet, would bring many long-sought amenities to the area involved.

Mrs Bradley, at this point, wriggled on her hard chair, and said 'Tchah!' very loudly. The Inspector cast her a look from under his heavy lids, but Mr Devon-Forbes continued quite unruffled.

His first witness, he said, would be the Planning Consultant of the authority, and he bowed politely to a short sandy-haired man who came forward thrusting a pair of horn-rimmed glasses against his face and clutching a sheaf of papers. Yes, indeed, he agreed, answering counsel's suave questions, the matter had been discussed at top level with the greatest attention. He began to unfurl a large scale map, and dropped his papers. Several people scuttled to retrieve them.

Might he pin up the map in full view, he asked? The Inspector said, 'By all means, by all means,' and indicated the beaver-boarding behind him. The map was pinned up and became the centre of attention.

The Planning Consultant then pointed out the present atomic centre, the distance involved in travelling to work from nearby towns, the need for more workers, and the impossible congestion this would cause in towns already overcrowded, and the perfect position of the site under discussion for a new, and, he emphasized, *attractive* small township which could bring added prosperity to the neighbourhood. The authority would do everything in its power to see that the countryside remained unspoilt and that the project would not industrialize or urbanize the area.

Mr Devon-Forbes nodded gravely at this pronouncement and his witness was about to sit down when the Deputy Clerk of the County Council jumped up and asked if he might cross-examine.

Had the planning consultant considered the value of the area in terms of agricultural worth?

Mr Devon-Forbes said that his next witness would answer that question if the opposing counsel would allow. The Deputy

Clerk sat down, and counsel called his second witness who was as he said, 'an agriculturist in general, and a soil surveyor in particular'.

Samples of the soil had been taken and statistics of the crop-yield from this area over the last twenty years had been made available, and it had been decided, after exhaustive discussion, that, agriculturally speaking, the loss would be negligible compared with the material advantages of using the site as a housing estate for people of the highest importance to the national effort.

Mr Miller here muttered something to his solicitor, who affected not to hear, but turned a very unbecoming beetroot colour.

The inquiry wound on. A formidable number of technical men were called and stated the case for the authority in varying degrees of clarity and audibility. Mr Devon-Forbes conducted his part in the affairs with firm politeness, keeping his witnesses very much to the point, but it was, as Mr Mawne had foreseen, a lengthy business.

Fidgeting became more general as the clock on the wall passed noon, and at half past, with still two more speakers to be called by Mr Devon-Forbes, and several more who had asked to be allowed to add their comments, the Inspector rose and adjourned the inquiry until after lunch.

'Terrible ol' chairs, ennum?' growled old George Bates who had worked for Mr Miller until last Michaelmas, to his crony, as they limped down the stairs. 'My bottom's fair criss-crossed!'

'Ah!' agreed his companion. 'You coming back after dinner?'

'Got to go to the dentist. He's taking out my last three, and I shan't be sorry to see they go, I can tell 'ee! One thing, I bet his chair'll have a sight more padding, whatever he does to me t'other end!'

But most of those who had attended in the morning turned up again for the afternoon session. One or two had prudently brought a cushion or a rug from the car and sat in comparative ease as the witnesses gave their testimony.

At ten to three the last speaker for the authority came forward. She was a welfare worker in one of the neighbouring towns which at present housed a large number of the employees at the power station. She spoke of the difficulties of overcrowded clinics and schools, the lack of proper playground facilities, and the incidence of childish diseases in these places. Gangs of young children, sent out to play in the streets, were already causing the local authorities headaches, and if this new estate could be built, some of the pressure in the towns could be relieved, with the consequent benefit for all concerned.

Mr Devon-Forbes then rose, cast a look around the room from under his distinguished eyebrows, and then made a short speech stating that the inquiry had now heard the authority's case, and that its evidence was now completed.

The Inspector adjourned the inquiry until the next day, and the assembly emerged into the grey October drizzle, with tea in mind.

The vicar drove Mr Mawne home to Fairacre in his rattling Ford. The drizzle became a downpour as they edged out of Caxley on to the road to Fairacre and beat in upon the vicar's clerical grey as he drove.

'Really I should have seen to this window, too,' said the vicar to his companion, 'but I so often need it open for signalling. What a good thing yours is staying up!'

He looked with pride at Mr Mawne's side of the car. A large knobbly flint, weighing two or three pounds, dangled from the end of a stout string. This was attached to the bottom handle of the window and exerted enough force to hold up the rattling pane against the weather.

'I thought of it myself,' said the vicar modestly.

Mr Mawne, who had received several vicious blows already from the swinging stone, feigned respectful surprise.

'Worthy of Leonardo da Vinci,' he assured the vicar, who glowed at the kind words.

They passed beneath the tunnel of great trees that gives Beech

Green its name. The nutty autumn smell of wet leaves mingled with the rain that came through the open window. They drove in silence, occupied with their own thoughts, until the vicar stopped with a flourish at Mr Mawne's gate.

'Coming in?' asked Mr Mawne. 'Oh, I forgot! My wife's got the Ladies' Sewing Circle here, I believe.'

'Thank you, thank you, no!' said the vicar hastily. 'I must be getting back.' He rested his arms across the wheel and looked at his friend. His expression was troubled.

'What do you make of it? They had a good case, you know. Very fair, I thought, really very fair.'

Mr Mawne straightened his shoulders.

'Our turn tomorrow, with a case as good as theirs! We'll rout them, never fear. Hope and pray for the best, my dear fellow!'

'I always do that,' said the vicar simply.

There were more people than ever, next morning, willing to endure the hardship of the R.D.C.'s chairs in order to hear the case put forward by the Deputy Clerk to the County Council, who was acting counsel for the local side of the affair.

He was a large, cheerful man, with a florid complexion and a merry blue eye. His bald, pink head fringed with silky white hair, shone with health and energetic soapings. He was clad in a shepherd's plaid suit, a blue shirt and blue spotted bow-tie, and looked hearty enough to take on all comers. Those about to be called as witnesses, and others who hoped for a reprieve for the downs, felt their spirits rise as they watched their spokesman.

He called first the County's Planning Officer who made a long and thoughtful statement about the objections to the scheme. The Planning Committee were not happy about the water supply for such a large number of people, probably used to urban life where water was more freely used. (Here a few eyebrows were lifted, as several country dwellers wondered if this might be an aspersion on their cleanliness.) The disposal of sewage was another problem. At the moment a fleet of up-to-date lorries adequately coped with the present need. (Long-suffering glances were exchanged by some Fairacre folk.) But if an estate, of the size envisaged, were to be built, a sewage system on a large scale must be faced.

The roads between Caxley and other near-by towns would need to be widened, and possibly lighted, to ensure safety for the increased traffic, and he was asked by the Finance Department to state that the expense involved could not reasonably be met, even in part, from the ratepayers' pockets.

He would like to point out too, that the Planning Committee had most definite ideas for that particular site. It was an area of great beauty, scheduled as an open space, and set on canvas many times by the noted local artist Daniel Crockford. (Here a pleased hum ran round the room and Mrs Bradley thumped vigorously on the floor with her umbrella. 'Order, please,' said the Inspector mildly.)

It should be kept as an open area for all to enjoy. An ancient road – of the Iron Age, he believed, but he was a bit hazy about this – it might be Bronze, he was open to correction – but *ancient* anyway, ran along the top of the downs, and he believed that more would be said about this by another speaker. He looked questioningly at counsel, who nodded his pink-and-white head vigorously, and said, 'That is so! Yes!'

The Planning Officer then folded his notes and added that the Education Department had viewed the scheme with concern, especially in the light of their own commitments already undertaken for the next financial year, and that the Director of Education would give further particulars. He turned towards the Inspector, who was making notes steadily.

'I do assure the Ministry, sir, that great hardship will come if this scheme goes through. Not only financial hardship, which will be heavy enough, but in losing a well-loved beauty spot to all, a valuable area of agricultural land and a certain gentleman's home for several generations. The whole balance and harmony of the two small flourishing villages will be thrown out. The repercussions on farming conditions will be serious and the social life of the present population will be hopelessly disturbed. I do earnestly beg the authority to reconsider their siting of the estate.'

He sat down, and the people stirred upon their uncomfortable chairs and felt that he had spoken well for them.

Mr Devon-Forbes, on being invited to cross-examine, intimated that he would prefer to do this at a later stage, and and the second witness, the Director of Education, was called.

The proposed new school on the housing site, he said, had given rise to alarm in the area affected, and he had had several visits from both parents and managers who had expressed their very deep concern at the possible closing of local village schools. He had been able to assure them that the schools in question would not close, but that if the new school were built, Fairacre School would have a different status – becoming a school for infants only, with but one teacher.

The closing of any village school was not welcomed by the Committee any more than the parents. In this case, Fairacre School had already lost its 'over-elevens' to Beech Green, an adjustment not without some feeling at the time, but if all the children of eight and over were to be taken from the village daily to the new school, which was what was envisaged, he had the greatest sympathy for the parents, managers and present staff of that admirable little school.

Apart from the humane side, the cost of the new establishment would be fabulous. He had estimates with him which would make painful reading to an audience already taxed beyond endurance. The Finance Committee had already passed plans for substantial improvements to Beech Green School, to be undertaken during the next six months, and any further expense would be out of the question.

He must stress too, he added, the importance of the two present schools to the existing communities. They were perfectly suited to the needs of the villages in question. Both Beech Green and Fairacre took a lively interest in their schools, pride in their children's attainments and had expressed every confidence in the educational arrangements made for them. He would be betraying their trust if he overthrew their wishes and attempted to force a comfortably working machine to a gear beyond it.

It might be as well to make one last point, went on the Director, studying his finger-nails minutely. The dwellers on the new estate would doubtless be drawn from urban areas, where educational conditions were different. '*Different*,' he stressed, 'but not necessarily *better*! However, they will have seen magnificent buildings, ample stock, a formidably large staff, and all the rest of it. For that reason alone, I am glad that they cannot, for reasons of space, send their children to Fairacre or Beech Green, for they would have made a great fuss about those two somewhat elderly buildings – and been as vociferous in their scoldings as they would have been silent about the excellent teaching and individual care possible with their relatively small classes. But even so they will bring a different standard to the area. They will want things – cinemas, a dance hall, a fried-fish shop possibly, which those who have lived there all their lives have not felt necessary or even desirable. They may well be difficult to digest into the slowly grinding system of village life, and I fear that they will not add to the sum of happiness which already exists there. They may cause resentment with their larger pay-packets. They may be bored with the sort of social life that a village can offer. They will be neither flesh, fowl, nor good red herring, but just a lost tribe on a lost, once-lovely hill. In my opinion, it would be better for the authority to make several smaller estates on the outskirts of existing towns, such as this one, where the children can take advantage of the present schools, and they and their parents can be assimilated into a way of life to which they are more accustomed.'

There was a considerable amount of throat-clearing and whispering as the Director resumed his seat. The room was growing very dark, as black clouds gathered outside, and the air grew uncomfortably close. The inquiry continued, the chairs grew harder, and it was with a feeling of general relief that they saw the inspector glance at the clock, rise and say, 'We will adjourn now for lunch, ladies and gentlemen.'

The vicar and Mr Mawne made their way to 'The Buttery' which stands conveniently near the R.D.C.'s offices.

A blast of hot air met them as they pushed their way against the heavy door.

'Beastly stuffy!' muttered Mr Mawne, undoing his coat and slinging it over the back of a pseudo oak settee. 'Hope there's something cold to eat.' He put his hand on the radiator beside the table, withdrew it with a regrettable exclamation, which the vicar affected not to hear, and called to a waitress 'to open a window and let in a bit of air'.

The vicar was studying the menu.

'Could you eat haricot mutton?' he asked.

'Good God, no!' exclaimed Mr Mawne, shuddering. 'Nothing hot, for pity's sake!'

'Then I fear it must be ham and salad,' said the vicar.

'Suits me,' said Mr Mawne. 'And an iced lager. For you too?'

'Yes, yes! Admirable!' agreed the vicar. 'It really is uncommonly close. Almost like thunder. Amazing in October.'

'Kept warmish most of the year,' answered his friend. 'The swallows were particularly late migrating this season. Ah! Here it comes!' He attacked his ham with relish, and neither spoke until he had finished.

But while the vicar ate a coffee ice, and Mr Mawne crunched celery with his biscuit and cheese, they turned to the business of the morning.

'A great deal of good sense spoken,' said the vicar. 'I wonder who is still to come?'

'The Ag. man,' said Mr Mawne elegantly, 'to tell us that that particular field is like gold-dust to the nation agriculturally. Then we're bound to get some old fogey for an hour or two about that prehistoric road along the top.'

'Heavens!' said the vicar, in some alarm. 'Do you think it might drag on till tomorrow? I've an early communion service and two churchings.'

'Never can tell!' said Mr Mawne, rummaging in his pocket for some money. 'Come on. We'd better be getting back.'

As it happened, old Mr Miller was the next to put his case, or rather, Mr Lovejoy, his much-tried solicitor, did his best, by judicious questioning of his client, to set Mr Miller's various losses before the Inspector. He had an uphill job. It had taken him twenty minutes to make his points about material losses in crops, and hard cash, and the depreciation of Mr Miller's remaining property if this estate were to be built, and he was flagging a little. Mr Miller, seated by him, looked about with button-bright eyes. He had missed his usual nap, but he was still fighting fit.

Mr Lovejoy had already given a heart-rending account of his frail client being wrested from his birthplace and tottering sorrowfully towards his grave, leaving a homeless family behind him. Mr Miller had listened with barely concealed impatience, drumming on his knee in a way which his solicitor found peculiarly tiresome. He took a deep breath and embarked on the last part of his case.

'Is it any wonder?' he asked, 'that my client's health has given way, his appetite has gone, and he can no longer get about as he did?'

'Fiddlesticks!' rejoined the crusty old gentleman, rising to his feet. 'I've just ate a partridge, drunk a pint of porter, and walked to "The Blackbird" and back, my boy!'

Mr Lovejoy did his best to retrieve the situation, amidst some laughter.

'As you can see, my client is a courageous man, as full of spirit as he is full of years. But, I can assure you, and his doctor can testify, if need be, that he is not the same man since the shadow of this project fell across his birthright!' He gave a polite bow and put a solicitous hand under Mr Miller's elbow, much to that gentleman's annoyance. Together they resumed their seats.

The 'Ag. Man', as Mr Mawne had so euphoniously called the officer of the Ministry of Agriculture and Fisheries, spoke next, and if he did not actually mention gold-dust he certainly made it clear that this was indeed a valuable agricultural area, farmed intensively by an enlightened owner who kept the land in good heart, and was a national asset. It would be a crime to see it built upon. He was sure too, that taking the long view, the building of a new town in this agricultural area would create a great deal of unemployment troubles for the farmers, already harassed by the shift to the towns of their erstwhile farm workers. It would be an unsettling influence for all concerned. He agreed with the Director of Education [that these people would be better placed near the existing towns.

Outside, the rumbling of thunder made itself heard above the steady drone of the traffic in Caxley High Street. The room was so dim that the lights had to be switched on, and despite the open windows the room was oppressively hot. The list of speakers, lying before the inspector, gradually shortened as the afternoon wore on.

Mrs Bradley had her say, and a very spirited one it was. No one, in her opinion, had really stressed the important point, which was that this was *artistically* one of the most important landscapes in England. She reminded her hearers, forcefully, of all Dan Crockford's many pictures of the spot. She adjured them to look once again at the splendours that hung – in far too dim a light, to be sure – in their own Town Hall. It would be a lasting disgrace to Caxley if this generation sold its birthright to a pack of – to the authority, for a pot of message – a mess of pottage, and denied its children their rightful inheritance. She sat down amidst some applause.

The proceedings wound on, statements, cross-examinations and answers, and nearer and nearer grew the thunder. The rain began to beat down, like straight steel rods, and the windows had to be shut. It was stifling as the last speaker rose. He was an official from the Council for the Preservation of Rural England and he was young, ardent and appallingly long-winded.

He agreed, at length, with Mrs Bradley. He reiterated, at length, the beauties of the range of downs involved, and he pointed on the map that still embellished the wall behind the Inspector's head, to the ancient green road that ran clean through the proposed site. That alone, surely, made the whole project impossible. He sat down as Mr Devon-Forbes rose to answer. The authority had as much feeling for the historic past as had the council which Mr Brown had the honour of representing. If he had troubled to look more closely at the map he would have seen that the ancient road was to remain as it had always been, with no building within a specified number of feet. If he remembered rightly, just such a situation had arisen in

Berkshire, at Harwell, where the authority had taken the greatest pains to preserve a stretch of ancient roadway – the Icknield Way, he understood – for posterity, although it ran through quite a large proportion of the authority's property. His tone implied that the recalcitrant roadway, like a wayward child, had had every consideration from a much-tried nursemaid.

The inspector looked at the Deputy Clerk, who rose and said that that brought the case for the County Council to a close.

The inspector thanked all those who had attended this necessarily lengthy inquiry, promised to put his report before the Minister with all possible speed, and began to put his papers together.

A devastating crack split the sky. There was a sizzling noise, and the lights went out. Through the murk came laughter, the clatter of those wicked chairs, and above all the voice of the inspector.

'And that,' he said loudly, 'ends our inquiry.'

There was a certain amount of confusion in the twilit hall below. The vicar waited for Mr Mawne, from whom he had become parted, and saw a very young man approach Mrs Bradley. They stood together, at the head of the steps down to the pavement, and effectively held up the flow of traffic.

'I thought you were wonderful!' said the young man, flushing pink. 'I'm Dan's great-nephew. Another Dan – but Dan Johnson.'

'No!' squeaked Mrs Bradley, in delight. 'Not Lucy's boy?'

'Lucy Crockford was my grandmother.'

'Wonderful! Yes, I can see you have her eyes. Come home to tea, won't you? Stay to supper. Stay the night. Stay a week or two –'

'I can't do that, I'm afraid,' he laughed. 'I'm due in Oxford next week. I go up on Tuesday.'

'Which college?'

'Worcester.'

'Near Mac Fisheries?'

The young man wrinkled his brow with mental effort.

'I don't think so.'

'No matter. I often shop in Oxford. You must have lunch with me at the Eastgate. Heavens, how rude people are, pushing like that!'

'We'd better move,' agreed the young man, and they walked together down the steps, and out of the vicar's earshot.

'What a scrum!' gasped Mr Mawne, arriving. 'I got cornered by some ass who wanted minute instructions on how to feed a captive tawny owl!'

'The price of fame,' said the vicar benignly, leading the way to the car park.

Rivulets chortled along the gutters of Caxley, and the good citizens picked their way among the puddles. The downpour had stopped with the same dramatic suddenness with which it had started, and, although black clouds still hung in the sky over the distant downs, the sun shone.

Sparkling raindrops slid along the telegraph wires, and awnings were beaded with diamonds. The vicar and Mr Mawne drove up Caxley High Street, splashing sedately through the water, and heading towards the black cloud that hung, like the threat which still lowered, above the two villages.

'Look, at that!' exclaimed Mr Mawne, ducking his head and peering up into the sky above the windscreen. The vicar followed his gaze.

Arched above them, a flamboyant and iridescent arc across the dark cloud, shone a rainbow. The vicar smiled at his friend.

'Let us hope it is an augury,' he said. And, stepping on the accelerator, he set the nose of his rattling car on the road to Fairacre.

PART FOUR

Calm after Storm

19. Mrs Coggs Fights a Battle

WHEN Joseph Coggs fled, in frantic despair, from the domestic hell of Tyler's Row, he had no plan in mind but escape from intolerable conditions. The wind howled in the trees above the road as he ran headlong, through the rain-swept darkness, towards the centre of the village.

He still burned with injustice, and was as frightened by the magnitude of his own rage as he was by the fury of the storm around him. Habit led his steps towards the school, and, still sobbing, he found himself at the school gate with the bulk of St Patrick's looming blackly against the dark sky.

All was in darkness, except for a faint ruddy glow from behind the red curtains of the school-house. But Joseph was in no mood to approach authority. Authority meant his mother, his father, scoldings, railings, and forced obedience to unbearable circumstances.

Joseph turned his back upon the light and looked, with awe, at the church. It would be dry in there, but nothing would induce him to find shelter in a building which, to his superstitious mind, might house the dead as well as the living. What should he do?

He became conscious for the first time of his own position. His clothes were so wet that he could feel the cold trickles running down his shivering body. He was dizzy with hunger and fatigue. He had left his home and there was no going back. He walked slowly and hopelessly to the school door. It was locked, as he had expected. The great, heavy ring which acted as handle to the Gothic door lay cold and wet in Joseph's hand, denying him entrance.

Joseph leant his head against the rough wood and wept anew. Tears and rain dripped together upon his soaked jersey, but as he rested there, abandoned to grief, a small, metallic sound revived his hopes. The rain was making music upon the empty milk crates beside the door-scraper. Those two milk crates, piled one on top of the other, would enable him to reach the lobby window and Joseph knew full well that that window had a broken catch.

He dragged the crates noisily along by the wall and struggled up. Sure enough, the tall narrow window tilted up under pressure and Joseph struggled through into the lobby closing the window behind him. Breathlessly, he made his way into his classroom, not daring to switch on the light lest he should be discovered.

It was warmer in here, for the tortoise stove still gave out a dying heat, but it was terrifyingly eerie. The floorboards creaked under Joseph's squelching canvas-topped shoes as he approached the stove. He held his thin hands over its black bulk and looked fearfully about him at the shadowy classroom. The moon-face of the clock gleamed from the wall. Its measured tick was the only companionable sound in the room. The charts and papers pinned to the partition glimmered like pale ghosts, and the ecclesiastical windows, gaunt and narrow, filled Joseph with the same superstitious terror that St Patrick's had done. He turned again to the comfort of the homely stove, and remembering the little trap-door at its foot which he had seen Mrs Pringle adjust, he bent to examine it through the bars of the fire guard.

He lifted up the metal flap and was enchanted to see a red spark fall from the embers. He crouched down beside it and with growing wonder watched the grey cinders glow again as the air blew through. His spirits rose as the warmth began to grow, and he set about making himself more comfortable.

He crept back into the windy stone-floored lobby and collected two coats which had been left there. He stripped off his wet jersey, his poor shirt and his heavy wet trousers, wrung them out into the coke scuttle and spread them to dry along the fire guard. His ragged vest was almost as wet, but modesty made him continue to wear it. He fought his way into a coat much too small for him, spread the other on the floor by the stove, and lay down, well content, where he could look straight into the minute cavern of glowing cinders inside the trap-door.

He was almost happy. In the arrangements he had made for his own comfort he had forgotten the past miseries which had led to his flight. Only one thing bothered him, an all-invading hunger beside which every other trouble dwindled into insignificance. His mind bore upon this problem with increasing urgency. What was there to eat in school?

He remembered Miss Read's sweet tin, but knew that the cupboard would be locked. Earlier in the evening he would have wept at this remembrance, but he was past tears now. To survive he must eat. To survive, to eat, he must think.

He sat up, looked around him, and relief flooded over him, for there in the shadows near the door was the nature table, and he himself had helped Miss Read to arrange 'Fruits of the Autumn'. He scrambled to his feet and ran towards this richness. A shiny cooking apple, as big as his baby brother's head, was the finest prize the table yielded, but there were a few nuts and a spray of blackberries.

Gleefully he returned to his coat on the floor and sat cross-legged. In the shadowy school room, his tear-stained face gilded in the glow from the stove, Joseph Coggs thankfully munched his apple, while the storm raged furiously outside.

In ten minutes' time, with every scrap of food gone, he lay curled up, sleeping the sleep of the completely exhausted.

He woke once during the night. The rain had ceased and a pallid moon shone fitfully between the ragged clouds that raced across the sky. A mouse, disturbed by his movement, scurried across the floor to its home behind the raffia cupboard, and Joseph caught a glimpse of its vanishing tail.

The stove had gone out and the room felt much colder. The draught from the window stirred the papers on the walls, and there was a little sibilant whispering from a straw which had escaped Mrs Pringle's broom, as it moved to and fro across the floorboard in which it was caught.

Joseph lay there quite unafraid. What had happened was too big, too important, too far-away to take in. He was drained of ill feeling. Nothing really mattered now except the fact that he was safe and at peace. Someone else must bother about his mother, the howling babies, the upturned lamp, the wretched chickens. He was too tired.

He rolled over again upon his hard bed, conscious only of the relief of being alone with enough room to stretch himself, in quietness and shelter.

It was there, fast asleep on the floor before the cold stove, that Mrs Pringle found him at eight o'clock the next morning.

At Tyler's Row Joseph's flight had had unexpected consequences. Before Mrs Coggs had had time to collect her scattered wits, her husband had entered. Work had stopped early on the building where Arthur Coggs was engaged because of the torrential rain. The overturned lamp was now upright and burning, but the children continued to whimper, awaiting their tea, and the house still reeked of paraffin oil.

'Where's the grub?' growled Arthur Coggs, slinging his wet cap and coat on to that same chair which had upset his first born. 'And shut your noise!' he bawled at the snivelling youngsters.

It was too much for Mrs Coggs. Years of abuse, hard words and hard blows, culminating in this disastrous day, made her suddenly and loquaciously bold.

'Shut your own!' she screamed at her flabbergasted husband. He began to raise a massive fist, but she advanced upon him, with such fire sparking from her eyes, that he stepped back.

' Jo's run off and I don't blame him. Any more of your tongue and I'll go after him, and you can look after the kids yourself!'

'Now then! Now then!' began Arthur Coggs, in a menacing growl. 'Mind what you're –'

'I mean it – straight!' panted his distracted wife. 'I can't stand no more. I'm off to the police!' She meant to ask for their help in finding Joseph, but her husband's guilty conscience construed this last remark as a reflection on his own wrongdoing. Alarmed at this fresh independence displayed by his wife, he became conciliatory.

'Here, don't take on like that! What if Jo has gone off? He'll be back for his tea, you see.'

'That he won't,' responded Mrs Coggs. 'I'm off after him!' She began to push past him to the door but Arthur Coggs stopped her.

'You make us a cup o' tea, gal, and I'll have a look round,' he said, gently. He put on his coat and cap again and went thoughtfully out into the downpour.

His wife watched him go grimly, arms akimbo. The worm had turned.

He returned fifteen minutes later. The children were seated at the table demolishing thick doorsteps of bread and margarine. His own plateful of baked beans and rasher stood ready for him.

'Anyone seen him?' cried his wife anxiously, hand on heart.

'No. But I told old Lamb at the Post Office and he said he'd keep a lookout.'

'Fat lot of good that was!' commented his wife. Arthur Coggs lied quickly.

'And I saw the copper on his bike. Going on home he was, so I let him know our Jo were out somewhere!' His wife looked at him suspiciously.

'It's the truth!' protested Arthur, beginning to bluster. 'And I'll tell you another thing – if he ain't home before bedtime we'll leave the doors unlocked so's the kid can get in.'

'I'll go out meself,' answered his wife resolutely, 'as soon as this lot's finished with.' She looked at her gobbling brood, at the poor, scanty meal, the cracked plates, the meagre fire and at her shifty, lying bully of a husband. The new-found fire burnt steadily within her and gave her unquenchable courage. She turned upon him again furiously.

'You've driven our Jo to this,' she told him shrilly, 'I went for him, I knows that, but only because I was that worried and fed-up. If I'd had a good man behind me all these years, there'd be no need for us all living worse than pigs. Things is going to alter here, Arthur Coggs, or, mark my words, you faces the lot on your own! I'm off otherwise, back to service, with good meals and decent people. I been a fool too long I reckons!'

The tears were running down her cheeks as she ended this tirade. The children watched her open-mouthed and Arthur Coggs, for once, was beyond speech.

*

Mrs Pringle presented Joseph Coggs to me just as I was about to lift my breakfast egg out of the saucepan. I had never seen a child look so exhausted.

'Asleep on the floor!' said Mrs Pringle dramatically. 'Lord! That give me a start! "What on earth can that old bundle of rags be adoing down there?" I thought to myself – when, all of a sudden, it moved!'

Mrs Pringle threw her hands up in astonishment.

'And been there all night, he says. What'll his poor ma be doing?'

'Be a dear and take a message down,' I begged. 'The stoves can wait. I'll give him breakfast while you're gone.'

Pleased to be the bearer of such momentous tidings Mrs Pringle hurried off with not the slightest trace of a limp, whilst I returned to my visitor.

'Do you like boiled eggs?' I asked him. He nodded dazedly. His eyes were puffy, his face and hands filthy and I led him to the sink while his two eggs boiled.

I stripped the child's dirty clothes from his waist up and gave him a thorough wash, as he stood silently impassive. He was pathetically thin, every rib showing and his bony shoulder blades protruding like a fledgling's wings. Here and there was an ugly bruise and the poverty-stricken smell of accumulated dirt and neglect hung around his fragile form. I wished that I had time to bath him properly, but after redressing him and combing his matted hair, I looked upon my breakfast guest with pride.

I let him eat before doing a little tentative questioning. The child seemed too listless, too dazed and too bewildered to do more than to grunt a 'yes' or 'no' to my few queries, but it was enough to give me a true and heart-breaking glimpse of all that Joseph had endured throughout his short life.

By the time his mother arrived I had already decided that someone in authority would have to tackle this family problem. I had foreseen a forlorn, negative hopelessness from Mrs Coggs, but was pleasantly surprised to find that, though red-eyed with weeping, she was in fighting trim. To my suggestion that the County Medical Officer should take a look at Joseph and his sisters in the school, and that he might be able to give some help, her face lit up.

'I only wants a hand,' she said. ''Tis that ol' house and all the kids. And Arthur's no help, as you knows, miss. If he brought his money home regular, us might've had a real house by now.'

I said that the Medical Officer might be able to pass their case forward to the housing committee. Something should be done, I promised her.

'I wouldn't know where I was!' she said wonderingly. She looked bemusedly about my kitchen, at the sink, the electric kettle, at the checked tablecloth and the breakfast food.

Joseph returned with his mother to Tyler's Row, there to sleep in his own bed.

'Let him come up to school dinner if he's awake by then,' I said to Mrs Coggs as they went down the path. 'And I won't forget to do what I can to help.'

And I should have done it long ago, I scolded myself, as I collected a pile of books and made ready to go over to the school. I made up my mind to get in touch with the vicar that same day. Two heads would be better than one, as Mr Willet no doubt would tell me, and between us the desperate conditions of Tyler's Row should be lightened by some hope from the county authorities.

Yes, I thought, remembering Mrs Coggs, the worm had turned indeed, and as it later transpired, the fortune of the whole Coggs family too. For before the end of the year the council house, which had been the home of old Shepherd Burton's family, became vacant, and the Coggs family was immediately moved in.

Mrs Coggs' new-found spirit glowed steadily in these surroundings. Arthur Coggs, in flabbergasted obedience to a court order, found himself handing over a fixed sum of money to his wife each week, and the whole of Fairacre voiced its approval. It was generally agreed that Joseph's rebellion on that stormy autumn evening had been 'a real blessing in disguise'.

20. *Miss Jackson Hears Bad News*

THE autumn term slipped by. The elm trees, overshadowing the school, now stood in gaunt majesty, the wind from the downs blew breathtakingly cold and the first signs of Christmas were abroad.

The children were busy preparing a nativity play, and during handwork lessons the pile of Christmas presents for parents, such as smudgy calendars, bumpy raffia mats and little hankies bearing here and there a needle-prick of blood from some hard-worked finger, grew apace.

In the village shop delicious boxes of crackers glowed on the shelves and further delights were to be found at the Post Office, which also sold sweets.

Cheek by jowl with the red sealing wax and foolscap envelopes stood pink and white sugar mice with string tails, chocolate watches and tiny jars filled with minute satin cushions, all waiting to deck some cottage Christmas tree.

The younger children, under Miss Jackson's care, grew daily more excited, and I dreaded to think of the pandemonium which would greet the ceremony of 'hanging up the paper for chains'. These grew at an incredible rate, scarlet linking yellow, yellow blue, blue silver, silver green, cascading down the sides of desks, lying in great rustling heaps on the floor and sending the makers into ecstasies. They plied their paste brushes madly, their faces flushed and their eyes sparkling. But Miss Jackson seemed unmoved.

I spent an evening with Miss Clare and our conversation turned to the girl. Miss Clare was busy knitting a pair of blue dungarees for Malcolm Annett's Christmas present.

'I hear that John Franklyn has found another attraction,' she told me, as her busy needles clicked. 'Mrs Fowler's niece who works at "The Bell".'

'Is it true, do you think?' I asked. Miss Clare lowered her knitting and looked steadily across at me.

'I'm quite sure it is. It seems to be general knowledge that the two are about together everywhere. Frankly, it seems the best thing for everybody. They are neither of them particularly likeable people, but they would suit each other very well and I'm sure she is a good-hearted woman who would welcome little Betty Franklyn if the aunt wanted to part with the child.'

'And what about Hilary?' I asked. 'Does she know?'

'I think she must have an inkling. I'm pretty sure that she doesn't see the man as often as she did. But she says nothing.'

'Well, if she doesn't know now,' I said, 'she will pretty soon, if I know anything about village life!'

Mrs Pringle had more to say on the subject as she washed up after school dinner. Miss Jackson had taken the savings money to the Post Office to buy stamps, and Mrs Pringle took advantage of her absence to probe into this delicate matter.

'Seems as though the wedding bells'll be ringing out again,' she said, with ponderous jocularity. She swilled down the draining board with a sizzling hot dish-cloth that would have scalded a less asbestos-like hand.

'Mrs Fowler was telling me she helped her niece write out an advertisement for her engagement for The Paper.' *The Caxley Chronicle* is always spoken of in this way for it commands well-deserved respect from its few thousand loyal readers.

'Be a shock to some, I dare say,' continued the old harpy, with morose relish, 'but best in the end. The Lord giveth and the Lord taketh away!'

I always find Mrs Pringle's invoking of divine support particularly irritating, especially when her mind is working maliciously. I tried to pin her down.

'Who do you think will find the engagement a shock?'

Mrs Pringle bridled self-righteously, tucking her three chins firmly against her black jumper.

'It's not my place to say. But this I do know. The gentleman – so-called – has been paying attentions to someone not a hundred miles from here. And there's no knowing what *she* might feel about it – the poor, put-upon, innocent soul!'

Mrs Pringle uttered this last with an affecting tremor in her voice and with her eyes upraised piously to the clouds of steam near the ceiling.

Luckily, the entry of Miss Jackson with the savings stamps called a halt to our discussion.

Nothing more had been heard officially about the new housing estate, but the matter hung ominously at the back of people's minds.

Dr Martin stood at Miss Clare's window looking at the brown furrowed beauty of Hundred Acre Field.

'I'd hate to think this is the last winter we'd see it like that,' said the doctor thoughtfully.

'Sometimes,' answered his patient in a far-away voice, 'I think I'd like this winter to be my last one.'

Doctor Martin turned and looked swiftly at her. Her blue eyes gazed serenely into space. He crossed to the chair where she sat, and looked down with mock severity.

'Now, none of that, Dolly. You'll see eighty yet!' Miss Clare smiled at him.

'What a bully you are! I'm very, very tired you know. I often sing that little bit of Handel to myself.

> 'Art thou weary?
> "Rest shall be thine,
> "Rest shall be thine."'

Miss Clare sang in a small voice, as sweet and clear as a winter robin's.

The doctor stood in silence, watching his old friend meditatively. When he spoke it was with more than usual robustness.

'Tonic for you tomorrow, my girl! A *large* bottle, with plenty of iron in it!'

'We must move,' said Mrs Mawne decisively to her husband, 'if this estate comes. The place won't be fit to live in!'

'I fear that we shall have to face much more responsibility,' said the vicar soberly to his wife, 'if our parish houses so many more souls. It is a very great trust – and we're neither of us getting younger, my dear.'

'Pretty well double my turnover, this will,' said Mr Prince, the baker at Fairacre.

'I shall have to give over the dining-room to Christmas cards next year,' commented Mr Lamb at the Post office, surveying his cramped stock.

'This hanging about will dam' well kill me!' exploded old Miller in his threatened farm house.

And thus spoke many in Fairacre and Beech Green as they chafed under this intolerable burden of suspense.

It remained for Mr Willet to sum up the matter.

'Ah! It's a bad time for us all, waiting and wondering. Which reminds me. I've chose my words for my gravestone. What d'you think of that, Miss Read?

> Good times
> Bad times
> All times
> Pass over.'

'For last words on a subject, Mr Willet,' I said, 'you couldn't do better.'

On the Saturday morning following my conversation with Mrs Pringle, I went to Caxley to buy Christmas cards.

As usual this was no light task. After overcoming the initial shock of staggeringly high prices (unconsciously I still expect something rather distinguished for fourpence!) I found further difficulties confronting me. Despite the plethora of cards on view in the stationer's they seemed to fall into comparatively few classes – arch poodles, ladies in crinolines and ringlets accompanied by mawkish verses, stage coaches hurtling through cheering spectators waving beaver hats, and cards of a religious nature bearing three camels and a star embossed in gold.

Whilst I was turning over morosely a pile of cards showing puppies in hampers and kittens in boots, someone spoke. It was John Franklyn's sister-in-law, the woman who was looking after his daughter Betty, in Caxley.

'I haven't seen you for a long time,' she said, and my mind flew back to the scene in the vicar's garden on the day of the fete. As though she could read my thoughts, she went on.

'Have you heard that my brother is engaged to the young lady we saw him with at the fete?' I said that I had heard, but had wondered if it were just a rumour. The woman's eyes grew troubled.

'No, it's no rumour. It'll be in The Paper this week.' She put her hand, in a sudden confiding gesture, on my arm.

'Break it to that poor girl,' she pleaded urgently. 'She was in a fair taking about him. Not that it's not all for the best, as it's fallen out – but it'll come hard if she sees it without warning.'

I promised to do what I could, shelved the comparatively simple problem of Christmas cards and left the shop pondering on this knottier one.

As any teacher will tell you, Monday morning is a hectic time. What with notes from mothers, dinner money, savings money, returned absentees, new children and other distractions, affairs of the heart, however pressing, have to take second place.

I was considerably perturbed about the best way to approach this delicate subject, and decided that after midday dinner would perhaps be a good time to make as casual a mention of it as I could. But it was not to be. Linda Moffat complained of severe stomach pains and looked so wretchedly ill at dinner time that Miss Jackson took her home to her mother.

It was not until school was over for the day and the children had run and skipped their way through the school gate to the lane that the opportunity occurred for an uninterrupted conversation.

Hilary Jackson came across to the school-house to borrow a book and, taking a deep breath, I made a cautious approach. I remembered our last catastrophic clash over John Franklyn, on that distant thundery day. The sound of that storm still echoed in my ears as I began reluctantly.

'I hope you will forgive me for asking you something very personal,' I said gently.

Hilary Jackson looked round from the bookshelves, wide-eyed.

'Good lord, no! What's that?' I began to feel like a baby-killer, but I stuck to it doggedly.

'It was about John Franklyn –' I began. Hilary drew in her breath so sharply, that I knew at once that I had no need to break any news to the girl. She already knew the truth.

She dropped the book she was holding, and with a dreadful despairing cry crumpled down on to the floor, pillowing her head in my armchair. Her shoulders shook with her sobbing and I stood there watching her, feeling powerless to help.

At last she lifted a blotched, woebegone face to me.

'Yes, I know, I know! And what's to become of me?' she burst out tragically. 'What's to become of me?'

21. The Problem of Miss Clare

THE *Caxley Chronicle* carried the notice of John Franklyn's engagement the next day, and Miss Jackson went sad-eyed about her affairs, the object of much sincere pity in the village. Although she had never made much effort to be pleasant to the parents and friends of the school, she was young and in love, and the romantic heart of the village was stirred. It rose to her support to a man.

'Enough to make your heart bleed!' announced Mrs Pringle lugubriously, laying a hand upon her 'afflicted member. Mr Willet, who was present, was much too delicate-minded to have mentioned the subject on his own, but was stung into speech by Mrs Pringle's dramatic excesses.

''Tis good riddance to bad rubbish,' he asserted sturdily, 'whatever you old women says, making sheeps' eyes over something that's none of your business. She'll get over it, and thank her lucky stars she's rid of him!'

Mrs Pringle bridled and looked to me for support.

'Broken hearts don't mend so easy, do they, Miss Read?' she said with dreadful meaning. I could only think that she was harping back to the long-forgotten affair of Mr Mawne and I replied with some tartness.

'I agree with Mr Willet,' I said with finality and watched Mrs Pringle retreat, registering extreme umbrage by her rigid back and sudden, severe limp.

But comfort was in store for Hilary Jackson.

The next day had dawned clear and bright, one of those sparkling December days all the more precious because they are so rare.

The bare black elm trees looked as though they were drawings in charcoal sketched delicately against the wintry pale blue sky. The smoke from the village chimneys rose in straight columns, the larks sang as though spring itself had burst upon them, and our spirits soared with them.

At morning playtime the children scampered eagerly outside with no prompting from their teachers. Cowboys, Indians, mothers-and-fathers, horses, spacemen and an occasional idle dreamer disported themselves in the playground, revelling in the warm sunshine.

Miss Jackson was taking playground duty, and even her sad heart appeared to be a trifle cheered by the weather.

I went indoors to put on the kettle for our elevenses and found the telephone ringing.

'I have a call for you,' said a distant voice. The line cracked and buzzed whilst I waited. Should I make a quick dash for the kettle, I wondered? It would be getting hot while I sat there.

'Have you finished?' asked a peremptory woman.

'No,' I answered aggrieved. 'I haven't even started!'

'Hold on!' commanded the voice. I held on whilst some violent clicking noises exploded against my eardrum. By this time I had imagined the worst. All my relatives had been taken ill, met with serious accidents, been wrongly imprisoned, and were, each and all, in urgent need of immediate help. I had mentally rearranged the timetable, enabling the school to be taught for the rest of the day by Miss Jackson alone, chosen a suitable wardrobe for travelling at a moment's notice in all directions, composed a note for Mrs Pringle about the household chores, and made arrangements for the cat's welfare, when another voice broke through the crackling.

It was, unmistakably, Miss Crabbe's.

'Is Hilary there?' she asked, sensibly going to the point at once and not spending ninepence of fatuous enquiries after my own health. I said I would fetch her at once, and fled to the playground.

'Miss Crabbe's on the telephone,' I said breathlessly, 'and wants a word with you.' If I had expected Hilary Jackson's face to light up I should have been disappointed. A distinctly sullen look was added to her dejected appearance.

'Oh! I'd better go, I suppose,' she answered resignedly, and departed into my house, while I remained outside among the hurtling bodies and ear-splitting shrieks of my pupils.

In a few minutes she returned, transfigured.

'She's wonderful —' she began.

'Miss,' shouted a child deafeningly, his face upturned by my waist. 'Miss, ol' George says there ain't no Father Christmas! NO FATHER CHRISTMAS!' he reiterated in an appalling crescendo.

'I'll see about it later,' I shouted back, above the din. With any luck, I thought cravenly, the dispute will be forgotten by then.

'Let's get the kettle on,' I said to Miss Jackson, 'and you can tell me in peace!'

'She's asked me to go to Switzerland with her, for the Christmas holidays,' burst out my assistant, and now her eyes were like stars, I noticed. 'The friend she was going with has been taken ill, and has had to cry off. I've always wanted to go to winter sports! Isn't it simply marvellous?'

It was a tonic to see the poor child in such good heart again, and I was glad too that at last she had made her peace with Miss Crabbe. This reconciliation and the wonderful holiday to look forward to should cure effectively the wounds made by John Franklyn.

'I'm absolutely delighted!' I told her honestly, and we fell to discussing ski clothes and kit, what to buy outright and what to hire, how much money one might need, the best method of travel and a hundred and one other matters whose discussion is as much part of the fun as the holiday itself.

I put the sugar and milk in our two cups, still chattering, and with one eye on the children whom I could see through the dining-room window. I raised the tea pot and poured a stream into Miss Jackson's cup. Shaking with laughter, she directed my attention to the liquid. It was crystal clear. In the excitement of the moment we had forgotten the tea.

The last few days of term sped by in an atmosphere of mounting excitement. The spring term, which normally lasts from January until early April, is acknowledged by the teaching profession to be the most gruelling of the three, but the two weeks at the end of the Christmas term, particularly in the infants' school, run a close second, from a class teacher's point of view.

The climax came with the customary Christmas party in the schoolroom on the last afternoon. Parents and friends joined in the time-honoured games. 'Cat and Mouse', 'Hunt the Thimble', and 'Oranges and Lemons', and Miss Clare came to play the ancient piano, a period piece with a filigree walnut front through which one had a glimpse of once-scarlet pleated silk. It must have been an object of great beauty in its early Victorian days, and even now adds an archaic dignity to our schoolroom, standing against the wall like a well-bred, elderly chaperon watching over our revels.

The yellowing keys tinkled plangently under Miss Clare's fingers as she played. Her face was pink with happiness at being among the children once more, and I began to wonder, for the first time, if loneliness perhaps, was the major cause of her general decline in health. Certainly, on the afternoon of the party, she glowed like an autumn rose. I determined to give the matter more attention during the holidays.

The vicar cut the presents from the sparkling Christmas tree, we all sang carols together, wished each other a Merry Christmas, and went out into the darkness.

Miss Clare, Miss Jackson and I watched the torches bobbing away down the lane, like fireflies, before we locked the school door upon the debris within, which was to await tomorrow's ministrations.

Later that evening I drove the two back to Beech Green and accepted an invitation to tea the next day.

It would be Miss Jackson's last meal at Beech Green before catching the night plane with Miss Crabbe to Switzerland, and she was as excited and as whole-heartedly happy as the children had been at their party.

As she chattered, Miss Clare and I exchanged secret smiles compounded of relief and extreme satisfaction. Franklyn was forgotten!

I spent the next day packing Christmas parcels and sending off my Christmas cards, jobs which have to be left until the whirl of end-of-term festivities are over. The house was refreshingly peaceful, and I pottered about enjoying my leisure and solitude.

It is deeply satisfying to me, after spending so much of my time among a number of energetic young people, to hear the clink of a hot coal and the whisper of flames in my own chimney, the purring of Tibby delighting in company, and the chiming of the clock on the mantelpiece. All these domestic pleasures tend to be taken for granted by the normal housewife, for they are her working conditions as well as her home, but they have an added appealing charm for the woman who is forced by circumstances to spend only part of her time at home. As I went happily about my small affairs I turned over in my mind the problem of Miss Clare. It seemed right to me that I should offer her a home with me at Fairacre school-house if she would like to come. I was beginning to see that she should not live alone, and that even if she had a lodger for some time to come, it would not be many years – or perhaps months – before that would become too much for her.

There were many factors to consider, I knew. Miss Clare would not want to give up her independence and her lifelong home any more than I, or anyone else, would. She would hate to feel that she was imposing on anyone, and I certainly might prove an awkward person to live with. I remembered wryly with what relief Miss Jackson had quit my portals, not so long ago! But I intended to make the offer. She would have companionship, someone in the house at night when she might be in urgent need, be within sight and sound of the children during the daytime, and have a house which would be probably more comfortable, if not as dear to her, as her own cottage.

A small faint regret about my own precious solitude I thrust resolutely and fiercely from me. I was getting downright selfish and it would do me a power of good to have someone else to consider. I went off to the tea party hoping for a chance to put my suggestion forward.

Miss Clare had drawn her round table close by the crackling fire. There were hot buttered crumpets under a covered dish and a very fine dark fruit cake covered with nuts.

As we ate the crumpets, with butter oozing deliciously over our fingers, Miss Clare poured tea. She had brought out the family silver teapot for this state occasion, a wonderful fluted object with a yellowed ivory knob like a blanched almond.

'I've made a large Christmas cake,' said Miss Clare nodding at the one before us, 'from the same mixture. You must sample this and tell me if it's good.' She began to recite the recipe, a list of so many mouth-watering ingredients including raisins, cherries, brown sugar and brandy, that it was like listening to a particularly luscious and fleshly poem.

Miss Jackson, resplendent in a new dark red suit, watched the clock eagerly. Mr Annett, who was going to meet his father-in-law at the county town, had offered to take her in to catch a fast train. He was due at half past five.

'Remember me to Miss Crabbe,' said Miss Clare, 'and I hope that she'll come down here again when the evenings are lighter.'

'I'm sure she'd like to,' responded Miss Jackson, warmly. She paused while she cut a piece of cake carefully into fingers and then looked from one of us to the other.

'She means a great deal to me. I'm beginning to realize that trouble shows you your real friends.'

Miss Clare nodded gravely, and it was at this moment that we heard the hooting of Mr Annett's car at the gate.

Miss Jackson fled upstairs for her things and we all escorted her down the garden path to the gate.

'Enjoy yourself!'

'Have a lovely holiday!' we called into the darkness, as we waved goodbye to the back of the disappearing car.

We washed up the tea things and settled thankfully one on each side of the roaring fire. The wind was rising outside, and though I should dearly have loved a holiday in Switzerland, I was glad that I was not setting off on such a long journey. An aeroplane seemed a very flimsy little thing to be conflicting with the mighty winds which were at large, sweeping the dark heavens.

I steered the conversation to the state of Miss Clare's health and her hopes for the future.

'Everyone worries far too much about me,' she said gently. 'I think I shall be able to manage here for some time yet. And I must say, that with Miss Jackson looking more cheerful, the outlook is much more hopeful for me. It's just at night sometimes – ' Her voice died away and she looked into the fire. Taking a deep breath I unfolded my proposals.

Miss Clare listened in silence. When I had finished, she leant forward and took my hand.

'I can't thank you enough, but I'm going to tell you something. George Annett has promised that if ever Miss Jackson leaves me he will find a really easy lodger from his own school to take her place – so that I have no financial worries. And if my health should fail, and I have to leave this little house, he and Isobel have another plan. But I won't speak of that. I hope I may be here for many years.'

She bent down and put two logs of apple wood on the fire. Their sweet outdoor fragrance began to creep about the firelit room.

'For a woman who loves solitude as much as you do,' she continued, 'and who gets so little of it – I think you have made a superhuman offer. But I don't think the need will arise for me to accept such kindness.'

'It will stand anyway,' I told her truthfully. Miss Clare stood up.

'Have a glass of home-made wine,' she said briskly. She went to a corner cupboard, high on the wall, and produced a deep red bottle that glowed like a ruby.

'Plum,' she said with satisfaction, 'and two years old!'

She trickled it into two wine glasses, brought mine over to me, and then raised her own.

'I'm thinking of Hilary's remark,' she said. 'To our friends!'

We sipped, smiling at one another.

22. Fairacre Waits and Wonders

THE Nativity Play, which took place in St Patrick's church three days before Christmas, had occasioned almost as much comment as the proposed estate. This was the first time such a thing had been attempted and the innocent vicar, whose only thought had been of his parishioners' pleasure in praising God in this way, would have been flabbergasted could he have heard some of the criticisms.

'Nothing short of popery!' was Mr Willet's dictum. 'Play acting in a church! I don't hold with it!'

'It's been going on for years,' I pointed out mildly. 'Churches were used quite often to perform plays for the people.'

'When?' asked Mr Willet suspiciously.

'Oh, a few hundred years ago,' I replied.

'Then it's about time we knew better,' was Mr Willet's unanswerable retort.

The children had been practising their part in it for several weeks, and I knew that Mr Annett as choirmaster had been busy with the singing which was to form part of the play. Several parents had spoken to me, rather as Mr Willet had, expressing their grave concern about what one called 'doing recitations in the Lord's House'. The singing passed without comment.

But on the evening in question Fairacre's villagers turned up in full force and it was good to see the church packed. A low stage had been erected at the chancel steps and the setting was the stable at Bethlehem.

The church looked lovely, decorated for Christmas with holly wreaths and garlands of ivy, mistletoe and fluffy old-man's-beard. On the altar were bowls of Christmas roses and white anemones. Only candlelight was used that evening, and the golden flames flickered like stars here and there in the shadows of the ancient church.

The play was simple and moving, the country people speaking their parts with warm sincerity, but it was the unaccustomed beauty of the boys' singing that was unforgettable. Mr Annett had wisely set aside several passages for the boys alone and their clear oval notes echoed in the high vaulted ceiling, with thrilling beauty. Whatever may have been said about such goings-on in church before the play, everyone agreed, as they stopped to talk afterwards in the windy churchyard, that it was a moving experience.

'The vicar could've done a lot worse,' conceded Mr Willet. And that indeed was high praise.

The holidays slipped by with incredible speed and early in January I was facing the school again at our first morning of the New Year.

There were thirty-six children now on roll and I wondered, as I watched them singing, how many I should see before me at the same time next year. Would all these older children, now making the partition rattle with their cheerful voices, have been wrested from Fairacre and be adding their numbers to those at the new school, standing on what had once been Hundred Acre Field? Would I have a handful of infants, and remain here, the sole member of staff, with one of the rooms empty of children after nearly eighty years? It was a depressing and disturbing thought and it had occurred to me more often then I cared to admit to anyone. This was my life, as satisfying and rewarding as ever a woman could ask for, and the thought of change distressed me.

Mr Willet would say 'Cross that bridge when you get to it!' I told myself, and I put these upsetting conjectures from me resolutely and determined to live for the day alone, although it was not easy.

Miss Jackson had returned in high spirits. Miss Crabbe was in the ascendant, and had evidently done her best to make the girl forget the unhappy love affair which had so unsettled her. She told me some interesting news.

'Miss Crabbe is starting a small school this summer. It's to be a kindergarten school quite near the college and she's running it on progressive lines, of course.'

'Of course,' I echoed gravely.

'She's got two other friends who are helping her with the money – people who are *quite sure* that her teaching methods are revolutionary – and she's asked me if I would like to be appointed to the staff.'

'And would you?' I asked unnecessarily. Hilary's face was radiant.

'I can't think of anything that I'd like more. There will be a house attached as there are going to be a few boarders – the really difficult cases – and I should live there with Miss Crabbe. Won't it be lovely?'

I said that it sounded a most hopeful venture and thought, privately, what a good thing it would be for the girl to get into another new post after all that had happened in Fairacre.

'She wants to open it next September and is already getting out prospectuses.'

'Then you'll have to give in your notice here about Easter-time,' I said.

'That's right,' agreed Hilary ecstatically. 'It will all fit in quite well, because by that time I expect the older children will have been sent on to the new school, and you won't need an assistant with just the infants.'

I was a trifle shaken by this calm acceptance of Fairacre's future plans, and hastened to point out that even if the estate were built, the school could not possibly be ready to house children by next September.

'In that case,' said Miss Jackson off-handedly, 'they would have to get another teacher in my place.'

'I suppose so,' I agreed. For one dreadful minute my old

doubts engulfed me again. Supposing that there was no assistant to be had this time? Could I tackle the whole school for any length of time? Could I even tackle the infants if the older children had been whisked away – to Beech Green perhaps – if the new school were not ready? Would it be best for everyone if I tendered my resignation too? I thought of all the tedious business of writing out testimonials, filling in endless forms, asking people if they would stand as referees. I thought too of all that Fairacre and its folk had come to mean to me. No, I told myself firmly, I couldn't face it. For Fairacre's good or not, I should do my best there, and be happy to stay if I were deemed fit for the job. I came back to earth from this swift day-dream to hear Miss Jackson speaking with great earnestness.

'I couldn't let Miss Crabbe down, you know. It would be unthinkable!'

It seemed to me, in the weeks that followed, that Miss Jackson's acceptance of the housing scheme, as a foregone conclusion, was shared by others in Fairacre and the neighbourhood. It was as though the prolonged waiting had numbed the anti-estate feeling which had been so ferocious earlier in the affair. The people had lived with the idea for so long now that a fatalistic resignation to what might transpire had affected quite a number of them.

'We must get a more efficient heating system in the church if we have to house the new people,' said the vicar to his wife. 'The back of the church is never really warm.'

'I'll have to think of an extra delivery van and an extra driver, this time next year,' said Mr Prince, the baker, to his assistant.

Even Mrs Pringle was beginning to soften towards the project.

'Poor things must live somewhere!' she pointed out reasonably. 'Do 'em good to get out into decent houses and a bit of fresh air!' From the way she spoke one might imagine that they were living, at the moment, huddled together in sewers.

But the flame still burned brightly in some breasts. Over at Springbourne old Mr Miller looked out at his unchanged view and the first tiny spears of his new crop in Hundred Acre Field.

'They'll not shift me!' he said grimly to his wife, wagging his frosted head. 'We'll still be here when they've gone elsewhere, mark my words!'

The vicar, on hearing that Mr Miller had planted his field as usual was much impressed and said so to old Mrs Bradley who was present at the time.

'It is an act of faith, dear Mrs Bradley. A true act of faith!'

'Plenty of spunk there,' agreed Mrs Bradley spiritedly. 'Keep fighting! That's the way to gain your ends, and fight with all the weapons you can find! I myself sent a telling Christmas card to the Minister at his home address.'

'Really?' said the vicar, somewhat alarmed. He would not have put sending a bomb past this fierce old lady.

'A reproduction of "The Dew Pond on the Downs",' continued Mrs Bradley. 'One of Dan's best pictures. And I signed it "Adelaide Bradley – Lover of Fair Play and Our Downs" and added "Remember Dan Crockford!" for good measure!'

'It may well have helped,' said the vicar politely.

'Too much waiting about is making far too many fainthearts,' announced Mrs Bradley shrewdly – '"Up and at 'em" is my motto! We'll see 'em off yet!'

Amy brought much the same news of Caxley's reaction to the scheme when she came to spend an evening with me. Resentment had largely been replaced by a philosophic acceptance of the affair as a necessary evil, and, in fact, the shopkeepers were beginning to speculate on the increase in their business which so many extra families must inevitably bring.

Amy herself, however, was as militant as Mrs Bradley.

'I've sent four letters already to the *Caxley Chronicle* and two more to *The Times* about this business,' she asserted.

'I haven't seen them,' I said innocently.

'For some reason they haven't been published yet,' replied Amy, not a whit disturbed, 'but it's the *writing* that matters. We mustn't give way and let things slide. Which reminds me!'

She scrabbled in her large crocodile handbag, a gift from

James after a week's absence at a mysterious conference at a place unspecified, and handed me a book.

'It's a lesson to you!' said Amy firmly. 'It's about a woman, living alone, just as you do, on a small income with a regular working day, who never Lets Herself Go! It impressed me very much. Quite a nice little love-story too,' added Amy, in a patronizing tone.

'Any picture strips?' I asked acidly, putting the book on my shelf.

'It's that sort of remark,' said Amy coldly, 'that reveals what a frustrated woman you really are!'

'That be blowed!' I answered inelegantly. 'Don't come the Integrated-Married-Woman over me, my girl. I've known you too long. What about scrambled eggs on toast for supper?'

United in common hunger we went cheerfully together to raid the larder.

23. The Village Hears the News

MARCH that year was one of the coldest that Fairacre had ever known. The nights were bitter, and cottage fires were kept in overnight with generous top-sprinkling of small coal dampened with tea leaves, and stirred into comforting life first thing the next morning.

All growth was at a standstill. The small buds on the hedges were brittle to the touch and the spearlike leaves of those hardy bulbs which had already sent them aloft grew not a whit. The birds were particularly hard hit and not a day passed without a child bringing in a small pathetic corpse, its frail claws clenched stiffly in its last agony.

The vicar grieved over the inadequate heating of St Patrick's. Mr Roberts, Mr Miller and all the neighbouring farmers chafed at the delay to their crops, the children came to school wrapped up like cocoons in numberless coats and scarves, and I suffered my seasonal stiff neck from the draught from the skylight above my desk.

Despite continuous stoking, on my part, of the tortoise stoves, the school seldom seemed really warm because of villainous draughts from ill-fitting doors and windows. The coke pile in the playground began to dwindle visibly and Mrs Pringle was affronted.

'Good thing the Office can't see the rate we're using up the fuel!' she said darkly.

'Must keep warm,' I replied equably.

'What some calls *warm*,' replied Mrs Pringle, loosening the buttons at her neck, 'others calls *stifling*. Proper unhealthy in here with the stoves blazing away like that! Shouldn't be surprised if we had the chimney afire.' She limped off, outraged, before I could answer.

'It won't get no warmer till the snow's down,' said Mr Willet, surveying the iron-grey sky behind St Patrick's spire. 'And that won't be long now. You take your shovel indoors with you tonight, Miss Read. Wouldn't mind betting us has a bit of digging out to do tomorrow.'

Mr Willet was right. The first few flakes began to flutter down early in the afternoon. I was putting a writing copy on the blackboard, and wishing that my own handwriting were as elegant as Miss Clare's had been, when I heard the excited whispers behind me.

'Snowing! Look, 'tis snowing!'

'Smashing!'

'Reckon it'll settle?'

''Tisn't *half* snowing too! Coming down a treat!'

The children were bobbing up from their seats the better to see this wonder through the high windows. Their faces were radiant. Here was drama indeed, and, with any luck, they might be sent home a few minutes early! Their day was made.

Within ten minutes the snow was falling steadily, whispering sibilantly along the window sills outside and covering the playground, the coke pile and the roofs with a white canopy. As the children finished their writing, they were allowed to go to the window to watch. They gazed entranced, looking up at the whirling flakes as they swirled down and making themselves deliciously dizzy with the sight.

'Miss!' burst out Eric, 'they's black coming down! *Black* snow flakes! Come and look!'

The scene outside might have come from a Christmas card. The bare black trees stood out starkly against their grey background and the bulk of the church loomed larger than ever against the heavy sky. The church windows glowed with lights within the buildings and I guessed that Mr Willet was stoking up the stove again. Along the lane I could see two small figures bent against the onslaught. They each carried a shopping bag and I suspected that the Coggs twins, ostensibly absent from school with unspecified ailments, had been sent 'up shop' by their mother. I watched their red coats vanish round the bend and realized that the only spot of vivid colour had now gone. The thatched roofs, the gardens, hedges and ground were all in muted shadings of grey, black and white.

At playtime the children had a few delirious minutes out among the flakes. I watched Patrick scoop up a handful of snow from the window ledge and eat it rapturously.

'S'lovely!' he shouted to the others, looking up with sparkling eyes and a thick white fringe round his wet, red mouth The rest skimmed round and round like swallows, screaming as shrilly, and kicking up the wonderful stuff with their flying heels.

When they came in they stood apple-cheeked, warming their pink cold hands over the stove and chattering away about the joys in store for them, 'if it only lays'.

It continued to snow heavily and Miss Jackson and I sent the children home ten minutes early. It was settling, even then, to a depth of two or three inches and I feared that it would be over the top of some of the smaller children's shoes. We wrapped them up as best we could. They stood, chafing at the delay, as we buttoned coats and tied bonnet strings, and the minute that they could break away from our grasp they rushed ecstatically out into this glorious new world which had miraculously been transformed from everyday Fairacre.

There was an orchestral rehearsal that evening and I made my usual trip to Beech Green to mind Malcolm Annett while his parents went to Caxley. The snow lay thickly on the verges of the road, in the crooks of the trees and along their branches, but the road itself was easily traversed.

Malcolm had become a vivacious toddler with only one thing in mind – farm machinery. He was as elated as the school children were about the snow, but this did not deflect him from his usual obsession and whenever the sound of passing vehicles was heard he bolted to the window, shouting hopefully: 'Tractor!'

His dearest possession was a red model tractor which accompanied him everywhere. Teddies, golliwogs, soft animals and all the other former loves now languished in the toy cupboard. To my enquiries after their well-being and his own health and interests, he answered brightly: 'Tractor!' holding up the object for my inspection.

'I must say it's a bit tedious,' said his mother plaintively, 'and when I mislaid it the other day I thought he'd have apoplexy.'

The conversation turned to Miss Clare, while Malcolm shunted the tractor blissfully back and forth between our feet on the hearthrug.

'We loved having her with us on holiday last summer,' said Isobel, 'and George and I talked it over with Dr Martin when she was groggy again later on, and we suggested that she might like to come and live here, if ever she found her own house too much for her.'

'I'm very glad,' I answered, 'but did she accept the idea?'

'Not at first,' said George. 'In any case it is far better for her to manage on her own in her own home for as long as she can comfortably do so. I hear Miss Jackson's likely to go.'

I said it looked as though she would be leaving Fairacre at the end of the summer and told them what I knew of her plans.

'Lord!' said George Annett, with profound awe, 'think of Miss Jackson *and* Miss Crabbe on one staff!'

They went on to tell me about the provision of a suitable lodger for Miss Clare, as long as she wanted one.

'I can never find enough decent accommodation for my young

staff,' said George. 'Any one of them would jump at the chance of being with Dolly Clare.'

'And we're keeping a room ready here where she can have all her things and make her home,' continued his wife. 'She could let her cottage probably and that would bring her in a little income. It's all very much in the future we hope, but she has promised to come if she needs to, and we are all of us – and Dr Martin too – very much relieved.'

I said that it was a most satisfactory arrangement, and thought what thoroughly good hearted people these two Annetts were.

'Look at the clock!' exclaimed George, jumping to his feet. 'Come on, Isobel, we'll be late!'

The usual scurrying began with Isobel shouting last-minute injunctions about her son's needs as she dressed.

'Let him have plenty of supper – he won't bother to eat during the day. And when he goes to bed, don't forget that he always takes –'

'Don't tell me,' I said, 'I can guess!'

'Tractor!' said my intelligent and besotted godson.

The snow continued intermittently for over a week, much to the joy of the children and the annoyance of their parents as they struggled about their affairs in a white world.

It was during this bleak period that a meeting was held of the Rural District Council at the offices in Caxley. Muffled in thick overcoats and scarves, and beating their leather gloves together, the members made their way up the stairs to the committee room, among them Mr Roberts from Fairacre accompanied by a cheerful young reporter from the *Caxley Chronicle*. They little realized what momentous news they would hear, for although the agenda lay in their pockets, the Clerk to the R.D.C. had received that morning a missive from the Minister of Housing and Local Government, sharing that honour with the Clerk to the County Council and the representative of the Atomic Energy Authority who had also received similar messages. It was this delicious letter which the Clerk looked forward to reading to his fellow councillors.

Within an hour the meeting was over and down the stairs

tumbled the councillors with most gratified expressions. Mr Roberts' great laugh shook some flaking plaster from the hall ceiling as they emerged and the young reporter tore along the snowy streets to the offices of the *Caxley Chronicle* with the biggest scoop of his brief career. This, surely, he could sell to a national daily and win himself, not only approval from his own local editor, but a guinea or two from the lords of Fleet Street!

Mr Roberts drove through the black and white lanes to Fairacre in roaring good spirits. As he passed Hundred Acre Field, a sheet of unsullied whiteness stretching to the misty obscurity of the downs behind, Mr Roberts gave it an affectionate wink and a smile.

His wife was making dripping toast for tea when he entered the farmhouse kitchen. He kissed her boisterously, told her the good tidings, and inspected the toast. It was a delicacy of which Mr Roberts was a connoisseur.

'Plenty of that brown goobly from the bottom, my dear, and a good sprinkling of salt,' he directed, as he made his way to the telephone. Anxious as he was to let one or two intimates know his good news, Mr Roberts recognized that there was a time and a place for everything. Dripping toast has as much right to respect as parish affairs, and at tea-time on a winter afternoon it must take pride of place.

'I'll go,' said the vicar, when he heard the telephone bell. He heaved himself from his shabby leather armchair by the fire and hurried into the draughty tiled hall where the vicarage telephone was housed.

'I can hardly believe it!' Mrs Partridge heard her husband say. 'Indeed, Roberts, it's almost more than I can take in! Thank you a thousand times for telling me.' She heard the tinkle as the vicar replaced the telephone, and a moment later he appeared in the doorway. He held out both hands to her and looked strangely moved.

'There is to be no housing estate. The Minister has made his decision known. It will be in the *Caxley Chronicle* the day after tomorrow.'

Mrs Partridge gripped her husband's hands thankfully. Tears, which did not come easily to the robust Mrs Partridge, filled her eyes as she felt relief flooding her.

'It is a direct answer to prayer,' said the vicar gently. 'I shall give public thanks in church next Sunday.'

'If that's a baby arriving,' said Dr Martin, setting down his unsipped tea as he heard the telephone, 'it can dam' well wait half an hour.' He lifted the receiver that lay within arm's reach on top of the bookshelf.

'Ah, Roberts,' he smiled across at his wife. 'Stand back a bit from the blower, man. You're deafening me!'

The roaring noise which Mrs Martin could hear subsided slightly. The doctor's face grew more and more pleased as he listened.

'Best news I've heard this year!' exclaimed the doctor delightedly. 'It solves a lot of my problems as well as everyone else's. Many thanks for letting me know!'

He put down the receiver and beamed at his wife.

'You can put all those plans about moving out of your head, my dear. The housing scheme is off!'

He took a long, satisfying draught from his tea cup.

'Thank God for that!' said Mrs Bradley when she heard the news. 'If anything had happened to Dan Crockford's field I think it would have killed me.'

She paused to listen to Mr Roberts's booming voice giving further particulars of the Minister's decision.

'Well, all I can say is this,' cackled the old lady mischievously, 'it was that Christmas card of mine that did the trick! I told you we must keep fighting – and now, you see, we've won!'

George Annett heard the news later that evening when the vicar telephoned to him about some arrangements for the next Sunday's anthem.

He rushed at once to the sitting-room where his wife and Miss Clare sat listening to the news on the wireless.

'Switch that off!' ordered Mr Annett excitedly, 'and I'll

tell you some *real* news, that'll make that international stuff look pretty silly!'

The two women gazed at him in surprise, but Isobel obediently switched off.

'Now then, it had better be good,' she said warningly.

'It is!' responded her husband proudly. '*We're not going to have a housing estate!*'

And snatching two knitting needles from Miss Clare's lap, he set them crosswise on the carpet and executed a lively sword dance, complete with triumphant, blood-curdling cries, much to the delight of the ladies.

Over at Springbourne late that night, Mr Miller filled four glasses. He had heard the wonderful news earlier that day by letter from the Rural District Council, and he looked upon it as a personal reprieve.

His two distinguished sons were at home when the news came, and they agreed that their father had shed twenty years from his eighty, as he had perused the letter. They stood now, glasses in hand, smiling warmly upon their spritely father.

Old Mr Miller raised his glass to his wife.

'To our home!' he said simply.

24. Farewell to Fairacre

DURING the night a warm westerly wind blew across the downs and Fairacre folk woke to find that the thaw had started. The thatched roofs dripped under a warm sun, little streams began to trickle in the gutters, the thirsty birds rejoiced in the puddles and life began to stir again.

The thermometers rose steadily, and as the news of the Minister's findings began to circulate with the village's customary briskness, the spirits of all who lived in Fairacre and Beech Green rose too. Many a village quarrel was patched up that morning. With such sunshine and such news, such relief from iron-hard frost and restricting suspense, it was impossible to pass a neighbour, even if one had been on 'no-speaking' terms for months, without stopping for a lively gossip. At back-door steps, over hedges, in the village street, in the grocer's shop and at the post office the loosened tongues wagged. A great burden had been lifted and life in Fairacre rattled on all the more lightly and merrily.

''Twould never have done,' repeated Mr Willet. 'I said at the time that 'twould never have done! Fairacre takes a bit of beating as it is!'

'I'll believe it when I sees it,' was Mrs Pringle's comment. 'I've heard too many rumours flying about lately for me to put much store by a lot of idle chitter-chatter. I'll wait till I sees it put plain in the paper!'

We had not long to wait, for the *Caxley Chronicle* came out the next morning and had given pride of place to the youthful reporter's notice of the meeting.

'In view of the government's recent decision for stringent cuts in expenditure, and having given the objections raised by local bodies his earnest attention, the Minister has decided, with reluctance, that the present housing-estate scheme must be abandoned.'

As everyone in Fairacre, Beech Green and Caxley pointed out to his neighbour the Minister had put the less important factor first. Naturally, it was the fighting spirit of the local inhabitants that had forced the issue, but as the Minister had seen reason in the end no one was going to quarrel with him over this relatively minor point.

'And give the chap his due,' Mr Willet pointed out, reasonably enough, 'he do seem to have sat up there cudgelling his brains over this 'ere business ever since last October. Say what you like, after six months' honest thinking he's pretty well bound to have got the right answer.'

'And that he have!' agreed Mr Lamb from the Post Office with conviction. And all the neighbourhood, with rejoicing hearts, concurred.

The spring term had ended in a spell of warm sunshine

which looked as though it might well stay for the Easter holidays.

The children had run home, on that last afternoon, hugging their bright Easter eggs carefully to their chests, and chorusing cheerfully.

'Good-bye, Miss. Happy Easter, Miss!'

When I answered with 'Be good children and help your mothers,' and some wag had called, with well-simulated innocence, 'Same to you, Miss!' their delight knew no bounds. It was a retort which would doubtless go down in to Fairacre history.

The first morning of the holidays was so fair and sweet that I readily turned my back upon household affairs and set out for a walk on top of the downs. I chose the narrow little-used lane that winds steeply up the slope of the downs, beginning among trees which form a leafy tunnel in the summer and now showed the first small fans of breaking leaves, and later emerging into the bare open downland.

The scent of spring was everywhere, heady and hopeful, and as I gained the upper slopes I could hear the numberless larks carolling. I remembered Mr Mawne's remark: 'More larks to the square yard on those downs than anywhere else I know.'

Puffed by now, I arrived at a five-barred gate at the side of the lane, and leant gratefully upon it, looking down at the view spread below me. What an escape we had had, when the housing scheme had been abandoned!

A fine blue haze lay over the valley. Away to my right lay Beech Green. Miss Clare's cottage, tucked in a fold of the downs, was hidden from my view, but the reprieved Hundred Acre Field lay spread there tinged with tender green. Mr Miller had weathered his storm bravely, I thought. And for that matter, hadn't we all, during this last year? I remembered the anxiety of the vicar, of Mr Willet and Mrs Pringle and of all those among us whose lives would have been shaken by the advent of the new town. I remembered too Hilary Jackson's stormy passage, Miss Crabbe's brief passion, dear Miss Clare's fight for health, and Joseph Coggs' rebellion.

But that was behind us now. The storm had passed, the sunshine warmed my bare head, and I remembered, with an up-rush of spirit, that the barometer had said *Set Fair* when I had tapped it that morning.

I took a last look at Fairacre away below me. There it lay in a comfortable hollow of the sheltering downs, ringed with trees that hid many of the thatched roofs from sight. But the spire of St Patrick's pierced the greenery like an upthrust finger and, at its tip, the weather-cock, glinting in the morning sunlight, seemed to crow a challenge to all comers.

Well-satisfied, I turned my back upon Fairacre, happy in the knowledge that however far I journeyed, it would always be there waiting for me, timeless and unchanged.

MORE ABOUT PENGUINS
AND PELICANS

For further information about books available from Penguins please write to Dept EP, Penguin Books Ltd, Harmondsworth, Middlesex UB7 0DA.

In the U.S.A.: For a complete list of books available from Penguins in the United States write to Dept CS, Penguin Books, 625 Madison Avenue, New York, New York 10022.

In Canada: For a complete list of books available from Penguins in Canada write to Penguin Books Canada Ltd, 2801 John Street, Markham, Ontario L3R 1B4.

In Australia: For a complete list of books available from Penguins in Australia write to the Marketing Department, Penguin Books Australia Ltd, P.O. Box 257, Ringwood, Victoria 3134.

In New Zealand: For a complete list of books available from Penguins in New Zealand write to the Marketing Department, Penguin Books (N.Z.) Ltd, P.O. Box 4019, Auckland 10.